SCENE OF THE CRIME

What Reviewers Say
About MJ Williamz's Work

Exposed

"The love affair between Randi and Eleanor goes along in fits and starts. It is a wonderful story, and the sex is hot. Definitely read it as soon as you have a chance!"—Janice Best, Librarian (Albion District Library)

Shots Fired

"MJ Williamz, in her first romantic thriller, has done an impressive job of building the tension and suspense. Williamz has a firm grasp of keeping the reader guessing and quickly turning the pages to get to the bottom of the mystery. *Shots Fired* clearly shows the author's ability to spin an engaging tale and is sure to be just the beginning of great things to follow as the author matures."
—*Lambda Literary Review*

"Williamz tells her story in the voices of Kyla, Echo, and Detective Pat Silverton. She does a great job with the twists and turns of the story, along with the secondary plot. The police procedure is first rate, as are the scenes between Kyla and Echo, as they try to keep their relationship alive through the stress and mistrust."
—*Just About Write*

Forbidden Passions

"*Forbidden Passions* is 192 pages of bodice ripping antebellum erotica not so gently wrapped in the moistest, muskiest pantalets of lesbian horn dog high jinks ever written. While the book is joyfully and unabashedly smut, the love story is well written and the characters are multi-dimensional. ...*Forbidden Passions* is the very model of modern major erotica, but hidden within the sweet swells and trembling clefts of that erotica is a beautiful May–September romance between two wonderful and memorable characters."
—*The Rainbow Reader*

Sheltered Love

"The main pair in this story is astoundingly special, amazingly in sync nearly all the time, and perhaps the hottest twosome on a sexual front I have read to date. ...This book has an intensity plus an atypical yet delightful original set of characters that drew me in and made me care for most of them. Tantalizingly tempting!"
—*Rainbow Book Reviews*

Speakeasy

"*Speakeasy* is a bit of a blast from the past. It takes place in Chicago when Prohibition was in full flower and Al Capone was a name to be feared. The really fascinating twist is a small speakeasy operation run by a woman. She was more than incredible. This was such great fun and I most assuredly recommend it. Even the bloody battling that went on fit with the times and certainly spiced things up!"
—*Rainbow Book Reviews*

Heartscapes

"The development of the relationship was well told and believable. Now the sex actually means something and M J Williamz certainly knows how to write a good sex scene. Just when you think life has finally become great again for Jesse, Odette has a stroke and can't remember her at all. It is heartbreaking. Odette was a lovely character and I thought she was well developed. She was just the right person at the right time for Jesse. It was an engaging book, a beautiful love story."—*Inked Rainbow Reads*

Visit us at www.boldstrokesbooks.com

By the Author

SCENE OF THE CRIME

by

MJ Williamz

2019

CREDITS
EDITOR: CINDY CRESAP
PRODUCTION DESIGN: SUSAN RAMUNDO
COVER DESIGN BY JEANINE HENNING

Acknowledgments

There are so many people to thank for this book. First and foremost, I want to thank my wonderful wife, Laydin. Not only did she give me the awesome idea for this story, but because her very existence makes my world a better place. Her constant love, devotion, and understanding of my need to write make me a happier, better author.

I also want to thank my beta readers. Sarah, Sue, and Karen—thank you so much for your invaluable input as this book developed. I really enjoy working with the three of you.

Since this book is a little different from what I normally write, I had a ton of questions. I want to thank Carsen and VK for taking the time to explain things for me and for helping me get things right.

As usual, I'd like to thank all the people at Bold Strokes Books for their continuing acceptance of my stories and their never ending efforts to help me improve my craft.

Finally, a huge thank you to you, the readers, who make this and every journey worthwhile.

Dedication

For always and forever—for Laydin

CHAPTER ONE

Cullen Matthews navigated through the driving rain, putting her day at the advertising agency far behind her. She was on her way home where Sara would be waiting for her. Sara, with her golden hair and bedroom blue eyes. Cullen's heart skipped a beat just thinking about her.

Cullen had actually given up on love years before. She'd always wanted a relationship but had never managed to find just the right woman. Until Sara. She was everything Cullen wanted in a woman—strong, independent, successful. The fact that she was drop-dead gorgeous was simply icing on the cake.

Sara made her money helping entrepreneurs start businesses. She'd work for a while, make a chunk of change, then live off her earnings until someone else came along. She fascinated Cullen. Everything about Sara captivated Cullen's interest.

Cullen parked in the garage and let herself in just as Sara came down the stairs to greet her. Cullen took one look and grew concerned as Sara's nose was red, and her eyes didn't look good.

"Baby? Are you okay? Have you been crying?"

Sara smiled warmly.

"I'm fine. I haven't been crying at all."

But she sounded nasally, and Cullen didn't believe her.

"You look like Rudolph and you're all stuffed up. How can you tell me you haven't been crying?"

Sara exhaled heavily.

"Allergies," she threw over her shoulder as she headed toward the kitchen. "Are you hungry? I made dinner."

Cullen wasn't in the mood to argue. Allergies? On a rainy day in November? She didn't believe Sara, and this wasn't the first time she'd noticed her all stuffed up. She wondered what she did to make her cry, but if Sara wouldn't tell her, how could Cullen possibly make it better?

She cleared her mind as she followed Sara into the kitchen and sat at the kitchen table which had been set with a lovely vase with fresh flowers in its center.

"So what's the occasion?" Cullen asked. "Why did you make dinner?"

"I had time and was bored. So I went to the store to get the ingredients to try a new recipe."

Sara never cooked, so Cullen was delighted. They tended to either go out for dinner or order takeout much of the time. And while they could certainly afford that, it would be nice to have a home cooked meal.

"This looks delicious," Cullen said as Sara set a plate full of casserole in front of her.

"I do hope you'll enjoy it. Dig in."

After the first bite, Cullen did her best not to gag. It was terrible, over seasoned and undercooked. She noticed Sara hadn't served herself.

"Aren't you eating?"

"I'm not hungry."

"Are you serious?"

"I am. I have no appetite. How is it?"

"It's good." Cullen forced herself to take some more bites since she didn't want to hurt Sara's feelings. Sara was her world, she made life worth living, and Cullen would do everything in her power to keep her happy.

"You sure you're feeling okay?"

"I feel great. I'm going to use the restroom. I'll be right back."

Cullen watched as Sara made her way down the hallway. She loved her curves and the way her hips swayed so seductively as she walked. Cullen decided then and there to please Sara that night.

Sara was back and even more congested, and Cullen was worried but didn't say anything. Something was definitely wrong, but she didn't know what and certainly couldn't force Sara to tell her if she wasn't ready. She pushed back from the table.

"I've had enough," she said. "I'll go wash my plate and will meet you in the living room?"

"I'll get your plate. You go relax."

"But you cooked. I'd feel bad if you did the dishes as well."

"Nonsense. You worked all day. I didn't. You just help yourself to a beer and I'll meet you in front of the TV."

Cullen didn't argue. A beer sounded good. Hell, anything to wash away the taste of that dinner would do. She turned on the television and watched reruns of her favorite cop show. She'd watched two episodes when she realized that Sara still wasn't through washing her single plate from dinner.

Cullen went to the kitchen to check on her and get another beer. There were pots and pans all over the counter and Sara was on her hands and knees.

"What are you doing?" Cullen said.

"I decided to clean the cupboards."

"Now? Couldn't you wait until tomorrow or something?"

"Sorry." Sara smiled up at Cullen. "The urge just hit me."

"Would you like some help?" Cullen hoped she'd say no since she'd already worked hard that day and just wanted to relax.

"No, thanks. I'll be through in a little bit."

Cullen grabbed another beer and headed back to the couch. She shook her head in amazement and wondered where Sara got all her energy.

After two more episodes, Cullen was ready for bed. She was beat but had plans for Sara so went into the kitchen to get her.

"Hey, babe, let's go to bed."

Sara looked around the kitchen, which was still a disaster.

"I need to clean the place up. You go on to bed. I'll be in shortly."

"But I might fall asleep if you don't come with me."

"Then fall asleep. I'll wake you when I come in."

"Promise?"

"I promise."

Cullen kissed her good night and climbed into bed. She fought to stay awake, but exhaustion won out. She woke some time later, alone, and checked her phone. It was after two. Where was Sara? She wandered down the hall and saw the light on in the study. Sara was bent over a table with puzzle pieces strewn over it.

"What are you doing?" Cullen wasn't amused.

Sara spun and faced her.

"I couldn't sleep. Puzzles relax me. You don't mind, do you?"

She was acting weird again. It wasn't the first time she'd stayed up later than Cullen. Cullen wondered if they had a problem. Why was Sara avoiding her bed? She exhaled.

"Whatever." She turned off the light. "Just come to bed now please."

Sara walked up and wrapped her arms around Cullen.

"Okay. I'll try to sleep."

They walked down the hall to the master bedroom. Cullen climbed into bed and started to doze, but something didn't seem right. She opened her eyes to see Sara sitting up, eyes wide, staring at her phone.

"What are you doing?" Cullen asked.

"Just scrolling. I'm sorry, but I'm really not sleepy. Would you mind if I turned on the TV?"

"Suit yourself."

Cullen tried to fall back asleep, but she was too tense. Why hadn't Sara wanted to be in bed with her? Why wouldn't she lie down with her? It wasn't right. The anger that had seethed within gave way to fear. Maybe something really was wrong between them. She rolled over and faced Sara, whose eyes were wide and whose mouth was moving. Like she was grinding her teeth only multiplied a hundredfold.

"Are we okay?" Cullen was scared of the answer.

Sara looked genuinely surprised by the question.

"Of course we are, silly. Why would you even ask that?"

Cullen lay on her back and linked her hands behind her head.

"I don't know. It just seems like more and more often you don't want to come to bed with me. And now, when I finally do get you to bed, you won't lie down. I like to hold you, and more, or have you forgotten?"

"Oh, Cullen. Sometimes I can't sleep. It has nothing to do with you, honest. Now you get some sleep. You have to work tomorrow. We'll talk more about it tomorrow evening."

She gave Cullen a perfunctory peck on the lips. Not convinced, but knowing she needed her sleep, Cullen rolled back over and drifted off.

Cullen tried to wake Sara for a little morning fun, but she was dead to the world. She ran her hands all over Sara's body, but was greeted with nothing but snores, loud and deep, like she had a cold. Cullen again worried about the stuffy red nose she'd been seeing lately. Still, if Sara said she was okay, Cullen had to believe her.

The day was long, but it was Friday and Cullen couldn't wait to get home and start her weekend. She was hoping to spend the next day on the couch with Sara snuggled up against her watching football. She loved autumn for so many reasons, not the least of which was college football.

When the day finally ended, Cullen drove home. She smiled to herself. She really thought of Sara's place as her home now. She wondered if they should sell their houses and buy one together. Maybe she'd broach that to Sara, but perhaps it was too soon. She didn't know. Besides, it wasn't something that had to be decided right then.

She pulled into the driveway and waited for the garage door to open. When it did, she noticed that Sara's car wasn't there. Cullen wondered where she could possibly be? Cullen was starving and had hoped Sara would agree to going out to dinner.

Cullen let herself in and was crossing the living room when she saw Sara sitting on the couch with a glass of wine.

"Well, hey there." Cullen smiled and bent to kiss her.

"Hi you. How was your day?"

"Long. Slow. I couldn't wait to get home to you. How was yours?"

"It was okay."

"Just okay?"

"I was on my way to a meeting downtown when my car broke down," Sara said.

"I'm sorry to hear that. Why didn't you call me?"

"I didn't want to disturb you. I called a friend, Robert, and he came and picked me up."

"Where did you have your car towed to? What's wrong with it? When will it be ready?"

"Jeez. What's with the twenty questions?" Sara sounded defensive. What was up with that?

Sara left the room and walked to the kitchen with her empty wineglass. Cullen followed close behind.

"Pardon me for being concerned," Cullen said.

"I'm sorry. I didn't mean to snap. It was just a horrible experience. Let's talk about something else, okay?"

"Sure." She took Sara's glass from her and refilled it before helping herself to a beer. "Let's talk about dinner. I'm starving. Where shall we go?"

Sara laughed and patted Cullen's stomach.

"Food, food, food. I swear you have a one-track mind."

"Au contraire. I have a two-track mind and I'd be easily convinced to put dinner off and head to bed for a while."

Sara laughed again, this one from her belly.

"Okay. You're right. You have mostly a one-track mind."

They settled on the couch with their drinks. Cullen draped an arm over Sara's shoulders.

"So which will it be? Sex or food?"

Before Sara could answer, there was a knock on the door.

"Who are you expecting?" Cullen asked.

"No one. What about you?"

"Not a soul. Sit tight. I'll get rid of them."

Cullen glanced through the peephole then backed away. It couldn't be. She looked again. It sure looked like Julia Stansworth, the girl Cullen had crushed on hard all through high school. Sure, she was older now. Who wasn't? But the blond hair and piercing blue eyes brought back tortured memories. Cullen opened the door.

"Julia?"

"Cullen? Cullen Matthews? What are you doing here?"

"I belong here. I think the question is, what are you doing here?"

"You belong here?" Julia's expression hardened. "As in you live here?"

"Sort of. Not exactly. How can I help you?"

Julia reached into her jacket pocket and pulled out what looked like a leather wallet, opened it, and showed Cullen her badge.

"Actually, it's Detective Stansworth and I'm here to speak with a Sara Donovan. Is she in?"

"What do you want with her?"

"Is she in?" Julia repeated.

"Sure, come on in."

Cullen stood back and let Julia enter.

"Would you like something to drink?" Cullen said.

"This isn't a social visit."

"Fair enough. Have a seat and tell us why you're here."

Cullen glanced over at Sara who'd gone ashen. She quickly recovered, though.

"Yes, Detective," Sara said. "How can we help you?"

"Tell me how you knew Donald Montague."

"Who?" Sara asked.

Cullen looked between them. Julia's eyes were hard now. She looked pissed.

"I've never heard of him," Sara said.

"We both know you're lying, so save us all a lot of time and tell me how you knew him."

"Who's Donald Montague?" Cullen asked.

"Ask your girlfriend."

Cullen turned to Sara.

"Sara? Who is he?"

"I have no idea."

Julia opened her briefcase.

"I thought you looked familiar when I saw you at the station this afternoon but couldn't put my finger on why."

"Wait," Cullen said. "Station? What station?"

"We'll talk about it later," Sara said.

"No, I want to know now. And who is this Montague man and why is Julia asking you about him?"

"She didn't tell you?" Julia's eyes glimmered. "She was brought in for possession with intent to distribute and a DUI."

"What?" Cullen felt like she'd been punched in the gut. What the hell was going on?

Sara sank back against the couch. Cullen stared at her in disbelief, but Sara wouldn't meet her gaze.

"And Montague?" Cullen said.

"He was a two-bit coke dealer for some of the fraternities and sororities downtown," Julia said.

"Did you supply him?" Cullen asked Sara.

"I'm telling you I've never heard of him."

Julia handed Sara a folder she'd removed from her briefcase. "Take a look at these."

Sara opened the folder and went pale. Cullen walked over to see photos of Sara with some young guy.

"Is that Montague?" she asked.

"Yes," Julia said. "And quite obviously Sara with him."

"Quite obviously." Cullen glared at Sara.

"I didn't know his last name. I only knew him as Donnie."

"Well, whatever you knew him as, he was being investigated for selling the cocaine that killed another college student. I'm sure you read about that, where the kid overdosed at the fraternity house?"

Cullen nodded. She remembered reading the story online.

"We were so close to getting him to finger his supplier and then he ends up dead. Coincidence?" Sarcasm dripped from Julia's words.

"I didn't kill him." Sara sounded panicked.

"I'm not sure I believe you," Julia said.

Cullen slowly backed away from Sara and lowered herself into the chair.

"Sara…" But she didn't have the ability to put her thoughts into words. Sara was a drug dealer? And a murder suspect? It was all too much for her to absorb.

Julia stood over Sara.

"These pictures were taken right before he was shot," she said.

"I didn't shoot him."

"No, you couldn't have. The bullet came from the other direction. But someone snuck into his hospital room and finished him off. You had a lot to lose, Ms. Donovan."

Sara shook her head violently.

"I didn't. I had nothing to do with that."

"Say I believe you," Julia said. "Let's just suppose for one crazy minute I think you're telling the truth. If you didn't do it, you know who did. I can help get your sentences lightened for the two charges you're facing now if you help me."

"I swear, I'd help you if I could, but I don't know anything."

Julia took the folder back from Sara and slid it back in her briefcase.

"You're not making this any easier on yourself," she said.

"Please. You have to believe me."

"See? That's just it. I don't have to do any such thing."

CHAPTER TWO

Julia headed back to downtown Portland to her bungalow just off Hawthorne. She had a lot on her mind. Donovan was guilty of something, that was certain. But just how innocent was Cullen? Julia had been shocked when she'd opened the door. Julia didn't like the idea that someone she'd known since high school was involved with dealing drugs. But after talking to them together, Julia was fairly certain Cullen had been oblivious to Sara's activities.

But had Sara actually killed Montague? Julia believed in her heart of hearts that she had. As she'd told them, either she'd done it or she knew who had. How was Julia going to prove one way or the other?

She drove past her exit and kept going until she came to the station. She locked herself in her office and began poring over the tapes from the night Montague died again. The hospital had handed over all the security footage, but none of it had been helpful. Still, she went over it again in hopes of seeing Sara.

Julia watched as their main suspect came into view. Whoever it was wore baggy sweatpants and an oversized hoodie. There was no way to discern the gender of the person on the film.

She froze the film and stared hard at it. How tall was the person on the film? How tall was Sara? She'd been sitting down the whole time Julia had been there, so she didn't get an accurate height assessment. But she was leggy, very leggy, and sat up high on the couch. Julia guesstimated she was about five ten.

So how tall was the person she was looking at? About the same, she imagined. Now, more than ever, she was convinced Sara had been the mystery woman who was guilty of killing Montague. It was time to prove it.

The next morning, Julia drove back to Sara and Cullen's house. She felt like a dog with a bone and she wasn't about to let go. This time when she knocked on the door, it was Sara who answered. Sara, who in her bare feet looked to be exactly the height she'd calculated. She was wearing baggy sweats and looked like she hadn't slept much. Her nose was red and her pupils dilated. She'd probably been snorting coke all night.

"Can I come in?" Julia said.

"Why?"

"I have more questions for you."

"This really isn't a good time."

"Sorry for the inconvenience." She couldn't keep the sarcasm out of her voice as she pushed her way inside.

Cullen came out then. She looked rough, but not like Sara. Cullen had apparently gotten some sleep the night before anyway.

"Good morning, Julia." Cullen sounded like she was greeting an old friend. "Welcome back. To what do we owe the pleasure?"

Sara spun toward Cullen.

"How dare you? This woman is trying to ruin our lives and you greet her like some long-lost friend?"

"I'm just being civil. Now, come on, let's all go to the living room."

"You two enjoy your chat," Sara said. She turned to her left and took the stairs two at a time.

"I take it she won't be cooperating today?" Julia smiled at Cullen.

"Apparently not."

"I'll wait her out."

"You want to wait in the kitchen? There's fresh coffee there."

Julia was torn. Again, it wasn't a social visit. But coffee with Cullen didn't sound like a bad way to pass the time.

"Sure, coffee sounds good as I may be here a while."

"You may indeed."

Julia sat down and doctored the coffee Cullen set in front of her. She thought long and hard about her next words, but finally figured she'd better ask.

"So, Cullen, you seemed a little surprised to find out that Sara had been arrested yesterday."

"Arrested, a drug dealer, and a suspect in a murder investigation. To say I was surprised is an understatement."

"So you're not into cocaine at all?" She held her breath. Why? She didn't know, but knowing that Cullen was clean was somehow vitally important to her.

"Never done it myself. Never have and never will."

"Good answer. How'd you get mixed up with Ms. Donovan anyway?"

"We used to eat dinner at the same Chinese restaurant. Like every Friday night. We'd each be there eating alone, and one night she asked if she could join me. The rest, as they say, is history."

Julia absorbed the information as she sipped her coffee. She nodded slowly.

"And now?" she said.

"Now what?"

"I mean, now that you know about her? Will you stay with her?"

"Look, Julia…is it okay if I call you Julia?"

"Sure."

"Thanks. I'm not happy to hear I'm involved with a drug dealer, but I truly believe she can get help for that."

"And her involvement with the Montague murder?"

"Sara may have made some poor decisions, but I don't believe she's involved with murder."

"Can't believe? Or won't?"

"Can't. She's a gentle soul. Trust me."

"I wish I could."

"And outside of a few pics of her with the victim, what other evidence do you have?"

"I'm working on that," Julia said.

"Where did you get those pictures anyway? Have the cops been following Sara for a while?"

"No such thing. A sorority girl who had a crush on Montague was taking pictures of them that morning. She gave them to us as part of the investigation." Cullen nodded but didn't say anything. "Right after she took them, shots rang out and Montague crumpled to the ground. You want to know what your girlfriend did?"

"What?"

"She jumped in her car and sped off. Didn't check to see if he was okay or not, she just gunned it. Probably figured nobody would ever link the two of them."

"Hm."

"Sorry to be the bearer of bad tidings."

"Yeah, as great as it is to see you after all this time, I'm not really enjoying seeing you."

"I hear you," Julia said. "I sure wish the circumstances were different."

"As do I. You want me to see if I can get Sara to come downstairs now?"

"I'd appreciate that."

Julia helped herself to another cup of coffee while she waited. And she pondered. If Cullen wasn't involved in Sara's coke dealing, what did she do? Did she have a decent job? Did she make good money? Or did Sara support her and Cullen just not care about where the money came from?

Cullen was back without Sara.

"No luck, huh?" Julia said.

Cullen shook her head.

"I'm really sorry."

"I'd hate to have to get a warrant and search the house."

"I think we'd hate that, too."

"Yes. You definitely would." She didn't make a move to leave. She still had a cup of coffee and was really enjoying her time with Cullen. "Have a seat, Cullen. Let's give her a little more time."

"Are you sure?"

Julia smiled.

"I'm sure."

Cullen poured another cup of coffee and sat across from her at the table.

"So, what have you been doing with yourself, Cullen? I mean, outside of eating Chinese food and getting involved with criminals? What's kept you busy all these years?"

"I work for an ad agency," she said. "I've been with the Logan and Bremer agency for almost twenty years now."

Julia breathed a sigh of relief. So Cullen was an upstanding citizen after all. Still, Julia would run a background check on her. She had to know for sure.

"Do you enjoy it?" Julia said.

"I love it. It's a dream job. I wouldn't trade it for anything."

"That's great." She grew serious. "You know, Cullen, if you know anything at all about the murder, you need to tell me or you'll be an accessory."

"I don't know anything other than what I've read. I swear."

Before Julia could respond, Sara came into the kitchen. Julia's stomach turned at the sight of her. She had no use for criminals. No use whatsoever. Especially not murderers.

"I'm here," Sara said. "What do you want?"

"Where were you on the afternoon of October twenty-seventh?"

"How should I know?"

Julia watched as Sara poured herself a glass of wine. She arched an eyebrow at Cullen.

"It's a little early for wine, isn't it?" Cullen said.

"It's never too early if the cops are in my house."

"Think hard," Julia said. "Where were you?"

Sara sat at the table and stared into space. Julia assumed she was thinking, trying to remember, but after a few minutes, she interrupted her daydreaming.

"Sara?"

"Hm? Oh yeah. I don't know."

"That's not much of an alibi."

"What day of the week was it?"

"A Friday."

"I was probably with Cullen," Sara said.

"Cullen?" Julia said. "I would imagine she'd have been at work."

"I'm telling you. I don't remember."

"And I'm telling you to think harder. You better come up with an alibi and fast, for your own good."

Julia stood and Cullen did the same.

"I'll be back, Ms. Donovan. That's a promise."

Cullen walked Julia to the door.

"It was good to see you again," Cullen said. "I mean...well, you know what I mean."

"Right. If you can think of anything that might help either one of us, please call me." Julia extended her hand and their fingers met when Cullen took the proffered business card. Maybe they stayed like that too long. Julia wasn't sure. She extracted her hand, turned away, and got in her car.

Cullen went back into the house and found Sara filling her wineglass again.

"Are you going to drink the day away?" she said.

"What else should I do?"

"Talk to me."

"About?"

"Don't be that way, Sara. You locked yourself in the office as soon as Julia left last night—"

"Julia? *Julia*? What is she? Your best friend or something?"

"Sorry. Detective Stansworth, whatever. You locked yourself away as soon as she left. I think you owe me an explanation."

"For what?"

"Gee, let's see... Maybe the fact that you were arrested yesterday and weren't going to tell me?"

"I didn't want you involved."

"But I am," Cullen said.

"Not in that part of my life you're not, and I figured it was better that way."

"Well, at least it explains why you didn't call me when your car mysteriously broke down. How'd you get home from the police station?"

"My attorney, Robert, gave me a ride."

"Fair enough. So you're a coke dealer, huh? Do you do anything with entrepreneurs? Or is that all a big lie?"

"It's my cover. I needed to have some way to explain my money to you."

Cullen ran her hand through her hair and paced the kitchen.

"Wow. So this house, your car, anything you've bought me? All paid for by drug money, huh?"

"I make good money," Sara said quietly.

"I guess you do. And what about that college kid?"

Sara's eyes teared up.

"I had nothing to do with his death," Sara said. "You've got to believe me."

"I want to, Sara, I really do. But our whole relationship has been built on a lie. Where do those lies end? How can I trust you?"

"You can trust me. I've never lied to you."

"Uh, coke dealer?"

"That was an omission."

"Same difference. And your story of having a job?"

"A little white lie. I didn't know how you'd feel about drugs. I still don't know."

Cullen stopped pacing and turned to stare at Sara.

"So, all those nights you wouldn't come to bed? Last night? You were snorting coke all night?"

"I do have a bit of a habit. But I can quit if I need to, I promise."

Cullen let out a long breath.

"God, this is just so much to try to take in."

Sara got out of her seat and wrapped her arms around Cullen. Cullen didn't return the gesture. She couldn't.

"Sara, please."

"What?"

"Just don't." She unwrapped Sara's arms and took a step back.

"Don't reject me, Cullen. Please don't reject me. I need you now more than ever."

Cullen collapsed into a chair at the table. Sara sat across from her.

"You saw that kid get shot," Cullen said. "And you just left. He could have died."

"I was scared. What if I got shot? How would you like that? I didn't know who they were shooting at."

The dangerous side of Sara's job hit Cullen like a ton of bricks. There were wars between drug dealers. People tried to take out rival dealers on a regular basis. Was Sara in danger all the time?

"Did you really believe someone was shooting at you?" It was all too much to comprehend.

Sara broke eye contact and looked away.

"I didn't know. How could I have known? And I sure as hell wasn't going to hang around to find out."

"Did you visit Montague in the hospital?"

"Is that your way of asking me if I killed him? And his name was Donnie, not Montague."

"Donnie, Montague, whatever. The poor kid who'll never live to see his full potential. Did you visit him in the hospital?"

"No, I thought about it, but figured I'd caused enough problems for the poor guy."

Cullen nodded thoughtfully. Then she had another question.

"And when I read to you about the other kid? The one that OD'd at that frat party? You could have said something then."

"What?" Sara said. "What did you want me to say? Oh, by the way, I'm ninety-nine percent sure I sold the coke that killed him? Is that what you wanted me to say?"

"I don't know." Cullen struggled not to raise her voice. "A little heads-up would have been nice. So the police went after Donnie?"

"Yep. Cops were crawling all over him. I provided him with my attorney and told him to keep his mouth shut, but he was getting scared and thinking of naming his source."

"You."

"Me."

Cullen felt a chill creep up her spine. So Sara definitely had a motive for wanting to kill the guy. But did she do it? She swore she didn't, and Cullen tended to believe her. She had been honest when she told Julia she didn't see Sara as a murderer. She wouldn't hurt a fly, of that Cullen was certain.

"Let's go get breakfast." Cullen stood.

"I'm not hungry. I think I want to take a nap."

"You do that. I'm going out. I need to think, to clear my head. I'll be back."

She got in her truck and drove to her favorite diner. It was after eleven by then, so she ordered a chili burger and sat sipping more coffee.

Cullen reached into the pocket of her jeans and slid out Julia's card. She turned it over in her fingers. She had no more information. She had no reason to call her. She slid the card back in her pocket. She should hate Julia. Detective Stansworth. She should be angry at her for trying to pin a murder on Sara when Cullen knew she was innocent, so why wasn't she? Why was she looking forward to seeing her again, regardless of the circumstances?

CHAPTER THREE

Monday morning arrived and Julia was in her office rereading every report she could find on the Montague shooting and subsequent murder. He'd been in the hospital for two days when he'd been killed. Whoever had done it had been smart. They'd adjusted his morphine IV so he overdosed. They'd gotten in, opened it up, and left before he flatlined to avoid any suspicion. And no one at the hospital remembered seeing anyone entering or leaving his room.

Did the person in the video have scrubs on under their sweats? Were they able to fit in? To look like they worked there? How the hell could no one have seen anything? She was frustrated beyond words. She needed to catch a break. And then she got an idea.

That afternoon, Julia drove back to the hospital armed with the photos she had of Sara. Now that she knew who she was and how she was associated with the young victim, she could show her picture to the different nurses and attendants. Surely someone had seen her that fateful afternoon.

She approached the nurses' station on the sixth floor and showed her badge.

"What can we do for you, Detective?"

"I have some pictures of some suspects I'd like the nurses to look at. I'd like to know if anyone remembers seeing her here before."

The nurse buzzed Julia in. Julia took out the photos and showed them to the nurses who were busy charting.

"Let me know if any of these women look familiar to any of you, please. Pass them around."

Everyone took their time looking at the pictures, but one by one, they shook their heads.

"Isn't this the boy that was murdered here?" a nurse asked.

"Yes, that's him. And these are persons of interest, but that's all I can say."

"I wish I could help you, Detective, but they don't look even remotely familiar."

Damn. Julia had had such high hopes someone would remember seeing Sara.

"Thanks anyway."

She gathered the photos and went back to the station. She pulled up the video from the hospital again and froze it when she saw the person in sweats appear on the screen. The photos she had of Sara were mostly from the shoulders up as she was leaning on her open car door talking to Montague, but there was one full body pic, and she held it up next to the frozen frame. Try as she might, she couldn't be sure it was Sara on the hospital video. Sure, it could have been her, but then, it could have been anybody.

How had someone been able to slip into the kid's room unnoticed? Where had his family been? His friends? Anyone? How had he been left alone and how would someone have known he'd be by himself?

Unless someone sat in the waiting room watching the room. That had to have been what happened. But surely someone would have noticed that, right?

It wasn't making any sense. She had other cases that needed her attention, but this was the one she wanted to solve. Montague was killed because he was about to finger his supplier. She would have bet her life on that. And now that she knew who that was, she just had to find a way to put two and two together. But how?

Cullen Matthews. Somehow she'd help nail Sara, Julia was certain. Maybe not intentionally, but if she could trip her up, she'd spill the beans. She grabbed her coat and drove downtown.

The ad agency of Logan and Bremer was on the corner of Southwest Fifth and Stark, in an old building that had been renovated on the inside while keeping the old façade from the eighteen hundreds.

She read the directory in the lobby to learn which floor she'd find Cullen on and rode the posh elevator with green leather up to the fifth floor. She walked up to the receptionist.

"I'm looking for Cullen Matthews. Is she in?"

"Is she expecting you?"

"No. I'm an old friend and I'm here to surprise her." It wasn't exactly a lie.

"I'm really sorry," the receptionist said. "She's in a meeting right now."

"I'll wait."

Julia sat in a wingback chair in the reception area. It wasn't uncomfortable, really, but it certainly wasn't the most comfortable chair she'd ever sat in. It was bright blue to match the blue and red decor in the office. She slid her laptop out of its case and, glad her back was to the wall for confidentiality reasons, opened her files on Montague.

Sara had said she'd been with Cullen when Julia had originally asked her where she'd been. Had Cullen had that day off? Could Cullen provide Sara with a much-needed alibi? Julia shook her head. She was getting ahead of herself. Sara didn't need an alibi. Not yet, anyway. Soon maybe. Hopefully.

Julia was lost in her studies of the hooded person from the hospital when she was interrupted.

"You wanted to see me?" There was no ignoring the chill in Cullen's voice.

Julia stood.

"Great to see you again, Cullen. Do you have an office or somewhere we can talk?"

"I have an office, but I don't have much time. Come on back, but make it quick."

"Will do." Julia slid her laptop back into its case and followed Cullen down the hall to a large office. Cullen sat behind the mahogany desk and Julia took a chair across from her.

One wall of her office was covered in plaques and certificates.

"You look like you do good work," Julia said.

"I'm one of the best."

Julia arched an eyebrow. Had Cullen grown arrogant? Or was she simply confident? And why did it matter?

"What do you need?" Cullen said. "Or is this a social visit?"

"Unfortunately, no. This is a business visit."

"Okay. What do you want from me?"

"I need to know, Cullen. Did you take October twenty-seventh off work? It was the Friday before Halloween. Did you get a head start on the holiday?"

Cullen leaned back in her chair and laced her fingers behind her head.

"That's important, isn't it?"

Julia stared at her for a minute.

"Very. And, again, I'll remind you this is a murder investigation. Lying could make you an accessory."

"Sara didn't kill Donnie," Cullen said.

"Donnie?"

"Montague. Yes, she knew him. No, she didn't kill him."

"How can you be so sure?"

"I know her," Cullen said. "I know her very well. She's not a killer."

"You didn't know she was a coke dealer did you?"

Cullen shook her head slowly.

"No. I didn't know that."

"So you don't really know what she's capable of. Isn't that the truth?"

"I know she couldn't hurt, much less kill, another human being."

Julia could appreciate Cullen's loyalty, misguided though it was.

"You haven't answered my question."

"What was the date again?"

"October twenty-seventh."

"No, I didn't take it off. I love Halloween but didn't request extra time off for the holiday."

"So you don't know where Sara was all that day, do you?"

"No."

Julia barely heard Cullen's whispered answer. She started to stand.

"Wait," Cullen said.

"What?" Julia sat back down. "I thought you didn't have much time."

"Julia, you have to believe me. Sara's not the murderer."

"She's got the motive and the opportunity. She's looking pretty good in my book."

"Motive? What motive?"

"You know as well as I do," Julia said. "Montague was going to finger Sara as his dealer. She couldn't have that, so she killed him."

"You can't really believe that."

"Yes, I can."

Cullen thought back to Halloween weekend. She and Sara hadn't been seeing each other very long. Some of Cullen's friends were having a Halloween party Saturday night. Sara had suggested they go as a gangster and moll. She remembered meeting Sara for dinner at the House of Good Fortune that Friday night. How had Sara been? Had she been distant? Subdued?

All Cullen could remember was Sara's excitement at having found the perfect costumes for the two of them. She'd eaten a normal dinner, so she clearly hadn't been upset about anything. If she'd just killed someone, surely she'd have been remorseful. She'd have lost her appetite or something, right?

"I don't know." Cullen brought herself back to the present. "I saw her that night after work and she seemed normal. I can't imagine she'd have wanted to meet for dinner if she'd just killed somebody."

"Killers are cold-blooded creatures."

"See? Sara's warm, caring. Anything but cold-blooded."

"Tell me about that night."

"We had dinner then went back to my place. There's nothing more to tell."

"And the rest of the weekend?"

"I guess she seemed fine."

"What did you do?" Julia said.

"Let's see. I remember dressing in my double-breasted suit and fedora and picking her up. She was wearing a black flapper dress and looked adorable. We headed to a friend's house for a party." Cullen smiled at the memory.

"And at the party? How did she act?"

Cullen exhaled as she thought back.

"She was fine. She saw some people she knew. She would disappear with them for a while, then come back out to where I was hanging out on the porch. Um…then we went inside and danced for a while. She was all smiles, like she was really having fun."

"Was there food? Did she still have her appetite? Or had guilt settled in?"

Cullen remembered the buffet that she'd enjoyed. Sara had said she wasn't hungry. But Sara often wasn't hungry, which Cullen now attributed to her coke habit.

"Cullen?" Julia prodded her.

"She didn't eat. But for all I know, she might have been doing coke. I mean, that would make sense, right?"

"Sure, it would. Or she might have been dealing with guilt."

Cullen reminisced some more about the end of the night, when she'd told Sara people would be asking her questions about her, and Sara had asked what she'd say. Cullen had told her she would tell them Sara was her new lady. Sara hadn't responded right away. Why was that? She'd finally said that would be great, but it sure had taken her a while. Now Cullen wondered if Sara was thinking about protecting her. She shook her head. She was being ridiculous. Julia was planting illogical thoughts in her head.

"She sure wasn't acting guilty," Cullen said. "She seemed to be having fun. Honest, good, down-to-earth, innocent fun."

"I think you're blinded to the truth. How long have you two been seeing each other?"

"About five weeks or so."

"So you don't truly know her, do you?"

"I know her well enough."

"Cullen, I'm asking you as a friend. Please be careful with Sara."

"There's nothing to be careful about. Thanks for trying to watch out for me, but I can handle my life. And my life includes Sara. She may be a coke fiend, but she is not a murderer. Now, if you'll excuse me, I've got work to do."

Julia rose.

"I'll see myself out."

Cullen couldn't concentrate after Julia left. She tried to lose herself in her work but couldn't do it. She didn't need to be there. She needed to be with Sara. She called and Sara answered on the first ring.

"Hello?"

"Hey, babe. How does Chinese for a late lunch sound?"

"Aren't you working?"

"I think I'm going to take the afternoon off. You want to meet me?"

"I don't have a car, remember? Why don't you come pick me up?"

"I'll be right there."

Cullen disconnected and checked out for the afternoon. She got on I-5 which was a parking lot. Her stomach growled, and she told herself to be patient. She'd be home soon. It took forty-five minutes to go the twenty miles to Sara's house, but she got there and found Sara sitting on the porch swing.

It was a beautiful sunny day in Bidwell. It was crisp but nice, and Sara looked beautiful sitting there in her jeans and black sweater. She came down the step and got in Cullen's truck.

"You look amazing." Cullen leaned over and kissed Sara.

"So do you. But then, you always do."

"Thank you. You hungry?"

"I am."

Cullen drove to the House of Good Fortune, but it didn't look open. She parked her truck.

"You wait here. I'm going to go see what's up."

"Be careful, Cullen. That looks like police tape."

Cullen walked up to the front door. It was indeed covered in police tape; crime scene, it said. She put her hands on the door so she could see inside and there were cops crawling all over the place.

"Back away," a male voice said. "This is a crime scene."

"So I see." Cullen stepped back and turned to see a man who looked to be in his mid fifties with a pot belly and tight sport coat approaching. "What's going on?"

"You ever been here before?"

"I come here all the time."

The man handed her a card.

"I'm Detective Magnell. My partner Silverton and I are working the case. This place was big in drug trafficking. You mind if I ask you a few questions?"

Cullen felt a knot in the pit of her stomach. Drug trafficking? Was that why this was Sara's favorite restaurant? She thought back to the odd fortune she'd gotten there one night about a week before she and Sara had started seeing each other. It had said, "The drop will be at Mayfields at seven o'clock on the tenth."

Mayfields was a popular department store downtown. What sort of drop had they been talking about and, more importantly, who was the message for? Clearly, there had been some mix-up, she'd thought at the time. She remembered now that Sara had been waiting for a to-go order as well. Had the message been for her? Had it been about cocaine?

"Ma'am?" Magnell said. "You with me?"

"I'm sorry. Sure, I'll answer any questions you have."

"Have you ever seen any shady looking characters hanging around the place? Anybody who looked out of place?"

"No, sir."

"What about suits? Overdressed people? I don't mean just your regular Joe coming in after work, I mean, jewels, the works."

Cullen shook her head.

"I never saw anyone who looked like that here. Everyone seemed so normal. And their food was delicious. Maybe you guys have made some mistake?"

"No mistake, ma'am. Now, can I get your information for my records?"

Cullen gave him her full name, address, and phone number. He thanked her for her time and she walked back out to where Sara waited. Cullen had so many questions she didn't know where to start, but she knew she had to find out if Sara was involved.

"What's going on?" Sara said. "Who were you talking to? Why the police tape?"

"Apparently, they were running drugs out of the restaurant. You wouldn't know anything about that, would you?"

Sara turned in her seat so she faced Cullen.

"Of course not!"

"Okay. Just checking."

"Cullen, not all drug dealers know each other."

"I'm not saying they do. I'm just thinking you spend an awful lot of time here."

"I love their food, and you spend a lot of time here, too, yet you don't see me accusing you of being a drug runner."

"I didn't accuse you. I merely asked."

"Same same."

"Whatever. You can't blame me for being suspicious."

"Look, I made a mistake. Can we please just put this behind us?"

Cullen didn't answer. She wished she could move on but didn't know if she honestly could.

"You know, I once got a weird fortune cookie from here. I wonder if I should tell the cops about it."

"Weird? How so?"

"It said something about a drop. I wonder if it was referring to drugs. Wait here. I'll go tell them."

Sara grabbed her arm. Hard.

"I wouldn't bother them. When did that happen?"

"A few weeks ago."

"Then they probably know all about it. Come on, Cullen, let's get out of here."

CHAPTER FOUR

I'm still hungry and I still want Chinese," Cullen said when they arrived back at Sara's house.

"Well, we're still in the car. Why don't we go someplace else?"

"Because no place else in town is as good as the House of Good Fortune. And I don't feel like driving into the city or anything."

"How about Mexican?"

"Fine. Let's go."

They drove to their favorite Mexican restaurant in a nearby strip mall. It was decorated in brightly colored Mexican folk art and made Cullen think they should get away. Maybe hit the Mexican Riviera where they could forget their problems. Then she remembered that Sara wouldn't be allowed to go anywhere anytime soon.

How much time did one have to spend in prison for dealing cocaine? She'd have to look that up. She wasn't looking forward to being apart from Sara that long. Sara in prison? Could it really happen? Yes. It could and it would. Would Cullen have what it took to visit her? Would she even be close enough to visit? Would Cullen be strong enough to stay faithful to her during the length of her sentence? And why did Detective Julia Stansworth just pop into her head?

"Are you okay?" Sara reached across the table and took Cullen's hand. "You're awfully quiet."

"Rough day."

"Yeah? Is that why you came home early? What happened? Talk to me."

"If you must know," Cullen said, "Julia came by my office to question me today."

"Julia?" Sara's eyes hardened. "You mean that busybody detective?"

"The very same."

"Why do you insist on treating her as a friend?"

"I don't."

"You do. You act like it's a treat when she comes to visit."

"No, I don't, Sara," Cullen said. "She's trying to railroad you. I don't consider that something a friend does."

"Still, you get all puppy dog eyes whenever she shows up."

"I do not. Sara, drop it. We have enough problems right now without accusing me of something like that."

"Look, I really am sorry about my legal problems. I'd understand if you didn't want to see me anymore."

"Listen to me. I'm committed to you. I'll ride this whole thing out with you."

"It's my first count," Sara said. "I'll probably get off easy."

"I hope so." Cullen was tired of talking about it. They were in public and she had no idea how many ears were listening. "So, what would you like for dinner?"

"A margarita or three or four."

Cullen laughed.

"I'll get a pitcher."

"Or two."

"Or two."

"You go ahead and order. I need to use the restroom."

Cullen had poured them each a glass by the time Sara came out. Cullen didn't miss her wide pupils and the residue around her nostril.

"Wipe your nose." Cullen was disgusted. "Can't you lay off that stuff even for a little while?"

"I'm stressed and it calms me."

"It's an upper. It can't calm you. Whatever. The waitress will be back in a minute to take our order. Unless you were serious about drinking dinner."

"I'll get food. I'm hungry."

"Right."

"Cullen?"

"What?"

"I'll quit if it's that important to you."

"It is that important to me. I don't know that we'd ever have gotten together if I'd known you had that habit."

Sara's eyebrows shot up.

"Really?"

"Really. Look, it's not something I've ever been into. So I don't understand it."

"Maybe if you tried some…"

"What the fuck? Seriously? Don't ever suggest that again."

"Fine."

They ate their dinner in silence. Cullen was fuming, and no amount of margaritas was going to calm her down. They finished their second pitcher and Cullen paid. They left the restaurant and walked separately to Cullen's truck. Once inside, Sara turned to look at her.

"Cullen, please talk to me. I can't handle the silent treatment."

"You were out of line back there."

"I'm sorry. It was just a suggestion. One I won't make again. Please don't give me the cold shoulder anymore."

"Not only do I not want you pushing coke on me, I want you to quit doing it. Can you do that?"

"I can and I will. For you."

"Thank you."

Cullen started the truck and drove home. Once in the house, she headed for the refrigerator, as she wanted beer, lots of beer. She cringed when she felt Sara pressing into her back.

"What do you say we go to bed early?" Sara whispered.

Cullen pulled away.

"I'm not in the mood, Sara."

"What? How can you say that? You're always in the mood."

"Yeah? Well, I'm not now."

"I'll go put on something a little more comfortable and then we'll see."

Cullen took a long pull off her beer and listened to Sara's footsteps on the stairs. She didn't care what Sara put on, she wasn't going to make love to her. The timing wasn't right and it would take her a while to get over Sara suggesting she try cocaine. Did she want her to get hooked so she could make money off her? Her stomach roiled. She couldn't remember the last time she'd been that angry. What a day. What a lousy, fucked up day.

True to her word, Sara came downstairs wearing a cobalt blue baby doll nightie. Cullen had to admit, she looked like a million bucks. She was also sniffling, and Cullen knew she'd just snorted more cocaine. Sara tried to snuggle against her on the couch, but Cullen didn't want to be that close to her. She stood.

"I'll get you a glass of wine."

Cullen stormed into the kitchen and poured Sara another glass of wine before helping herself to another beer. She walked back out to the living room and handed Sara her glass. She took her beer and sat in the recliner.

"Why are you sitting way over there?" Sara pouted.

"I need some space."

"And yet you're here. You could easily go to your place if you need so much space."

"Is that what you want?" Cullen said.

"No. Is it what you want?"

"I don't know. I don't think so. Just don't throw yourself at me. Not tonight, please."

"What do you want from me, Cullen?"

"I want you to get clean. I want you to allow us to get back to normal."

"Look, I'm sorry I got caught. If I'd had my way, you never would have known about my business ventures."

"No? So you would have continued a relationship based on lies?"

"Why do you have to put it that way?" Sara said.

"Because that's the way it is." She stood and placed her bottle on the coffee table. "You know what? I'm out of here. Turns out you were right. I need more space."

Sara reached for her hand.

"Cullen. Don't go."

"I'll see you tomorrow. I'll come over after work or I'll text you. Good night."

Julia pulled up in front of Sara's house. She really didn't have anything new to ask her, and yet there she was, ringing the doorbell.

Sara opened the door looking almost excited, but her face fell when she saw Julia.

"You were expecting someone else?" Julia said.

"Yes. What do you want?"

"Can I come in?"

"Do I have a choice? Look, this is a really bad time. Cullen and I just had a fight and I'm not really in the mood to deal with you."

Julia took in the wide pupils and clenched jaw. Clearly, Sara was coked up again. She wondered, and hoped, that that was the reason she and Cullen had fought.

"Fine. I won't keep you. Just tell me this, do you have an alibi yet?"

"I'm still working on it."

"Work harder. And faster."

Sara closed the door in her face before Julia could ask where Cullen lived. No biggie. She'd look her up in the database. Not that she knew what questions she was going to ask, but the fact that she and Cullen had just had a fight might make her more vulnerable. Maybe she'd open up and say some negative things about Sara that might help Julia in her case.

She found Cullen's house and parked in the driveway. Her porch didn't have much of an overhang, and Julia knew she was going to get drenched waiting for her. Oh well. A little rain never hurt anybody.

Julia knocked on the door. There was no answer. The rain pummeled her and she thought about giving up, but she really wanted to question Cullen while she was still mad. She rang the doorbell again but still got no answer.

She fumbled in her pocket, pulled out her cell, and called Cullen.

"Hello?"

"Cullen? It's Julia. I'm on your doorstep and it's pissing down. Would you please open the door?"

The line went dead, and a few moments later Cullen opened the door.

"Sorry about that. I thought you were someone else."

"Like Sara?"

"Yeah. Come on in. I'll get you a towel and some sweats. We can dry your wet clothes while we chat."

"That would be great, thanks. It's really coming down out there."

"Welcome to Oregon in the fall."

"No doubt."

Cullen disappeared down the hallway and returned with gray sweatpants and an Oregon Duck hoodie. She motioned for Julia to follow her and led her to a large bathroom.

"The towels are in there." Cullen pointed to a cabinet. "Help yourself."

"Thanks."

She changed out of her wet clothes and hung them over the shower rod to dry. She went to the living room to find Cullen holding two beers.

"I know it's not a social call, but you look like you could use a beer."

"I'll gladly take it and we can turn it into a social call, I don't care. After I ask you a few questions anyway."

Cullen lowered herself onto the black couch and Julia sat in the leather recliner.

"So you and Sara had a fight, huh?" Julia said.

"Is that what she told you?"

"Yes."

"It wasn't really a fight. Look, I really don't want to talk about it."

"Ah, but I have to know. What did you fight about?"

"Let's just say my reaction to her arrest is less nonchalant than hers."

Julia raised her eyebrows.

"Her attitude is nonchalant?"

"Yeah. She seems to think it's no biggie."

"How much coke does she usually do?" Julia asked.

"Who says she does any? Maybe she's just a dealer."

"I've been a cop long enough to know the symptoms of cocaine use. Her pupils were like saucers tonight, she kept clenching her jaw, and her nose was red. How much does she do?"

"I have no idea. I wouldn't even know how to hazard a guess."

"Did she say anything about Montague? Because I'm sure confessing to murder would have been grounds for you to leave her."

To Julia's surprise, Cullen laughed, showing off two deep dimples in her cheeks. Cullen wasn't bad looking. She should smile more. All she ever did was sneer at Julia though.

"Nice try, but no, she swears she's innocent."

"Yet she has no one to corroborate her story."

"True statement. You ready for another beer?"

"Not yet, but go ahead and get one. I'll wait."

"No, I'm the one who'll wait. I don't need to pound them. Especially since I've got company now."

"Is that what I am?"

"Sure. You said we could chat while your clothes dry. Just let me know when your interrogation is over."

It was Julia's turn to laugh. Cullen was so easy to be around. She did a mental run through of her notes and couldn't think of anything really she needed to ask Cullen.

"Do you have anything, anything at all, you want to tell me, Cullen? About Sara and her habit? Her income? Her involvement in Montague's murder?"

"I've got nothing. Look, we went out to dinner and got in an argument and it just kind of escalated when we got back to her house, so I left. There's really nothing to tell."

"Well, I'd guess from the way she was dressed when I got there, that she was hoping you'd come back so you could make up."

"Oh, God," Cullen said. "Tell me she wasn't still in that baby doll?"

Julia smiled.

"She was indeed and she didn't look half bad if you're into femmy femmes."

"And you're not?"

"Not really, no."

"Okay, well, that's embarrassing. I'm sorry you had to see that."

"No worries. Okay, so, interrogation over. What shall we talk about?"

"Do you remember me from high school?" Cullen asked.

"Sure. You were the star of the junior varsity basketball and softball teams. I remember watching you play. Do you remember me?"

"Of course, you were a couple years ahead of me and the star of the varsity teams. I always admired you."

"Thank you, that's very sweet."

"What happened to you after high school? I lost track of you."

"I took some time off before college and traveled around the country. When I came back to town, you were gone."

"Ah, right, and I went straight from high school to Oregon. I couldn't wait to get out of Bidwell."

"And then you couldn't wait to come back?"

"What can I say? I got a killer job offer in Portland and couldn't pass it up."

"Good for you. I ended up at Portland State and got my degree in criminal justice. Landed a job with the Portland Police Bureau and never looked back."

"Who knew our paths would cross again someday?"

Julia grew serious.

"I really hope you're not involved in any of Sara's extracurriculars. I think it would kill me to have to arrest you."

"No worries, my friend. I'm as disgusted as you are at her activities. I guess it's finally sunk in how into drugs she really is."

"Do you get it, Cullen? Do you fully grasp the concept that she's the number one suspect in a murder investigation? *Murder*."

"I don't know. Like I told you, she wouldn't harm a flea. I don't see her killing anyone for any reason."

"I wish I had your faith in her," Julia said.

"Me, too." They sat in silence for a few minutes. "You ready for another beer now?"

"Sure. What the heck? I'm off the clock."

CHAPTER FIVE

Cullen spent the next day nursing a slight hangover and thinking about Sara. And Julia. They had had too many beers the night before, polishing off a twelve-pack between them. In a show of complete responsibility, Julia had crashed in her spare room rather than drive.

They'd had such a good time reminiscing. And after Cullen had had a few too many, she'd asked Julia what she was into if she wasn't into girly girls.

"I don't know," Julia had said. "I'm more into people than facades."

"How would you classify yourself? You're certainly not a femme."

"I think of myself as soft butch. Not a hardcore diesel dyke by any stretch."

Cullen had laughed so hard her stomach hurt.

"Is that what you think I am? Hardcore?"

"No. And you're definitely not soft either. You're just plain old butch I guess."

"Plain old, huh?"

"Yep."

Cullen smiled as she reflected on the time they'd shared. She'd almost had to pinch herself to believe it was real. Julia Stansworth. The Julia Stansworth had been drinking beer with her. She'd never in a million years have dreamed that would ever happen.

But the night of frivolity was over and Julia was back at work trying to prove Sara was a murderer. And Sara? Sara. She'd better call her and see how she was. But she didn't want to. She'd show up after work, just like she'd said she would. They'd talk things out, or maybe they wouldn't. Either way Cullen knew she'd spend the night. She needed Sara. It had been too long since she'd enjoyed that body.

Hopefully, Sara would be coke free and Cullen would be able to relax around her. Something had to give where her drug habit was concerned. She'd told Cullen she'd quit. So had she? Was she really trying?

The rest of the day dragged on for Cullen who managed to stay until quitting time. At four thirty, she hopped in her truck and drove through traffic to reach Sara's house, but Sara wasn't home.

Cullen used her key to let herself in and went to the kitchen to get a beer out of the fridge. She wandered into the living room, but then her curiosity got the better of her. She set her beer on the coffee table and took the stairs up to Sara's bedroom two at a time.

She felt a momentary pang of guilt, but soon got over it. She tore open the dresser drawers looking for Sara's stash but found nothing. She was about to give up and go downstairs feeling horrible for doubting Sara's attempt to get clean when she remembered Sara's little dressing table.

Cullen opened the sides and slid out the middle drawer. There was a mirror covered in white residue, a razor blade, and several vials. She briefly contemplated pouring the coke down the toilet but didn't. Instead, she hurried back down the stairs and opened the front door to leave.

Sara stood with her hand on the knob about to come in. She smiled brightly.

"Thank you for opening the door for me, sweetheart. I really appreciate it," she said.

"Where were you?"

"Picking up my car from impound."

She sounded so nonchalant that Cullen wanted to shake her. Like it wasn't any big deal that her car had been impounded. She slid her hands in her pockets and stepped out onto the porch.

"Good. I'm glad you got it. Look, I've got to go. I'll see you later."

"Where are you going?"

"Anywhere but here. Sara, I've got to know, do you care about me at all?"

Sara's brow furrowed.

"Of course, silly. Why do you ask?" She leaned against Cullen. "Want to come on in and let me prove how much I care?"

Cullen took a step back.

"No. Not tonight. And if you really cared about me you'd quit snorting coke."

"I'm trying."

"Not hard enough."

"What do you mean?" Sara asked.

"When was the last time you had some coke?"

"Last night. I don't even have any in the house."

Liar, Cullen wanted to scream at her but didn't want her to know she'd been snooping.

"Okay. Good. I'll be over tomorrow after work. I'm not in the mood to be here tonight."

"Cullen? What's going on? You can't still be upset about last night?"

"Maybe. I don't think so. I don't know. All I know is I don't want to be around you until you're clean. So let me know when that happens."

The dark sky and pouring rain suited Cullen's mood. She drove to her favorite pub, ordered a burger and a beer. She finished her burger and her beer, paid her tab, and drove home.

Alone in her house, she let her mind wander to a very dark place. What if Sara was so addicted to cocaine that she couldn't quit? What if their relationship was over? The thought made Cullen sad. She'd miss Sara, even though their whole relationship seemed to have been built on lies. She'd still enjoyed their time together. They'd had fun. There was no denying that.

And Cullen couldn't think of another lover she'd had who could compare to Sara in bed. Sara was so easy to make love to, so incredibly easy to please.

Was that over? Would she never hold Sara again? She was about to pour herself a whiskey to drown her sorrows when her doorbell rang. She almost ignored it since she really didn't want to see Sara at that moment. Something made her open the door, though, and there stood Julia with a twelve-pack of beer under her arm.

"I figured it was my turn to buy," Julia said. "May I come in or is this a bad time?"

Cullen desperately wanted to be alone but couldn't find it in her heart to turn Julia away. She stepped back, away from the door, and reached for the beer.

"Come on in."

"Thanks."

Julia shook off the rain in the entry hall. Cullen liked how Julia always looked so nice dressed in casual clothes. Sure, she always wore a blazer, like the navy one she had on, but she also usually wore jeans with them.

And she looked amazing that night. The blazer really brought out the blue in her eyes. Her blond hair was matted to her head, probably from standing on Cullen's front stoop. She was sopping wet.

"Let me get you a towel," Cullen said.

"I'm fine."

"Your hair though. Wouldn't you prefer to dry it? You're going to catch your death of pneumonia."

"That's an old wives' tale." Julia laughed. Cullen liked the sound of it. It wasn't tinkly like Sara's, whose laugh washed over her and caressed her. It was different, genuine. And it resonated with Cullen nonetheless. "But I'll still take that towel."

Cullen went into the bathroom and got a towel for Julia. She handed it to her and watched as she dried her hair. She came to her senses and realized she was staring.

"I'd better put these in the refrigerator," Cullen said.

She went into the kitchen and put the beer in her pathetically empty fridge. She'd better do some shopping soon. She could cook when she had to, and if she and Sara were kaput, she'd have to.

"I like your kitchen." The sound of Julia's voice startled Cullen, who almost dropped the beers she was holding.

"Jesus, woman. You almost gave me a heart attack. You must walk like a ninja."

Julia laughed again.

"Sorry. Hazard of the job. Sneaking up on people is kind of something I do."

"I understand. Just try to make some noise when you're here, okay?"

"Will do. Now, about that beer?"

Cullen popped the top and handed it to her. She opened her beer and followed Julia into her living room.

"So, seriously, why are you here? I don't have any more info on Sara, I swear."

"Why are you here and not at her place?"

"I needed a break."

"Yeah?" Julia looked around the living room. Her gaze landed on the bar. "Were you about to have some good stuff before I got here?"

"I was. Would you like some whiskey?"

"Not on a work night. Maybe this weekend?"

"Sure."

"Great." And she smiled at Cullen again.

"Yeah," Cullen continued. "I really need to clear my head and think a good long time about what I'm doing with Sara. You know, what do I want? What are my expectations? What am I willing to settle for?"

"And how long will you wait for her once she's in prison."

"It's her first offense, at least that's what she tells me. Surely her sentence won't be that long."

"I'm not talking about the coke charges, Cullen."

Cullen was confused, then the light dawned.

"You're talking about the murder charge."

"I am. I won't rest until she's behind bars."

Cullen was tired of talking about Sara. She didn't want to think about her anymore.

"It's my turn to ask you a question," Cullen said. "Why are you here? What possessed you to bring a twelve-pack to my place?"

"I hope you don't mind. I had so much fun last night. But figured we'd drunk all your beer, so I thought I'd show up with some. I mean, you seem okay with it?"

"Oh, I'm fine with it. I just wonder what you would have done if I was at Sara's."

"Gone home. Simple as that."

Cullen arched an eyebrow at her but didn't say a word. She took a drink of her beer and set it down. She liked Julia, always had. But she was trying to pin a murder on her girlfriend, and she didn't appreciate that. She was torn. She sure had enjoyed taking a trip down memory lane with her the night before, but what did Julia really want from her? She decided not to dig too deep. Instead, she'd just relax and have fun. What could it hurt?

"You're awfully quiet all of a sudden. Are you sure you're okay with me just showing up? Maybe we should exchange phone numbers so I can text you when I feel like a few beers," Julia said. Sure, she'd already looked up Cullen's number in the database, but she hoped Cullen wouldn't remember she'd called her once before.

She sat waiting with bated breath. She knew she'd been taking a chance showing up unannounced, but she'd really wanted to see Cullen again. Cullen had been two years behind her in school, so while she knew who Cullen was, and who wouldn't, they hadn't been close. Hell, they hadn't even been friends, just acquaintances. Fellow jocks flanking the outskirts of the student body.

But Julia had always noticed the way Cullen had looked at her with a mix of admiration and something else. Did Julia dare to think it was affection? And now Cullen was involved with a suspect in one of Julia's investigations. She was glad their paths had crossed again as she really liked Cullen. Though she didn't like the circumstances of their renewed acquaintance. Was it possible that a friendship could blossom under said circumstances? And why was it so important to Julia that one did?

"We can exchange numbers," Cullen said. "I think that's a good idea. Although you're welcome to bring beer by anytime I'm here. My door's always open."

Julia breathed a sigh of relief and took a swig of beer.

"Sounds good," she said.

She heard the front doorknob turn and instinctively reached for her weapon. Cullen stood and held her hand up so she lowered her own hand. She stood as Cullen walked to the entry hall.

"What are you doing here?" she heard Cullen ask.

"Whose car is that in the driveway?"

That voice was unmistakably Sara's.

"None of your business," Cullen said. "You need to leave."

"Are you two-timing me, Cullen Matthews?"

"Hell, no. You're the one with a mistress, not me."

"That's bullshit and you know it," Sara said.

"No, I know that cocaine is your mistress. Now, go back home."

Sara stormed into the living room where Julia stood shell-shocked. She had no idea what her presence would do to Cullen and Sara's already fragile relationship.

"You! What in the hell are you doing here?"

"I came over to have a beer with Cullen." Julia struggled to keep her voice calm. She couldn't explain it, but she felt like she'd just gotten caught with her hand in the cookie jar.

"So now she's your best buddy?" Sara whirled on Cullen. "You do realize she's trying to frame me for murder?"

"I'm not trying to frame you." The words were out before she could stop them. Damn it. Why hadn't she just kept her mouth shut?

"Are you going to help her?" Sara said. "Are you working with the enemy? Is that why you're avoiding me? Guilt?"

"No such thing." Cullen's voice was like ice. "You need to leave. Now."

"I'll go," Julia said.

"You're not going anywhere," Cullen said.

"Is she you're new girlfriend?" Sara said. "Butch on butch. Ew."

"Leave." Cullen took Sara by her upper arm and guided her roughly to the door. "And don't come back all coked up again. It doesn't help your cause."

She slammed the door and locked it.

"Doesn't she have a key?" Julia said.

Cullen jumped.

"Damn it. Don't sneak up on me. And no. She doesn't have a key."

"Okay, well, the mood is pretty much soured. Maybe I will just go home."

"Negatory. I need a drinking buddy now more than ever. Come on back to the living room."

Cullen draped an arm over her shoulders and walked her back. Julia lowered herself onto the couch and reached for her beer. Cullen sat in the recliner.

"I'm sorry," Julia said. "I feel like I've really messed things up for you two."

"Nope. She's the one messing things up. You're fine, honest. Let's not talk about her anymore. I'd like to forget about her, at least for a while."

"Great. Well, I'm sure I can help with that. Hey, do you still play poker?"

Cullen smiled, her dimples prominent.

"Oh, my God. Do you remember the poker games we'd play on the bus? I didn't think you paid any attention."

"I remember. I just never knew if you were any good."

"I wasn't." Cullen laughed. "But I've gotten better."

She got some cards and poker chips out from behind the bar.

"Come on. Let's go to the dining room and play."

Nothing in the world sounded better to Julia as she grabbed their beers and joined Cullen.

CHAPTER SIX

E arly the following morning, Julia was at the evidence room at the precinct.

"Good to see you, Detective. What can I get for you?"

"Good morning, Marge. I'd like to take a look at the evidence from the Montague case. The items from the hospital, please. Specifically, the IV pole, morphine bag, and drip line."

"You're like a dog with a bone, Detective. Sign here and I'll go get them for you."

Julia signed the form and waited impatiently while Marge brought out the items.

"Are you going to have them long?" Marge asked.

"I'll try to have them back in a few hours."

Everything was bagged and tagged to seal them from contamination. Julia didn't care; she'd bag it all again when she was through. She took everything up to the lab.

"Hey, Mike." She greeted the young man working with the test tubes. "I've got a favor to ask you."

"Sure thing, Detective. What do you need?"

"I want you to go over these items again, to make sure we didn't miss any fingerprints. We've got a suspect now so I want to be sure we didn't miss anything."

"Sure thing, when do you need it by?" Julia stared at him flatly. "Got it. I'll work on them right now."

To protect the chain of evidence, Julia stayed in the lab and watched Mike meticulously go over every piece.

"Hey, Detective, I think I found something."

Julia hurried to his side. She looked through the magnifying lens and saw, without a doubt, that there was a partial fingerprint on the drip. It was on the small switch that had been opened to release the morphine that would kill Montague.

"Excellent." She patted Mike on the back. "You do such good work. Now lift the print for me, please."

When she was through with her successful trip to the lab, she bagged everything up and took it all back to Marge, who breathed a sigh of relief when it was returned.

"Told you I'd bring it back." Julia winked at Marge, who could have been her mother.

"I never know with you. Is it even worth putting them back or are you just going to make me get them out again?"

Julia laughed. "Go ahead and put them away. I think I have what I need right now."

Julia ran the print herself and came up empty. No matches. How was that possible? She knew Sara was a match. She knew it in her heart. She looked at the print. Damn it. She hated to admit it, but the print was too much of a partial. She'd need more if she was going to nail Sara.

She took her laptop to a local diner and ordered coffee and a greasy breakfast. She needed to watch the amount of beer she'd been drinking as she couldn't let it affect her work or replace her workouts. She also couldn't get used to sleeping in Cullen's spare room, regardless of how comfortable it was.

Comfort. That was the big problem. She was too comfortable with Cullen. Far too comfortable. As she finished her breakfast, she made a vow not to go back to Cullen's for a while. She had a case to investigate and she didn't need to be hanging around with a suspect's girlfriend.

She tossed some cash on the table, grabbed her still unopened laptop, and headed back to the office. She poured herself a cup of the tepid brown liquid that passed for coffee and settled in at her desk.

Julia pulled up the still photos from the hospital again. She enlarged one and zoomed in on the shoes. Surely she'd be able to tell if the person was male or female based on their shoes, right? But the tennis shoes were nondescript. Frustrated, she took a sip of coffee and stared at the screen. She was missing something; she just didn't know what.

Then she had an idea. She took a screen print of the shoes and printed it off. She called a judge and requested a search warrant. In a few hours, she had the warrant in hand. She had two uniformed officers come with her and she drove out to Bidwell.

She rang the doorbell.

"Go away! Leave me alone!" Sara was obviously in no mood for visitors.

"Open up," Julia said calmly. "Don't make us break down the door."

"Give me a minute."

Julia looked at her watch. Three minutes later, she rang the doorbell again and, to her surprise, Sara opened the door.

"Ms. Donovan, how are you?" But she really didn't need to ask. Sara's pupils were like saucers, her nose was red, and she had telltale red wine stains on her lips and teeth. She looked horrible.

"What do you want?"

Julia handed her the search warrant and turned to the officers. She had given each of them a copy of the picture before they left the station.

"You know what you're looking for," Julia said. "Tear the place apart if you need to."

"Wait," Sara said. "No need to tear anything apart. Just tell me what you're looking for."

"We're looking for a pair of white Nike Fingertrap training shoes. Do you own a pair?"

"I have no idea. What do they look like?"

Julia showed her the picture of the shoes with the crosshatch over the arches.

"These look familiar?"

Sara blanched.

"Sure, I have a pair. What of it?"

"I believe they were worn by whoever killed Donald Montague."

"I've told you I didn't kill Donnie."

"And what? I'm just supposed to take your word for that? Why don't you go get the shoes for me to take to the station?"

Sara glared at Julia before turning down the hall. Julia nodded at one of the uniforms to follow her. They were back in no time with Sara's shoes and Julia slid them into a plastic evidence bag.

"Wait. When will I get those back?"

"I have no idea and, to be honest, that really should be the least of your worries right now."

Julia took the shoes and the other officers and left the house. Back at the station, she went up to see Marge.

"What do you have there?" Marge asked.

"Shoes. They're evidence in the Montague murder case."

"You act like that's the only open case we have right now."

"I know we have others, but I'm very close to solving this one. I can feel it."

"Suit yourself. Sign your life away and I'll put these with the rest of the evidence that's sitting there collecting dust."

Julia laughed.

"You're funny. It won't be collecting dust for long. I'll have my perp behind bars soon."

"So you say. Have a good afternoon, Detective."

"You do the same."

Julia went back to her office and wondered what else she should do with her day. She checked her watch. Three thirty. She could leave. Hell, she'd earned it. She'd just gotten in her car when her pocket buzzed. She checked her phone. It was a text from Cullen.

You coming over tonight? I'm heading home now if you want to meet at my place. I'm buying tonight.

That was odd. Shouldn't Cullen be trying to make up with Sara? Of course, Sara probably wasn't in much of a mood for company at that moment. She shot a text back.

I'm on my way.

Cullen had just put the beers in the fridge when Julia knocked on the door. She answered it and greeted Julia with a smile.

"Glad you could make it."

"I can't say no to free beer."

"A woman after my own heart."

They took their beers into the living room and were chatting about their days when Cullen's phone rang.

"Shit. It's Sara. I need to make some decisions there."

Julia shrugged.

"Are you going to answer it?"

"I should, huh?"

"Put her on speaker."

Cullen did just that.

"Hello?"

"You sound like you're far away."

"I'm kind of busy so you're on speaker."

"Take me off."

"No," Cullen said. "Look, I'm sorry I'm not coming over again tonight. I swear I'll be there tomorrow."

"What are you doing tonight? Hanging out with your new girlfriend?"

"Sara, you're the only girlfriend I have."

"You sure don't act like it."

"I'm trying to give you time to get yourself clean."

"You know what your little friend did today?"

"What?" Cullen said. "No comment about getting clean?"

"I'll tell you." Cullen wondered if Sara could even hear her. "She came by and took my favorite pair of workout shoes. I hope she gets athlete's fingers from handling them."

"Why'd she take them?"

"Evidence or some bullshit."

"Did you put up a fight?" Cullen looked over at Julia who shook her head.

"No, I gave them to her. I don't know why she is so focused on me. Except I think she wants to split us up. That way she can have you to herself."

"Sara, you're the only one who can split us up. And Ju— Detective Stansworth is an old friend from high school. We've just been playing catch up."

"Whatever you say. I'm too pissed to talk. Come over tomorrow and tell her to go to hell."

The line went dead. Cullen put the phone back in her pocket, embarrassed by Sara's outburst.

"I'm sorry about her," she said.

"Don't be. I'm about to arrest her for murder. She has every right to be pissed at me."

"You really think she did it, don't you?"

Julia, who was taking a drink from her beer, merely nodded.

"What can I do to convince you otherwise?"

"You can't. The evidence will show she's guilty. Or it won't, which I highly doubt."

"I don't know, Julia. Maybe we shouldn't hang out until this whole situation is over."

What was it Cullen saw in Julia's eyes? Fear?

"I don't think that's necessary. Drinking beer with a buddy isn't going to influence the outcome of my investigation."

"It might if your beer drinking buddy is the girlfriend of your main suspect."

Julia laughed.

"Well, when you put it that way..."

"Right? That's okay. Besides, after tonight I really should make an effort to make amends with Sara. You know, help her get clean and all that."

"She was a coked up mess when I saw her today."

"She was?" Cullen couldn't fight the disappointment that washed over her. "Are you sure?"

"Positive. And she'd had enough wine to stain her mouth. I don't know, Cullen, I honestly don't see what you see in her. I mean, she must have redeeming qualities, but I sure haven't seen them yet."

"Let's talk about something else," Cullen said. "Like... I don't know. Anything."

"Let's talk about food," Julia said. "Is there a decent pizza delivery in this town?"

"Oh, my God. Pizza sounds great."

"Cool. Give me the name of a place and I'll order."

After they'd eaten, Julia finished her beer and stood.

"I should get going."

"What? You're not going to stay here again?"

"No. I've been thinking about what you said. Maybe we shouldn't hang together until this whole Montague mess is over. I really think it would be best."

"Hey, Julia, I was half joking."

"Right. But that means you were half serious. And I think you're right. I'll see you at the courthouse I guess."

"Yeah, I guess."

Irritated in a way she couldn't put her finger on, Cullen decided to turn in for the night. She was up early the next morning and working hard when her phone buzzed at ten. It was Sara calling.

"Hello?"

"What are you doing?"

"Working," Cullen said. "What are you doing?"

"Begging you to come over tonight."

"I told you I would. You don't need to beg."

"I just don't want you to forget."

"I won't. I'll see you around five or so."

"Sounds good. Should I make dinner?"

"No, thanks. I'll take us out for Mexican again."

"Oh good. I can't wait. I miss you, Cullen," Sara said.

"I miss you, too. Will you be coke free tonight?"

"I will."

"Good. Okay, babe. I'll see you soon."

"Okay. Bye, Cullen."

Cullen ended the call and tossed her phone on the desk in front of her. What the hell was wrong with her? She had a beautiful woman begging for her attention and she dreaded seeing her. Sure, finding out about Sara's coke habit had been a turnoff, but shouldn't she be over the initial repulsion by now?

Was it the murder investigation? Is that what was bothering Cullen? No, she knew Sara was innocent. She didn't need to worry about that. She just needed to get over herself. She was acting ridiculous and needed to straighten up and fly right.

She left the office at three and headed over to Sara's. She stopped and bought some beer for herself, wine for Sara, and flowers. There was a spring in her step as she let herself into Sara's house.

Sara came out to greet her wearing a yellow ankle-length sundress. She looked amazing. Cullen couldn't wait to kiss her.

"Let's get these in some water." Sara took the flowers and Cullen followed her into the kitchen to deposit the beer and wine. When Sara had the flowers just how she wanted them, she turned to face Cullen. "They're beautiful."

"Good. I'm glad you like them."

Cullen pulled Sara to her and reveled in the feel of Sara's body pressed into hers. She looked into her blue eyes that were dark with desire. Cullen dropped her gaze from Sara's eyes to her lips, so full and ripe and ready for her. Sara's lips parted and Cullen dipped to taste them.

CHAPTER SEVEN

The kiss intensified and Cullen knew if she didn't break away soon she'd end up taking Sara right there in the kitchen. But it felt so wonderful to be kissing her again, to feel Sara's tongue smooth and wet against hers. She wanted her with every ounce of her being. She was throbbing with need but told herself to be strong. Cullen needed proof that Sara could stay clean before she would make love to her.

"Wow," she said when the kiss finally ended. "That was some kiss."

"Yeah, it was. Let's skip dinner and head upstairs for dessert."

Sara turned to the hallway and tugged on Cullen's hand. But Cullen didn't budge.

"Not yet," Cullen said.

"No? I have to wait until after dinner? But, Cullen. I need you now."

"You have to wait until you've been off coke for a while."

"What? Look, I know you want me to stop using, but it's going to take time. Surely you're not going to make me wait that long?"

"Ah. But I am. Now, come on, let's get some dinner."

Sara crossed her arms over her chest and pouted.

"That's not fair."

"Sure, it is. You want me to make love to you and I want you to quit coke. We both have something we want. We'll each do something for the other."

"You can't go that long without sex. I know you."

"I can go as long as I need to," Cullen said.

She held out her hand and Sara took it. They walked out to the truck together. The ride to the restaurant was in silence. Cullen finally spoke as they got out of the truck.

"Are you going to make me regret coming over tonight?"

"No. I'm sorry. It's just…I don't think you know what you're asking of me."

"And I'm sorry. You're right. I've never done drugs so I have no idea what it's like to quit them. But I need you to do it. I can't stay with a drug addict."

"You say it like it's a bad word. I'm still me, Cullen. That's what I don't think you get."

"But you're not. You used to come to bed with me and we'd make love. Lately you've been staying up snorting coke until God knows when. Then you finally pass out and I can't even wake you up in the morning for pleasure."

"Well, I'm here now. I'm offering myself to you. Take me."

"No. I can't. I'm sorry. Now, let's get inside. I'm starving."

After dinner, Sara got out of the truck and slammed the door. Cullen exited her side and had to practically run to catch up with her before she got in the house.

"What's going on?" Cullen said.

"Aren't you leaving?"

"I wasn't planning on it. I thought I'd come in and have a few beers."

"What's the point? If we're not going to make love, why even bother coming in?"

"Maybe because I like your company?"

"Spare me. Go home, Cullen. I'll see you tomorrow."

"Are you going to snort coke?" Cullen asked.

"What if I am?"

"You're not helping our cause."

"Whatever. Good night."

Cullen lost herself in thought on the drive to her house. What the hell was she doing? Was Sara worth pursuing? Would she ever get clean? Was she guilty of murder?

The last question snuck in unbidden. Where had it come from? She didn't doubt Sara's innocence any more than she doubted her own. So why even think like that?

She stripped and climbed into bed. It was early, but she was tired, emotionally, mentally, and hormonally. She needed to forget everything and everyone and let herself relax. The sound of the rain hitting her roof relaxed her and lulled her to sleep.

Friday was a long day for Cullen. Sure, she'd fallen asleep early Thursday night, but she hadn't been able to sleep until her alarm. She was wide awake at three thirty and finally gave up and got out of bed at four. She went to her office and booted up her computer after starting her coffee.

She waited for her browser to load, then searched "cocaine addiction." The first article she found proclaimed cocaine highly addictive and warned the addiction should not be taken lightly. Apparently, those who were addicted to cocaine kept snorting more and more as their tolerance grew. According to the article, they were always in search of that high.

Another article claimed that cocaine was a highly addictive drug that could change the chemical makeup of a person's brain with regular use, making it challenging to quit using the drug without help. So Cullen was right. Sara needed help. How could Cullen help her?

She did a search and was pleased to see there were several recovery centers in Portland. She'd broach the subject to Sara that night.

By one o'clock, Cullen was dragging. She'd gone through so many of the office's Keurig cups she'd lost count. She found herself in her office reminiscing about the first time she'd actually met Sara.

She had been exhausted as she pulled into the parking lot of the House of Good Fortune that Friday night and was looking forward to some good food and quiet time. She walked in and was seated at her usual table, the one in the back by the fountain. She noticed the same regular woman she'd seen the week before at her usual table as well. Cullen nodded to her, then took her seat.

She was surprised when the woman walked over to her.

"Do you mind if I join you?"

Disagreeable as Cullen's mood was, the idea of the company of an attractive woman appealed to her nonetheless. She stood.

"Please. Sit down."

The woman sat and extended a perfectly manicured hand. "I've seen you here for years but have never introduced myself. My name is Sara."

"I'm Cullen. It's nice to meet you." She shook her hand.

"I hope you don't think me too forward," Sara said.

"Not at all. I feel like I should know you by now anyway."

Sara smiled.

"I know the feeling."

The waitress arrived and took their drink orders, then left them to get acquainted.

"So what do you do, Cullen?"

"I'm in advertising. And you?"

"I'm an entrepreneur. I start up businesses, get them running, then move on to something else."

"Sounds exciting."

"I like it."

The waitress brought their drinks. Cullen raised her gin and tonic to Sara. "To new friends."

"To new friends." She clinked her wineglass against Cullen's.

They ordered dinner and passed the time in pleasant conversation. When they were through, Cullen picked up the tab.

"You're a fun person, Cullen. I'm glad we finally met."

Cullen looked into the deep blue eyes across the table from her and was sad the evening was coming to an end. "This has been a very nice evening, indeed."

"Why don't we go over to Layla's and keep the night going?"

Layla's was a women's bar in Bidwell that Cullen had occasionally visited to fight off loneliness. The fact that Sara knew of it was a good sign for Cullen, who was enjoying her company far more than she'd anticipated.

"Layla's sounds wonderful."

"Shall we take my ride?" Sara said.

"Why don't we meet there?" Cullen was adverse to leaving her truck parked at the restaurant.

"Sounds good." Sara stood, and Cullen admired the way her tailored skirt clung to her curves. Sara was a looker, of that there was no doubt.

She followed Sara into the night and walked her to her car. Sara surprised her with a tight hug.

"I'm sorry," Sara said. "I just felt like doing that."

"No need to apologize. I enjoyed it." Cullen struggled to keep her hands on Sara's waist. She was tempted to kiss her. The sight of her full lips so close combined with the heady scent of her perfume and made Cullen dizzy. She quickly stepped back.

"I'll see you at Layla's then."

She got in her truck and took a deep breath. That had been close. She could have really blown something there. She followed Sara's Mercedes through town to the club.

The sounds of the band could be heard in the parking lot. Sara took Cullen's hand and they cut through the crowd to an empty table. They ordered drinks, then Cullen led Sara to the dance floor, where they danced to several songs.

Cullen enjoyed watching the way Sara's body flowed with the music. She was so languid, it was as if the music took hold of her and moved her this way and that. Cullen was used to being taller than most women at five eleven, but Sara didn't stand much shorter than her. Of course, she was wearing heels with her business outfit.

Pleading thirst, but mostly wanting more time to get to know Sara, Cullen led her back to their table.

And from there, the night had progressed and Cullen had taken Sara home with her. She'd never forget that night and, remembering it now, she knew she had to fight to keep Sara. What they had was too good to throw away.

❖

Julia was frustrated. She'd gotten a call about a murder in the Pearl District and had spent the day interviewing people, following leads, and overall playing detective. There wasn't much to this particular case, though. It was a clear-cut example of domestic violence. It was just too bad a thirty-seven-year-old woman had to lose her life because some asshole lost his temper.

Still, he wasn't at the scene when they got there so she'd had to interview neighbors, coworkers, anyone who might know where he'd be. She found out the name of his favorite dive bar and there he was, playing pool like he hadn't just murdered his wife of eighteen years.

She'd questioned him about his whereabouts at the time of the murder and, not knowing she'd already spoken to many of his friends, he gave several impossible answers. She'd finally heard enough and arrested him.

It had been an open-and-shut case, but that wasn't what had frustrated her. What had frustrated her was the fact that the case took her away from the Montague murder, and she'd wanted to spend the whole day on it. She'd wanted to watch the videos again. She knew she was missing something important, but she'd be damned if she knew what.

By the time she got him booked and questioned him some more, daylight was waning. She gathered up her laptop and headed home. She let herself in her bungalow and poured a glass of scotch. She was tired, frustrated, and irritated. She took a sip of the drink and fought the urge to drive to Bidwell to ask Sara some more questions. At this point, it could probably be construed as harassment and, if truth be told, she'd only be doing it to get a glimpse of Cullen.

Cullen was drop-dead gorgeous and had been even as a high school sophomore. Her easy smile, twinkling eyes, and laid-back manner had had Julia fantasizing about her years ago. And now they were older, more mature, and had enjoyed spending time together. Like, really enjoyed it. And while Julia didn't delude herself into thinking Cullen was at all interested in her, she still missed her, even though they'd only hung out a couple of times.

She wondered if, once Sara was in prison, Cullen might be willing to pursue something more than friendship. She hoped Cullen didn't think she was too butch. She wasn't, really. She just had to dress and act the part for work. Sure, she didn't wear skirts and dresses, but she was all woman and could be soft when she wanted to. She just needed to figure out how to convey that to Cullen.

Julia was fantasizing again. She needed to get her head clearly in reality. She'd have plenty of time to deal with the future once it arrived. She opened her laptop and went to work. The first thing she did was reread the statements of the witnesses from the day Montague was shot. No one saw a thing except Sara talking to him, but Julia knew Sara couldn't have shot him since he was shot in the back. She carefully perused each statement in case she'd missed something. Had anyone seen a car? A suspicious person down the street? No. She was left with nothing but Sara talking to him, presumably warning him to keep his mouth shut.

Feeling like she'd never catch a break and not wanting to give up, she checked the records of Montague's arrest. His attorney's name was Robert Allen. How could a college kid afford a high-level attorney like him? Unless Mommy and Daddy were footing the bill. But something about Allen's name struck a nerve with Julia. What was it?

She pulled up Sara's arrest. Sure enough, Robert Allen was her attorney, too. He wasn't known for defending low-level drug dealers, yet there he was. He usually defended millionaires and the like. If Julia could peg Sara as Montague's drug dealer, she might be able to get her for accessory to murder for the young man, Bruce Payne, who'd died of an overdose of cocaine that started this whole mess.

Julia smiled to herself. This was a good thing, a very good thing. She made a note to call Robert Allen first thing Monday morning. She had to find out who was behind his defending two regular people. Someone with a lot of money obviously. She just needed to find out who.

She thought about how good it would feel to bust a drug ring. That would be a feather in her proverbial cap for sure. But still, it would pale in comparison to locking Sara up for murder. That was her main goal and she couldn't lose sight of that.

CHAPTER EIGHT

Sunday morning dawned cool and crisp. Tired of eating out all the time, Cullen and Sara were going to go grocery shopping. They had planned out the week's meals, and Cullen hoped against hope that Sara would eat some of the food instead of just snorting her life away.

Cullen had spent the last couple of nights at Sara's house. It had been nice to get back into their routine. It was killing her to sleep with Sara without getting physical, but she was sticking to her guns. No sex until Sara was good and clean.

They were walking through the aisles at the grocery store with a million other people when Sara brought up the subject of her addiction.

"I think I'll need help," she said.

Cullen simply looked at her.

"I mean, you're great and all, but I think I might need professional help."

It was time to broach the subject Cullen had been too nervous to mention.

"There are lots of treatment facilities in Portland. I think we should look into one of them."

"Or a few. You know. Compare and contrast sort of thing."

"True. Find the one that's the right fit."

"You'd really stick by me if I chose to do that? You wouldn't think I'm a loser?" Sara said.

"Never, babe. I'm here to help, and I think a treatment facility is just what you need."

"Great. So, next week, we'll look together?"

"You've got it."

Cullen was walking on air as they put the groceries away. Life was looking up for them, and she couldn't stop smiling. When everything was put away, they snuggled together on the couch while Cullen watched her beloved Seahawks destroy the Patriots.

When the game was over, it was time to get ready for the wine and food festival going on in Portland.

"Please shower with me," Sara said. "Please?"

"No can do." She took her hand. "As much as I'd love to, you know the rules. I think waiting motivates both of us to help you get the help you need."

Sara pouted.

"But I promise to do that. Please?"

Cullen patted Sara's ass.

"Nope. Now, get in the shower so I can take mine."

Cullen washed their breakfast dishes while Sara showered, then took her turn. When she walked out to the bedroom after with her towel wrapped around her waist, she found Sara at her dressing table.

"What are you doing?"

"Just waiting for you. I'm putting on my jewelry and brushing my hair. Do you think I should wear makeup?"

Her speech was hurried, and Cullen felt the pit of her gut clench.

"Sure," she said. She walked over and placed her hands on Sara's shoulders, loving the feel of her cashmere sweater. What she didn't love were the dilated pupils and the white residue around her nostrils. Damn, would she ever be able to trust her? "Maybe we should think about getting you into treatment right away. Maybe tomorrow?"

"Please, Cullen. Don't even joke like that. I'm not ready yet. But I will be. I promise."

"Fine. Wipe your nose and let's finish getting ready."

Sara teared up.

"I'm sorry, Cullen."

"No need to cry. You've got an addiction, a serious one. And I know you'll break it. I just wish it was easier."

"Me, too." She placed her hands over Cullen's and leaned back into her.

Cullen exhaled heavily and squeezed Sara's shoulders.

"We'll get through this. I'm going to get dressed now. Are you ready?"

"I think I will wear makeup. I'll be ready in a minute."

And just like that, things were back to normal. Cullen's new normal where she was in a relationship with a coke addict. She wished she could just leave her, but she cared far too much for that. She slid into her black blazer and straightened her kelly green tie and felt Sara wrap her arms around her from behind.

"I'm crazy about you, Cullen."

"I feel the same. You ready?"

"Let me just use the restroom and we can walk out."

Cullen walked out to the entryway to wait. She hated that she questioned whether or not Sara was using the facilities for what they were designed for or if she was snorting coke to boost herself for an evening out. Cullen was pretty sure she knew the answer and it made her sick. Yes, she'd sworn she'd be there for Sara, but that didn't mean she had to like her cocaine abuse.

They walked into the Heathman downtown and were surrounded by women. The annual lesbian event to help raise money for Pride was one of Cullen's favorites. She loved how everyone dressed up and how the reception hall had been decorated with pumpkins and leaves of every color. It felt like fall and that was Cullen's favorite season.

Cullen and Sara sampled wine and fare from several different places. Cullen was surprised how many people knew Sara. Cullen saw many old friends, but it seemed every time she turned around, someone was hugging Sara and dragging her off. At first Cullen wondered how Sara knew so many people, but then an unpleasant thought hit her. Was she dealing to these women? She wondered but didn't really want to know. She wanted to believe the best in Sara.

She hoped she'd learned her lesson about selling cocaine even if she hadn't quit using it.

It was one of these times that Sara had been pulled away that Cullen heard a familiar voice.

"Fancy meeting you here."

Cullen turned and saw Julia dressed in a blue pantsuit that really brought out her eyes. She looked stunning.

"Hey, Julia. How are you this evening?"

"I'm doing well, thank you. Where's Sara? Or are you stag?"

"I don't know." Cullen let out a rye laugh. "She's here somewhere. She knows more people here than I do."

Julia's smile disappeared.

"Interesting."

"Not really. She just knows a lot of people. Let it go."

"I don't know if I can."

Cullen motioned to the glass of wine in Julia's hand and arched an eyebrow.

"Looks to me like you're off duty."

"Fair enough. I'll let it go. You look very nice tonight, by the way."

"As do you."

"Hey, sweetheart." Sara walked up. "Who are you talking to? Oh, never mind."

"I was just setting off to mingle," Julia said. "Please excuse me."

Cullen watched her walk off before turning her attention to Sara.

"What can I get for you, babe? More wine? More food? Just name it."

"Let's sample some more wine."

"Great." Cullen took her hand. "Are you having fun?"

"I'm having an absolute blast. Thank you for thinking of this."

"I've been coming for years. I have to ask, though, how do you know so many people here?"

"I was a single lesbian for years before I met you, Cullen."

"I suppose that's true."

Let it go, Cullen told herself. Don't pick a fight. Not here, not now. But she knew Sara hadn't lived in the metro area that long, and she could dig deeper when they got home. If she really wanted to know the truth.

They got to the wine sampling and were helping themselves to a local red when Julia walked up. Sara whirled on her.

"Stop stalking me," she hissed. "Leave us alone."

"Look, I didn't come here to run into you. I'm here just like you, trying to relax and have some fun. So, back off."

Sara took her wine and stormed off. Julia and Cullen stared after her.

"I'm really sorry," Julia said. "Maybe I should leave."

"Why? You have as much right to be here as we do. Now, if you'll excuse me."

Julia watched Cullen go after Sara. Her heart ached. She hated to see Cullen mixed up with a criminal. A drug dealer was bad enough, but Julia knew Sara was a murderer as well. Cullen needed to disentangle herself from Sara, the sooner, the better.

She thought about going home but didn't want to give Sara the satisfaction. Instead, she kept her focus out for Cullen and Sara, ostensibly to avoid Sara, but deep down she couldn't complain about watching Cullen.

Still, after a couple more hours, she'd had enough fun and took off. She drove home and stripped out of her getup. Cullen had said she'd looked good. Had there been any deeper meaning there? She needed to stop. It was her idea to quit hanging around with Cullen rather than to see where things might go, so she needed to get a grip and accept life as it was.

The following morning, Julia was at the station early, researching every news article and website she could find that discussed Robert Allen. As she'd expected, his website was perfectly done and well presented and she didn't learn much from it.

She did, however, learn much from the newspaper articles she found. Allen rubbed elbows with Portland's elite, from politicians to athletes to actors and actresses. He'd represented a ton of people, and he usually won. But she couldn't find any history of him representing a murder suspect. Maybe it would be unchartered territory for him; maybe he'd refuse to represent Sara. Only time would tell. Assuming she could gather enough evidence to try her.

At nine o'clock, Julia called Allen's office. She explained who she was and asked to set up an appointment for later in the day. She was put on hold and was preparing herself to get mean when the receptionist came back on the line and said Mr. Allen would see her as soon as she could get there.

Julia thanked her lucky stars that Allen's office was not far from the station. She checked her reflection in the rearview mirror, adjusted her collar, and went into the high-rise. Allen's office was on the tenth floor, and Julia wasn't surprised to find the reception area decorated with leather furniture and rich, colorful paintings. It reeked of money, money she assumed was dirty.

"Detective Stansworth?" The receptionist had opened the door to the back offices for her. "Would you like to come back? Mr. Allen will see you now."

"Thank you." Julia was nervous and excited. She was nervous because if Robert Allen had agreed to see her so readily, she figured he was up to something. She was excited because, well, she just might learn something.

The receptionist led her down a long hallway to a conference room where a fifty-something-year-old man sat in a dark suit and red power tie. He looked completely at ease.

"Mr. Allen?" Julia said.

"Yes. Detective Stansworth?" He stood and they shook hands. "Please have a seat. Can I have Nadine get you anything? Coffee? Water?"

"I'm fine, but thank you." She sat across the table from him.

Allen nodded his dismissal to Nadine, who closed the door behind her.

"How can I help you today?" Allen said.

"I'm investigating the murder of Donald Montague, and by extension, that of Bruce Payne."

"I don't believe Bruce Payne was murdered."

"Someone sold him the coke he OD'd with."

"Stores sell guns all the time. They aren't charged with murder."

Julia stared at Allen. She had a feeling she wasn't going to get anywhere with him.

"Be that as it may. I couldn't help but notice you represented Montague and are currently representing his presumed drug supplier, Sara Donovan."

"And?"

"I'm more inclined to believe Donovan can afford you, but don't believe Montague could."

"Your point?" Allen said.

"I want to know who was paying you."

"You know I don't have to tell you that."

"You don't have to, but I think you should. I'm going to find out, so you should just make it easy on us both and tell me."

"I'm not going to make anything easier on you, Detective. That's not my job and it certainly isn't in my best interest." He stood. "I think this meeting is over."

"One more question. Are you going to defend Donovan on a murder charge?"

"I didn't know she'd been arrested."

"It's only a matter of time. Thank you for your time, Mr. Allen."

"Good day, Detective."

Julia left disappointed but not disheartened. She didn't know what she'd expected from Allen. She knew he wouldn't give up who was paying him. It had to be a big-time drug lord, but she'd hoped he'd give her something to go on.

She got back to her desk and put her head in her hands. She'd had so much more she'd wanted to ask Allen but had gone for the jugular too soon. She should have paced herself and now she wouldn't get another chance.

She watched the video from the hospital for the umpteenth time as she still felt like she was missing something. There was something about the shoes that should have given her a clue. What was it? The shoes. Sara's shoes were in the evidence locker. She needed to get them tested.

Julia went to see Marge.

"Good morning, Detective. Let me guess. You want to see the hospital evidence again."

Julia smiled at her.

"No, today I want the shoes that I brought in the other day."

"Okay, sign your life away and I'll be right back."

Marge returned and handed Julia the baggie that contained Sara's shoes. Julia took them to the lab where Mike was working on a project already.

"Good morning, Mike."

"Detective. Let me guess, you, too, have a rush job."

"Not really a rush job. I just need these shoes tested when you have a chance."

"Tested for?"

"Morphine in particular, but I'll take any residue of saline as well."

"Testing shoes for morphine? That's an odd request."

"I'm hoping some morphine might have dripped onto them in the completion of a crime."

"I understand," Mike said. "I'll try to get to them this afternoon."

"Thank you."

Julia was just sitting down to work on the case some more when her phone rang.

"This is Stansworth."

"Detective, we've found a body. We need you to come investigate it."

"Where?"

She jotted down the location in the Mount Tabor neighborhood. She grabbed her jacket and headed out.

CHAPTER NINE

It was rainy and cold when Julia pulled up at the scene. She wished she'd brought a coat but was hoping to check things out then delegate work and get out of there. She walked up to a uniform.

"So, what happened? Fill me in." She had to shout to be heard over the wind.

"Not sure really. Victim was apparently killed by a blow to the head, but no weapons around, not even a big rock. It's probably a robbery gone wrong. There's no money on her at all. No purse, no wallet, no nothing."

Julia surveyed her surroundings. It was a nice park that was empty, presumably due to the weather.

"No eyewitnesses, I suppose?" she said.

"Not a one."

"I wonder why she was down by the water on a day like today. I'm curious if she was meeting someone."

"Maybe, I don't know."

"Thanks for your help. I'm going to check out the body now."

She walked down to where the crime scene investigators were working.

"You got anything I can go on?" Julia said.

"Not yet. Looks like an altercation that went a little wrong. Maybe a robbery victim who wouldn't give up her purse? I'm guessing the murderer picked up a rock and hit her in the temple with it."

Julia looked down at the victim. Sure enough, the only visible mark so far was the gash on her head. She looked down at the ground. There were a couple of sets of footprints.

"Be sure and make models of the footprints," she said.

"They both look small. Like maybe it was her and another woman."

"Maybe so." And then Julia knew what she'd been missing in the Montague murder investigation. "Do you need me?"

"No, not unless you have any specific requests."

"I want an autopsy done on the victim ASAP."

"Yes, ma'am."

"We've got no ID on her at all, right?"

"No."

"That's probably her car in the lot. I'll run the plates."

"Yes, ma'am. Any further instructions for us?"

"You guys just do your thing and let me know if you find anything."

"Will do."

She didn't have time to deal with a robbery. She was sorry for the victim for being in the wrong place at the wrong time, but she had bigger fish to fry. She'd follow up accordingly, of course, but she had something to check out. Yes, it was a murder as well, but she was obsessed with another case at the moment. One she couldn't wait to get back to.

Excited to test her theory, she opened up the picture from the hospital as soon as she got back to her desk and zoomed in on the shoes again. She'd been so obsessed with finding the shoes she hadn't really paid any attention to the size of them. They were small. The person in the video was almost certainly a woman. Finally. She was that much closer to arresting Sara.

She sat at her desk gloating and almost forgot to run the plates of her latest victim. The car belonged to a Sherry Bergstrom, and the photo on her driver's license was clearly the victim. So they had a name. Julia decided to see what else she could find out about her and get back to Sara's shoes later.

Sherry Bergstrom was a housewife and mother. She had no police record. She had been married for twenty-four years and had been active in the PTA when her kids were in school. She seemed like a model citizen.

So what was she doing at the park on a cold, wet, windy day in November? Julia's interest was piqued. She wondered if maybe the perfect Mrs. Bergstrom wasn't so perfect after all.

Her ringing phone interrupted her musings.

"This is Stansworth," she said.

"Detective. It's Mike. I'm through with the shoes. There was some salt on them as well as morphine. I don't know if that helps or not, but I'm through with them."

"Did you find anything else?"

"You didn't ask me to look for anything else."

"True. Thanks, Mike. I'll be right down."

She hurried down to the lab. Mike had found saline and morphine, which was incriminating. Maybe some of the saline solution from Montague's IV had dripped on her feet. Or she could have worn those shoes to the coast. Damn it. But where else could the morphie have come from? It felt like it was the break she needed and she felt confident things were moving in the right direction.

"Where did you find the drops?" she asked Mike.

"Just one little spot of each on the top of the shoe. Odd, really."

"Great work, Mike. Thanks."

Julia returned the shoes to Marge and decided to call it a day. She had nothing to go on in the Bergstrom murder and nothing new in the Montague case. She'd have to wait until the next day to make any more progress.

She went home and slipped into some sweats, took a beer from the fridge, and curled up on the couch. Maybe she'd watch a movie. She needed something to take her mind off Sara and, by default, Cullen. She turned on *Law & Order: SVU* and took a sip of beer which was just what the doctor ordered.

Her cell phone rang.

"Stansworth."

"Hello, Detective. It's Mike. They're about to do the autopsy on the murder vic and I wondered if you wanted to observe."

"Already? I thought they wouldn't be able to do that until tomorrow."

"Nope. They've got time this afternoon."

"I'll be right there."

Julia brushed her teeth, dressed, and headed back to the station. She didn't know why it was so important for her to observe the autopsy, but it was. She just had this niggling feeling that there was more to the murder of Sherry Bergstrom than met the eye.

She suited up as soon as she got to the lab. The medical examiner nodded at her and she stepped up to the table as he began to cut.

"Her heart's enlarged," he commented.

"True, but she looked to be in decent shape."

"May be congenital."

"Or could be drug related."

"We won't get the tox screen back for a while, you know."

"I want a test for cocaine run now."

"Detective…"

"That wasn't a suggestion."

"Yes, ma'am," he said.

He drew some blood from the femoral vein and her heart and started the test.

"Any other special requests?" He looked annoyed.

"How does her nose look?"

He shined a light up her nostrils.

"Inflamed. Okay, you win. She looks like a heavy cocaine user."

"Thanks. I think I've seen all I need to see. Go ahead and finish without me."

She hurried up to her desk. She had to find a connection between Bergstrom and Sara. She knew she was grasping for straws, but she just had a gut feeling and her gut hadn't failed her yet.

Julia knew Sara drove a Mercedes so she pulled up the picture of it and printed it out. She headed out to the Mount Tabor neighborhood again. The rain had let up slightly, but it was still cold and windy. She pulled into the entrance of the park. Pulling her coat high around her neck, she crossed the street to the expansive houses and started ringing doorbells. She wasn't surprised that no one was answering. She figured most families had two working adults in order to be able to afford those houses. Houses she'd never be able to afford unless she won the lottery.

Cold and discouraged, she was just about to give up when she knocked on the door of a cute two-story house right across the street from the park driveway. Julia noted the large front windows overlooking the entrance and held her breath that someone might be home and might have seen something.

An elderly woman slid the curtain aside on the front door and peered out. Julia held up her badge and the woman cracked the door.

"Are you really a police officer?" she said.

"I am. Do you mind if I ask you some questions?"

"I don't mind if you'll answer some of mine."

Julia grinned.

"Fair enough, I'll do my best."

"Then please come in."

"Okay, Mrs....?" Julia began.

"Burke. I'm Rita Burke. But I get to ask you questions first."

"Shoot." Julia lowered herself onto the couch.

"What happened at the park today? Is Mrs. Bergstrom okay? Why did they tow her car? Why were all the police over there?"

Julia sighed.

"That's a lot of questions."

She knew the police had notified the next of kin, so she proceeded as gently as possible. "No, ma'am. Mrs. Bergstrom is not okay. She was attacked in the park today."

"By that blond lady?"

She now had Julia's undivided attention.

"What lady is that?"

"The one that came in after her and then burned rubber as she was leaving. That lady. Did she hurt poor Sherry?"

"We don't know who did it. We're investigating all leads, though. Now tell me about this woman you saw. What color car did she drive? What make? Do you know?"

Mrs. Burke shook her head.

"I didn't get a good look at her and I didn't notice the kind of car. It was silver and fancy. That's all I know."

Julia took pictures of several silver cars from her briefcase, one of which was Sara's. She showed them to Mrs. Burke.

"Was one of these cars it?"

"Oh, yes. This one." Mrs. Burke held up the picture of Sara's car. "I'm sure of it."

Julia's heart soared, but she played it cool. She needed to keep a calm exterior.

"Did you see anything else? Anything at all? It might help us in our investigation."

Mrs. Burke shook her head.

"I'm sorry, Detective. That's all I saw."

Julia stood and handed Mrs. Burke her business card.

"If you think of anything, even if you think it's minor, you call me, okay?"

"What are your hours?"

"Mrs. Burke, you can call me any time."

Julia drove the few blocks to her house and called a judge. She needed an arrest warrant. Then she sat back and waited.

Cullen was in a great mood when the workday ended. Even traffic couldn't dampen her spirits. She was heading home for the evening. All of which would be spent with Sara who seemed to be really trying to extricate herself from the grip of cocaine. And once the weekend was over, she'd go into rehab. Life was looking up.

She got to Sara's house to find her fidgety. She seemed on edge and Cullen could only assume it was the cocaine wreaking its havoc again.

"Are you okay?" Cullen said.

"I'm fine."

"How much coke have you had today?"

"Some. Not a lot, I swear."

"Good, at least it's not a lot. Are you going to be able to eat dinner?"

"Sure."

"Great. Let's go to McKenzie's. I want a burger and some beer."

"I could handle that. Let's go."

They drank beer, played pool, and ate burgers and fries. Cullen was having such a good time. She knew then that she and Sara were meant to be together. Everything just felt right. They were solid and she'd stick with Sara through anything.

After dinner, they were on the couch watching television when the doorbell rang.

"I got it," Cullen said.

She opened the door to see Julia flanked by two uniformed police officers.

"What are you doing here?"

"Is Sara home?" Julia said.

"Of course. What's this about?"

"We need to speak with her, Cullen."

"Come on in. Is it necessary for all three of you to be here?"

"Yes."

Cullen stepped aside and invited them in. She walked them down the hall to the living room where Sara was still curled up on the couch. She saw Julia and jumped to her feet.

"What are you doing here? I'm going to sue you for harassment."

"I have a couple of questions to ask you, Ms. Donovan."

"What?" Sara demanded.

"Where were you today between eleven and one?" Julia asked.

Fear gnawed her gut. Cullen really hoped Sara wasn't in more trouble with the police. She didn't know how much more she could take. Yes, she'd just declared to herself that they could get through anything, weather any storm, but she'd been thinking of the cocaine. Not of the legal issues. Surely Julia was just fishing.

"I was home. It was too ugly of a day to go anywhere."

"Was anyone here with you?"

"I'm sure you know Cullen was at work. So, no. I was home alone. What is this about?"

"Someone saw you at Mount Tabor Park during that time."

Sara's face blanched, but she quickly recovered.

"Whoever that was is mistaken. I didn't leave the house today."

"How do you know Sherry Bergstrom?" Julia continued.

"I've never heard of her."

"So, you're denying ever selling coke to her?"

"Yes, I do deny it."

"And I suppose you deny killing her today." It was a statement, not a question.

"Would you get over it, Julia?" Cullen raised her voice. "I've told you, Sara is not a killer."

Julia didn't look at her.

"Sara Donovan, you're under arrest for the murder of Sherry Bergstrom. You have the right to remain silent…"

Cullen didn't hear the rest. Everything was a blur as Julia had one of the other policeman handcuff Sara and lead her out to the car.

"Call Robert Allen," Sara called over her shoulder. "His number's in my phone."

CHAPTER TEN

Cullen looked around for Sara's phone but didn't see it anywhere. She grabbed her purse and looked through it and found her phone as well as several baggies of cocaine. Was Sara still dealing? Julia seemed to think so. Could she have been selling to that dead woman?

She tossed the purse on the couch and pulled up her contacts. Before she looked for Robert Allen, she looked for Sherry Bergstrom. There was no one called Bergstrom in her contacts, but there was a Sherry whose address said Mount Tabor. Shit.

She shook herself out of her dismay and found Robert's number.

"Hello? Sara?"

"Is this Robert Allen?"

"Who's asking?"

"My name is Cullen Matthews. My girlfriend, Sara Donovan, was just arrested for murder and she asked me to call you."

"I'm on my way. Meet me at the station."

The line went dead. Meet him? Oh, yeah, she supposed she should head downtown to be there for Sara. But where the hell was the police station? She searched on her phone and found it. She mapped it and drove off.

With almost no traffic at that hour, Cullen pulled into the police station twenty minutes later. She had no idea where to go or what to do. She opened the front door and saw a uniformed officer sitting at a desk.

"Can I help you?" she asked without a smile.

"I hope so."

The officer simply stared at her.

"What did you need? Do you need to see someone?" She sounded annoyed when she finally spoke again.

"I don't know. My girlfriend was just arrested so I'm here."

"This ain't like a hospital, lady. There are rules and regulations about visiting."

"I understand," Cullen stammered. "I'm not sure why I'm here. Her attorney just told me to meet him here so here I am."

"Have a seat. If he needs you, he'll come out here to find you."

"Thank you."

Cullen sat on a hard, plastic chair. Maybe she should just leave, but then how would Sara get home? Could Robert give her a ride? Would she even be coming home?

Cullen shuddered. The thought of Sara in a prison cell was too much for her to handle. She didn't deserve that. But what if she'd killed that Sherry person? Could she have? Surely not. But since Julia arrested her, they must have pretty strong reason to suspect her unless Julia was just on a witch hunt and Sara was a fall guy. But then, why did she have Sherry's name in her phone?

Maybe it wasn't the same woman. Sherry was a pretty common name. There could be several of them in the Mount Tabor neighborhood. It was probably all some crazy coincidence. She hoped Sara's lawyer would get everything straightened out.

A door opened then and a relatively short man with graying hair who was dressed in a navy suit with a red tie walked up to her.

"Are you Cullen?"

She stood and shook his outstretched hand.

"I am. You must be Mr. Allen."

"Please call me Robert."

He motioned to her chair and she sat back down. She looked at him expectantly, hoping for good news.

"What's going on, Robert? Can Sara come home now?"

He glanced at the officer behind the desk and lowered his voice.

"The evidence they have on her is pretty circumstantial. We're meeting with a judge in a little bit and I'm hoping he'll let her go home."

"What evidence do they have?" Cullen wasn't sure she wanted to know the answer.

"They have a witness who claims to have seen Sara drive into the park where the victim was murdered. She didn't get a good look at Sara, but ID'd her car."

"There must be millions of Mercedes in that neighborhood."

Robert shrugged.

"They say they'll have more evidence in a day or two. They did say the victim was a heavy cocaine user, and with Sara's reputation, that really doesn't help."

Cullen nodded. She felt herself going numb. It was all too much to take in.

"So, she could come home soon?"

"Yes, she should be able to post bail and get released. Bail will be high, but since Sara's not much of a flight risk, I don't see a problem. You just sit tight and I'll bring her out to you as soon as I can."

"Okay."

And just like that, he was gone, leaving a trail of expensive smelling cologne drifting behind him.

Cullen sat there for another couple of hours before the door opened again and Robert came out escorting Sara.

"Here you go," he said to Cullen. "Safe and sound."

"Thank you, Robert."

"Yes," Sara said. "Thank you."

"You stay out of trouble. I want you in my office at nine in the morning," Robert said to Sara.

"I'll be there."

"Good girl. You two go home and get some rest. Oh, wait a minute. Cullen, can I get your number so I'll have it in my phone in case you call me again?"

He entered her number in his phone. Cullen placed her hand on the small of Sara's back and guided her out to her truck.

"I'm so sorry, Cullen." Sara broke down in tears as soon as they were in.

"For what? You didn't do anything, right?"

"Of course not. You believe me, right?"

"You'd better believe I do." She pulled Sara into her arms. "Try to calm down. We'll be home in no time."

They pulled into Sara's driveway. It was late and all Cullen wanted to do was get some sleep and forget the whole horrible night. Sara spoke to her before she could turn off the engine.

"Hey, Cullen? I think I'd like to be alone. I need to process what happened, what's happening. Is that okay?"

"Sure, babe." Cullen's heart ached to see Sara in such pain. "I'll see you tomorrow night then."

"Count on it."

"If you need me for anything, anything at all, reach out, okay?"

"I will."

And with a brief peck on the cheek, Sara got out and went inside. Cullen felt selfish at her happiness, but she really needed her sleep. Sure, she would have been there for Sara had she needed her, but she was grateful to get to go home to her own bed.

The following morning, Cullen's phone buzzed several times while she was in a ten o'clock meeting. Several was an understatement. It buzzed throughout the whole meeting. She could barely focus, assuming Sara needed her desperately. When the meeting finally ended, she went back to her office and slid her phone out of her pocket.

She was shocked when it wasn't Sara's name on her display. It was Robert Allen's. She called him back and was put right through to him.

"Hello? Cullen?"

"Yes. What is it? Why are you calling me? Is something wrong?"

"How was Sara this morning?"

"I don't know. She said she wanted to be alone, so I slept at my place last night. Why?"

"She never showed up for our appointment this morning. She's not answering her phone either."

Cullen's heart sank. Something must be seriously wrong with Sara.

"I'll go to her house right now," she said. "I'll find out what's going on."

"Thank you. And please have her call me."

He ended the call and Cullen grabbed her laptop, checked out with the receptionist, and drove to Bidwell. Traffic wasn't moving even though it was the middle of the morning so it took her forever to get there.

She tried to let herself into the house, but her key didn't work. What was that all about? She rang the doorbell and pounded on the door, but there was no answer. She peered in through the living room window. All the furniture was there, but the artwork was all missing from the walls. What was Sara up to?

She punched in Sara's number on her phone. No answer. She left a voice mail begging her to call back. She used her garage door opener to check the garage. She was shocked. Normally, Sara's car and Cullen's truck fit in the three-car garage, and the other part was filled to the ceiling with boxes and stuff. Cullen had referred to it as junk once, but Sara had corrected her by saying it was stuff. Still, it was gone. Sara's car and all the stuff, gone. The garage was completely empty. Cullen started to feel sick.

Not knowing what to do, she called Robert.

"Hello, Cullen. Where's Sara?"

"I don't know. She's not at home and the place looks cleared out."

"Shit."

"Exactly."

Julia was busy collecting more evidence with which to convict Sara. She whistled while she worked, comparing the size of the shoe at the latest scene to Sara's Nikes. They were a perfect match. When she was through, she took the shoes back to Marge.

She requested a search warrant to collect the rest of Sara's tennis shoes to find ones that matched the tread exactly. She had just hung up the phone when her cell rang. It was Cullen. Julia figured she was the last person Cullen would want to talk to. Still, she was curious so answered the phone.

"Cullen?"

"Julia, can we meet for a beer?"

"It's barely after twelve."

"I need a beer."

"I tell you what, I'll meet you at Kell's for lunch at twelve thirty. If you choose to have a beer then, be my guest."

"Thanks, I'll see you then."

Julia's heart twisted. What was eating Cullen? Why would she seek Julia out now? Had Sara confessed something to her? Was Cullen going to admit her little Sara wasn't perfect?

So many questions swirled in her mind, but she had to focus. On what? She was in a holding pattern. She'd take a long lunch. There was no harm in that. She called the judge back and left her cell number. She grabbed her coat and headed outside.

It was bone-chilling cold that day. The sky was a light gray, and there were some forecasters calling for snow. That would be fine. Julia liked snow and they didn't get it often in Portland. She loved the quietness of a blanket of white powder on the ground.

She walked into Kell's at twelve twenty-five, and Cullen was already at a table, a pint of Guinness in front of her. Julia shed her coat and slid into the chair across from her.

"Rough day?"

"You could say that."

"What's up?"

"Get a beer first. You're going to need it."

"No beer for me. I'm on the clock."

"Suit yourself."

She went up to the bar and got a Coke. She sat back down.

"Now, what's so important?"

"Sara's gone."

"What?"

"You heard me. She's gone. She wouldn't have run if she was innocent, would she?"

"Hold that thought."

Julia forgot her coat as she stepped outside into the bitter wind. Her finger trembled as she called the station.

"This is Stansworth. I need a wanted alert. All information is in the system. Suspect is Sara Donovan. She was arrested for murder last night. She also has a pending court date for drug charges and a DUI. She's the prime suspect in the Montague murder. You'll find pictures of her, her car, her license plate, the whole bit. Do it ASAP. I don't know how big of a head start she got, but we need to find her."

"Yes, ma'am, I'm on it."

"Thank you."

She hung up and walked back into the restaurant.

"Did you let loose the dogs?" Cullen said.

"I did." She took a sip of Coke. "Why did you tell me, Cullen? I wouldn't have found out for a very long time. She would have gotten a head start. Could have even gotten away."

"Like I said, she wouldn't have run if she was innocent. And if she's guilty... I mean, if she actually killed those people... Well, then, she deserves to be in prison."

Julia reached across the table and placed her hand on Cullen's folded hands.

"Thank you, Cullen. I know it wasn't an easy decision."

Cullen stared at their hands for a few minutes before she spoke. "Actually, it wasn't that hard."

"Good. Because you did the right thing."

Cullen nodded and drew a shaky breath.

"I know."

"Did you really want to eat?" Julia said. "I mean after the morning you've had. Do you have an appetite?"

"Not much of one. But I'm going to drink so I figured I should eat something."

"Let's go back to my place. I'll stop and get some Guinness. We'll order a pizza and eat and drink to our heart's content."

"You wouldn't mind?" Cullen said.

"Not at all. I think it would be good for both of us."

CHAPTER ELEVEN

"Here." Julia handed Cullen the key to her house. "So you can let yourself in since you'll be there before me."

"Are you sure?"

"Of course. Now, let's get out of here."

Cullen let herself in to Julia's small, well-appointed house. It was sparsely decorated in neomodern style. The decorations that were there were chrome and glass. Somehow the place fit her. And Cullen felt comfortable there.

She wandered from living room to dining room to kitchen in her socks, taking it all in. The kitchen was small with stainless steel appliances. The living room was painted periwinkle with a gray dining room and kitchen. She liked it.

She made herself at home on the couch and ordered a pizza. She remembered that Julia liked the meat special so she ordered a large. She was checking her social media pages when Julia walked in with a case of beer.

"A case?" Cullen laughed. "Of Guinness? We'll be hammered."

"There's no rule saying we have to drink them all in one sitting. Now, grab us each one and I'll put the rest in the fridge."

Cullen did as she'd been asked and followed Julia to the kitchen.

"Where would I find a bottle opener?" she said.

"On the fridge. Just give me a second."

Julia closed the refrigerator door and took down a PSU bottle opener. She popped the tops off and took the one Cullen handed her.

"Now, let's talk pizza," she said.

"Already ordered."

"Really?" She raised her eyebrows and Cullen nodded at her. "That's great. Thank you."

Julia slid off her jacket and folded it over the back of a dining room chair. She laid her shoulder holster on the table. Cullen watched her untuck her shirt and get comfortable. She still had a killer body. There was no denying that.

Cullen took a big swig of beer and looked away from Julia, not sure if she wanted to ask the question burning in her brain. She finally decided to go for it and turned to face her again.

"Have you heard anything?"

"Hm?" Julia was kicking off her shoes and settling in on the couch.

"Have you heard anything? About Sara, I mean."

"Oh, no. It's too soon. I mean, sure, it would be great if we'd already found her, but we have no idea what time she left. Or do we?"

Cullen shook her head.

"No clue. When we got back to her place last night, she said she wanted to be alone, so I went home. It wasn't until her lawyer called to say she'd blown off her appointment with him that I went to her house."

"And what time was that?"

"About ten thirty."

"What did it look like? Did you check all the rooms? Were there any clues?"

"I couldn't get in," Cullen said. "She'd changed the locks."

"Well, she couldn't have left too early then. I wonder how early locksmiths open."

"No clue. And who's to say she waited around? She might have just left some money under the mat or paid by phone or online. You know? We don't know how that worked."

"I like the way you think. You would have made a good cop, Cullen."

"No, thank you. You deal with dead bodies and stuff. I couldn't handle that."

"You never know."

"Trust me. I know. I'd rather deal with ad campaigns than murder mysteries."

Another thought hit her and she wondered if she should tell Julia. She supposed she should. She owed Sara nothing, less than nothing.

"There are a couple of other things I should tell you," she said.

"Yeah? What's that?"

"When you were taking Sara away last night, she told me to call her lawyer, remember?"

"I remember."

"So, her phone was in her purse."

"That's logical."

"And also in her purse were baggies of white powder."

"I'm sure that was hard to see."

"I knew she was still snorting coke," Cullen said. "But I'd hoped she'd learned her lesson about selling."

"And I'm sure Sherry Bergstrom was a drug deal gone bad."

"That's the other thing."

Julia took a chug of beer.

"What other thing?" she asked casually.

"There was a contact in her phone, no last name, but it was Sherry in Mount Tabor."

"Damn, I wish I'd known that last night."

"Shit. Does that make me an accessory? Because I knew?"

Julia clasped Cullen's hand.

"Let's just assume there could be more than one Sherry in Mount Tabor."

Cullen breathed a sigh of relief.

"Thank you, because I really don't want to go to prison."

"And I'd hate to send you there."

Cullen grew warm all over. There was something in the way Julia was looking at her, something had shifted. She had the overwhelming desire to kiss her. What was going on? She didn't want to overthink things. This was Julia Stansworth after all.

The doorbell rang and they both started. Julia stood.

"I'll get it."

"I'll find some plates in the kitchen."

"The cabinet right above the sink." Julia called over her shoulder.

Cullen found them and, on shaky legs, set the table. Had Julia wanted her to kiss her? Was it just Cullen's imagination? Not that it mattered. She'd been single for less than twelve hours. She sure as hell didn't want to rebound.

Julia kept the conversation light as they served themselves dinner, thus convincing Cullen their little moment or whatever had never really happened. Thank God. But still, she couldn't completely shake the edge of desire cutting through her.

They reminisced about old classmates and shared information on who they'd seen. Cullen had worked on an ad campaign for their homecoming queen.

"Sondra Mouton? I remember her. Is she still gorgeous?" Julia asked.

Cullen laughed.

"She looked good, though her enormous boobs have drooped a little bit."

"Imagine that."

"Who have you seen lately?" Cullen said.

"Do you remember Mike Martin? The stoner? I arrested him the other day for the millionth time."

"What for?"

"You name it. Mostly domestic abuse though."

Cullen shook her head.

"That's not good."

"No, definitely not. But she keeps taking him back."

"Who's she? Anybody I know?"

"No. She's not a local."

They finished half the pizza.

"I could eat more, but I know better," Cullen said.

"I hear ya. Let's leave it out though, in case we get the munchies later."

They moved back to the couch where Cullen pressed herself against the far end. She needed as much space between herself and Julia as possible.

They sipped their second beers, and Cullen wondered if she should hit the road. She didn't want to be out too late.

"You know," Julia said. "For a shitty day, this has been fun."

"I know what you mean. I'm just sorry for the reasons behind needing to drink."

"Are you going to move on, Cullen? Or will you stay with Sara even after we arrest her?"

"Would I have told you she was gone if I was planning on staying with her?"

"No, I suppose not."

Cullen laughed wryly.

"You need to be smarter than that, Detective."

"I shouldn't need to be on my game after a couple beers and half a pizza."

"You never need to be on your game around me, Julia."

"Thank you."

Their gazes met and Cullen forced herself to look away as she took a final mouthful of beer. Shit, what was she doing? What was she thinking? And most importantly, what was she feeling?

"Speaking of beers," Cullen said. "Would you like another one?"

"I'd love one, thanks. I love how you've made yourself at home at my house."

"It's cozy. I like it here."

Julia watched Cullen walk to the kitchen and checked her hormones. They were running rampant, but she needed to cool her jets. She had the feeling that Cullen was into her, but she had no way of knowing for sure. Besides, Cullen had just been burned. Bad. Julia didn't need to be a vulture swooping in to pick at the remnants. She wanted Cullen to be one hundred percent if she came to her. And she could wait. She was patient.

Her phone rang just as Cullen walked back into the room.

"Stansworth here."

"Detective, it's Officer Fabian."

"What's going on? Did we find her?"

"No, ma'am. I just showed up to relieve Officer Tim McHugh who was posted at Donovan's house."

"And?"

"And the place has been shot up. And I just called nine-one-one for McHugh. I don't think he's going to make it though."

"Shit. Okay. I'm on my way."

She slid her phone back in her pocket and stood.

"What's going on?" Cullen asked.

"Come on. You need to stay in the car though. Do you hear me?"

"Where are we going?"

"Sara's house has been shot up. They got one of my men, too. Buckle up, Cullen. It could be a long night."

When they pulled up at Sara's house, the street was filled with cop cars and police were crawling all over the property.

"Stay here," Julia said to Cullen.

Her heart was heavy where she saw the outline of McHugh's body. Poor guy. She didn't know him well, but he was just a kid and his loss of life was for no reason.

"What have we got?"

"Bullets everywhere. We're collecting them and setting up a perimeter. Wish McHugh was around to tell us who did this."

"Yeah, I hear that. Listen, I want every bullet you find compared to the bullet in the Montague shooting. Do you understand?"

"Yes, ma'am."

"Thank you."

Julia gloved up and walked into the house which had been unlocked. She wandered around, careful not to step on the broken glass or any of the bullets scattered about. She went upstairs and found Sara's bedroom. It was in disarray with things thrown all over. She looked in the closet which was empty save for Cullen's clothes. Her heart tightened. Suppose Sara hadn't left? Suppose Cullen had been there that night? She could have been killed.

She shook it off and examined the bathroom before further checking out the bedroom. The drawers of the dresser had been pulled out and were tossed on the bed. She saw a little dressing table along the far wall. She opened it and pulled out the middle drawer. It was empty, but there was white residue all over the inside.

When she went downstairs, several other officers were there collecting more bullets.

"There's a residue in the dressing table upstairs. I want it tested for cocaine."

"Yes, ma'am."

Something was bugging her, so she went back upstairs. The room was large, but there was a lot of furniture in it. Where did Sara hide the coke before she sold it? She wandered through the other rooms but didn't see any likely hiding spots. She went back to the bedroom. She pulled the dresser away from the wall and there it was, a safe in the wall just above the floor. Bingo.

She made a note to call the locksmith again in the morning and went back downstairs.

"What can I do?" she said.

"We've got this under control, Detective. Do you have any more orders for us?"

"I don't think so. If I think of any, I'll let you know."

"Have a good night, Detective."

"I'll do my best. Keep up the good work."

"What's it like in there?" Cullen asked when Julia slid back into the car.

"You still have some clothes here." Julia started the car. "And thank you for staying put."

"I know. You were gone a long time."

"I have a job to do."

"Understood. Do you think I'll be able to get my clothes any time soon?"

"I doubt it."

"Fair enough."

They rode in silence back to Julia's house.

"Have you given any thought to the fact that you could have been in that house tonight?" Julia finally spoke.

"Shit. You're right. Damn. Now I don't know how to feel. Relieved?"

"Relieved?"

"Yeah. I'm glad she bolted so I wasn't there. I could have been killed, Julia."

"Yeah. I know." She didn't trust herself to say anything else.

Julia let them in her house.

"You want another beer?" she asked.

"At least."

"I hear that. You sit down. I'll get the beers."

Julia went into the kitchen. She prided herself on being calm and collected and cool under pressure. But as she reached for the bottle opener, she couldn't ignore her shaking hands. She rested her head against the fridge and took a deep breath. She easily could have lost Cullen tonight.

"You okay?"

Julia jumped when she heard Cullen's voice.

"I thought you were in the living room."

"Sorry, I don't mean to intrude. I just wanted to check on you and I'm glad I did."

"Can I ask a favor?"

"Anything."

"Will you hug me?"

"Now?"

"Yes, please."

Cullen opened her arms and Julia stepped into them. She wrapped her arms around Cullen's neck and held tight, trying to steady herself. Cullen's arms around her waist felt amazing. Everything felt right. Maybe they had a future, maybe not. But she wasn't ready to lose her. That much she was sure of.

CHAPTER TWELVE

Cullen stepped back before she did something stupid.
"You sure you're okay?"

"I'm fine. Some days the job is harder than others."

"I guess."

They walked back to the living room, and Cullen sat back on one couch while Julia sat on the other. Cullen wondered what she was thinking.

"You want to talk about it?" Cullen said.

"Nothing really to say. We lost a good man out there tonight. For no reason. And we could have lost you."

"But we didn't. Lose me I mean. I'm still here."

"Thank God."

"I didn't realize you lost someone tonight."

"Yep. The officer standing guard over Sara's house was killed in the gunfire."

"I don't know what to say."

Julia smiled weakly at her.

"There's really nothing to say."

"No, I suppose there's not."

"Damn. That beer went down fast. Are you ready for another one?"

"Give me a minute."

Cullen chugged the remainder of her beer then handed Julia her empty. Their fingers met briefly and again Cullen felt washed in heat, but she felt like a total heel. Julia had had a rough night and really needed a friend. If she couldn't be that, she should just leave.

"I should get going after this one," Cullen said.

"Nonsense. I'm a cop and I can't, in good conscience, let you drive after five beers."

"You just drove."

"After two. And maybe I shouldn't have, but you're staying here tonight."

Cullen smiled at her.

"Oh, I am, am I?"

Julia smiled back.

"Yes. Yes, you are."

"Well, okay then. Cheers."

They clinked bottles and Cullen took a long swig. It tasted good and helped soothe the fear at how close she'd come to being killed. But it did nothing to put out the flame burning inside. She wondered for a brief second in which room she'd be staying. Julia's? She took another drink and her phone buzzed. It was a text from Sara.

"What's wrong?" Julia said.

"I just got a text from Sara."

"Are you going to read it?"

"I don't really want to."

"Maybe she'll tell us where she is. Please, check it."

"Fine." She read it out loud.

I'm okay. Just wanted you to know. I'm sorry we didn't get to say good-bye.

"Okay," Julia said. "Ask her where she is."

"She won't tell me."

"You'll think of a way."

Cullen sat quietly for a minute before texting Sara back.

I'm glad you're okay. Where are you? Can I see you?

"Ooh. That's good. You're devious. I like it."

"I don't really want to see her, you know."

"I didn't think you did. Oh. I just heard your phone. What did she say?

I can't tell you where I am. I'm safe though. They'll never find me here.

But I want to see you, Sara.

That's not going to happen. I'm sorry, Cullen. We had a good run. Thanks for the memories.

"Shit," Julia said. "She's hiding and she's not giving anything away. Not even to you."

Cullen sat silently drinking her beer. She'd really fallen hard for Sara. Had Sara ever cared about her at all? Had it all been a big game to her? Like life? She didn't like feeling used, especially by a drug dealing murderer.

"Well?" Julia seemed impatient.

"Well, what?"

"Text her back."

"What can I say? I have nothing to say to her." Cullen was feeling bitter and didn't care who knew it.

"Say something. Maybe she'll text you again if you do."

She swallowed her pride and texted back.

I'll miss you. Take care.

"There. You happy?"

"Very."

Cullen tossed her phone on the coffee table. She couldn't help but notice Julia could barely sit still. Cullen finished her beer.

"Ready for another one?" she said.

"Yeah. I'll get them. You look like you've lost your best friend. We'll talk about it when I get back."

Cullen handed Julia her empty and sat back against the couch. Why had Sara texted her if she'd never cared about her? Maybe she had in some way. That made Cullen perk up somewhat. Only somewhat though because deep down, she really didn't believe it.

"So why so morose?" Julia handed Cullen another beer.

"I'm not. I'm fine."

"Bullshit, you're upset. Are you mad I made you text her?"

"No."

"No? Then what?"

"I don't know."

"Yes, you do. Now talk to me."

"I just wonder if Sara ever had feelings for me, that's all. I feel like I've been played, and I don't like it. Not one bit."

"I'm sorry. It's got to be hard. Do you think you'll pine for her for long?"

"I don't pine for her." Cullen laughed sardonically. "I'm glad it's over. I'm just sorry she wasn't prosecuted before she got away."

"It's okay. You can be honest with me. I'm sure it'll take a while for your feelings for her to die down, even with all you know. You two were together how long?"

"Like six weeks." Cullen laughed again. "Not a major relationship by anyone's standards."

"Did you love her?"

"How am I supposed to know? I thought we were heading that way, but it was way too soon to know that."

"I don't know, Cullen. I feel like when you know, you know."

"When was the last time you were in love?"

It was Julia's turn to laugh. Hers wasn't dry or cold. It was deep and real.

"We're talking about you now."

"Ah yes, but cheer me up. Tell me who broke your heart."

"Oh, aren't you sweet?" Sarcasm dripped from her words. "Wanting to know all about my broken heart."

"Oops. So I take it you weren't the one to call it off?"

Cullen struggled to sound calm, while she churned inside over the thought of someone hurting Julia.

"Not even. Although, I must say I wasn't completely surprised. Still, it hurt."

"I'm sorry. We can talk about something else."

"I'm just picking on you. It all happened seven years ago. I'm fine. She wasn't right for me. I can see that now."

"Was she butch or femme?"

"Is that important? Relevant?"

"No, I'm just curious what your type is."

"She was like me. Not butch but not into dresses or makeup either."

"How long were you together?"

"Only two years," Julia said. "But I really thought she was the one."

"I'm sorry."

Julia sighed.

"Thanks. But it's all good. I'm over her and hoping to move on someday. What about you? Do you think you'll ever be ready to move on?"

I could move on tonight, Cullen thought.

"Oh, yeah. I'll move on. Sara didn't take a chunk of my heart. I've been protecting it far too long to allow that to happen."

Julia pondered what Cullen had said. So Cullen had been hurt. The thought made Julia sad.

"Talk to me. Tell me all the sordid details."

This time when Cullen laughed it was genuine and was music to Julia's ears.

"Not much to tell, really. We were together ten years. She cheated on me with my best friend. The rest is history. Which is why finding out Sara hadn't been honest with me was so hard to take."

Julia's heart was breaking for Cullen. She'd been deceived twice now. Would she ever be able to trust again? Julia truly hoped so. She had plans for them. Someday. Not now, of course. But someday when Cullen was ready to try again.

"That sucks. Big time," she said.

Cullen blew out her breath.

"It is what it is. I just need to be even more vigilant next time. If there ever is a next time."

"Do you think you'd be willing to try again? Or do you think you'll be too gun-shy?"

"I like to think I'll be able to try again. I mean, I want to find that special person, you know? I want my happily ever after and I think I deserve it. Not to sound egotistical or anything."

"Don't worry, you don't," Julia said.

"I think I'd make some woman a good wife."

"I agree. You've got a lot to offer, Cullen. I just hope you find a woman who can see that and will be open and honest with you."

"Me, too."

"I'm getting hungry again. Don't ask me how because this beer should be filling me up. You ready for round two?"

Cullen laughed again.

"Sure, why not? Let's eat."

Julia thought while they devoured more pizza. She had a lot of work ahead to get Cullen to fully trust her. She'd have to make a point of proving how honest and upfront she was at every opportunity without being obvious about it. It wouldn't be easy, but she truly believed it would be worth it.

When the last piece of pizza had been consumed, they grabbed more beer and went back to the living room.

"I may call in for tomorrow," Cullen said. "I'm not going to be in any shape to work."

Julia laughed.

"Good call. I wish I could do the same. But we'll be busy tomorrow. Too much stuff going on with Sara's case. Maybe I'll be able to just work in the morning, though. You know. Go in and check on things then leave around noon. Maybe we can do something tomorrow afternoon? There's an indoor miniature golf course in Beaverton. Would you like to check that out?"

She held her breath waiting for Cullen to answer. She'd essentially just asked her for a date. Something besides drinks. Would Cullen freak out? She'd probably just graciously decline. That was more her style.

"Heck yeah," Cullen said. "That sounds like a lot of fun. I'll head home to shower and change and then I'll meet you there."

"Okay." Julia fought not to let her overwhelming relief show. "That should work. I'll text you in the morning to let you know what time I'll be able to sneak away from work."

Cullen looked at her phone.

"Did you get another text?" Julia shifted into cop mode.

"What? No. Just checking the time. It's after one. Not that I'll turn into a pumpkin or anything, but it's past my bedtime. And you need to get up in the morning."

"True. Okay, come on. I'll show you the guest room."

"Before you do that, your coffee pot looked rather space age. Since you'll be gone before I wake up, will you show me how to use it?"

Julia laughed. Cullen was cute. So damned cute.

"I tell you what, I'll make you a pot before I leave. Fair?"

"Thanks, that would be great."

Despite the late hour, Julia had a hell of a time falling asleep. Knowledge that Cullen was in the bed across the hall was making her crazy. She considered going into her room and crawling into bed with her just to see what would happen. Maybe they'd only have a night, maybe they'd have more. But she stayed put. It wouldn't be fair to Cullen. She needed to mourn the loss of her relationship, fucked up though it was.

When Julia's alarm went off, she wanted to throw her phone across the room. She felt horrible. She was tired and marginally hungover, and her stomach was protesting all the pizza she'd eaten. She turned off her alarm and promptly fell back asleep. She awoke a half hour later panicked and hurried to the kitchen, cussing the whole way. She'd be late and that wouldn't be good.

She poured a cup of coffee then headed for the shower. She let the hot water pound her until she remembered she was running late. She dressed quickly and went to the kitchen to fill her travel mug.

There stood Cullen in boxers and an undershirt. Julia paused in the dining room and just enjoyed the vision before her. Cullen was tall and lean and muscular. Her lithe body beckoned to Julia. She knew if she got too close, she'd touch the merchandise and that could blow everything.

"You're up early," she said.

Cullen jumped and whirled to face her. Her small breasts were clearly outlined by the undershirt, her nipples at attention. Julia longed to take the morning off and make Cullen forget all about Sara.

"Shit. I thought you'd be gone by now," Cullen said.

"I'm running late. I'll pour myself one for the road then I'll set it up for you, okay?"

"Sure. I'll go put some clothes on."

"You don't have to." The words were out before she could stop them.

Cullen arched an eyebrow at her.

"What's that supposed to mean?"

"Look, Cullen, you don't have anything I haven't seen before." She hoped she sounded calmer than she felt, and she hoped Cullen didn't notice her blush. "And you look comfortable, so don't change for my benefit. I'm out of here anyway."

"If you're sure."

Cullen leaned her ass on the kitchen counter and crossed her ankles. She looked absolutely delectable. Julia shook herself from her reverie and took care of the coffee pot.

"I'll text you," she said. And, fighting the urge to kiss Cullen good-bye, headed to the station.

CHAPTER THIRTEEN

The station was subdued when Julia finally arrived. They'd lost one of their own the night before, and it was weighing heavily on everyone's mind. She checked her email first to read the reports from the guys the night before. The rest of the night had gone smoothly. They were boarding up the windows on Sara's house later that morning. No more incidents were reported so Julia closed her email and took the stairs two at a time to the lab.

She found Mike bent over a microscope.

"Morning, Mike," she said.

"I expected you earlier." He looked up from the microscope.

"Sorry. What have you got for me? I really need you to look at something."

"If it's about the bullets, save your breath."

"I won't. I need that comparison done ASAP."

"I figured. I've already done it. The bullets from last night's shooting were from the same gun as the one who shot the Montague kid."

"Seriously?" Julia wanted to hug him. "You've already run the tests?"

"I have." He smiled. "And they're a match. You want to see?"

"Hell yeah."

He stepped away from the microscope and she peered through it. She didn't need Mike to tell her what she was looking at. The striations were identical. So whoever shot Montague shot up Sara's house. Why? Were they trying to kill her or just send a warning? And who was behind the shootings?

"Thanks, Mike." She patted his upper arm. "Great job. Now get me the report sooner rather than later, please."

"I'll type it up by the end of day."

"Thanks."

She went back to her office. She was really getting somewhere. She just didn't know where and it wasn't a pleasant feeling. Julia went down the hall to check on the unit who were tracking Sara.

"Any info on Donovan?" she asked.

"Not a thing. No one's reported her license plate anywhere. We don't even know which direction she went in."

Julia wanted to punch a wall.

"She texted her girlfriend last night. Check to see where the call came from. That should help."

"Got it."

"Also, I want you to go through her house with a fine-tooth comb. I mean, check her garbage cans, everything. She must have left a clue behind as to where she was going."

"Yes, ma'am."

She watched as the team headed out then went back to her desk. She'd received an email from the powers that be telling her to go see McHugh's widow. Ugh. Not her idea of a good time, but it was necessary. She cleaned out his locker, placed his belongings in a box, and made the long, slow trek out of the station.

All activity stopped as everyone watched her make her way to the parking lot. Police officers were in danger any time they were on duty, but they couldn't obsess about that. They had to push it out of their thoughts as they did their jobs day in and day out. So when one of their brothers or sisters was killed, it really hit home. They could be next and the thought was sobering.

Small white flakes hit her windshield as she drove to Bidwell, where McHugh had lived with his wife. They were young and hadn't started a family yet which was some relief. She pulled up in front of their nondescript, two-story house and retrieved the box.

The flakes stung as they hit her face, but she refused to change her expression. She kept a serious face as she approached the front door. The door opened before she could knock, and Mrs. McHugh wailed at the sight of Julia.

Julia stood firm and let the widow pound on her chest and shoulders.

"This is all your fault," she screamed.

The blows didn't hurt, necessarily, but they certainly didn't feel good. Yet Julia did not flinch. She felt responsible for the young officer's death so took the hits as part of her punishment.

When Mrs. McHugh ran out of steam, Julia set the box down and enveloped her in her arms. She held her while she sobbed.

"I can't believe he's gone," Mrs. McHugh said. "He was much too young to die."

"It's a great loss to everyone."

"Thank you for saying that. I don't believe you feel that way though."

"It's the truth. I'm very sorry, Mrs. McHugh."

Mrs. McHugh stepped out of the embrace.

"What do you need from me?"

"I need you to sign a form that you received his belongings."

"Fine. Where's the form?"

Mrs. McHugh was suddenly as cold as the weather.

"It's right here. Would you mind?"

Julia handed her her phone and she squiggled her signature with her finger.

"Thank you for bringing his things. I just wish they'd have sent someone else. If I never see you again it'll be too soon."

Her words stung, but Julia knew she deserved it. She handed her a business card.

"When you're ready to hear about benefits and all that, you give this officer a call. Don't worry, there's no hurry. Just whenever you're ready."

Mrs. McHugh nodded, obviously biting back tears.

"When can I get him?" she asked.

"Soon. Hopefully, by the end of the day."

"Hopefully? How much of an autopsy needs to be done to determine he was shot to death?"

"I'm sorry. I'll try to get them to release him to you as soon as possible."

"I appreciate that. I have arrangements to make, you know?"

"I understand," Julia said softly.

"You can leave now. I don't like looking at you and you'd damned well better not show up at his funeral. I don't care what the damned procedures say."

That one hit Julia hard, but she didn't let on. If that was her wish, she would abide by it.

"His box is pretty heavy. Would you like me to take it inside for you?"

"I'm stronger than I look."

"You'd have to be. Call us when you're ready." Julia walked back to her car. She sat in it and thought about going back to the office. She really didn't want to and she was already in Bidwell where Cullen lived. She texted her to let her know she was nearby.

Hey. I'm in the neighborhood and don't want to go back to the station. Can I come over?

Sure! I'm ready for some golf. You're off early. Everything okay? I'll be right there.

Julia didn't feel like going into everything she was feeling over text. She was upset and excited at the same time. She knew Cullen would help her feel better and be a sounding board. She could get used to Cullen being in her life.

She rang the doorbell and Cullen answered looking sharp in faded Levi's and a green Oregon Duck hoodie that made her eyes look like emeralds.

"Come in," Cullen said. "It's freezing out there. Is that snow falling?"

"It is. And, yes, it's cold."

Cullen closed the door behind her.

"How was your morning? I didn't expect you for a couple of hours."

"It was a mixed bag."

"How so?"

"We don't have any information on where Sara went. The same gun that shot up Sara's house shot the Montague kid. And the wife of the officer who was killed last night was none too happy to see me. I know I shouldn't tell you these things. I don't know why I do."

"You need someone to talk to. Let me be that someone." Cullen wrapped Julia in her arms. "I'm sorry. I didn't realize you'd have to see his widow. Didn't someone notify her last night?"

"Yes, but I cleaned out his locker and took his belongings to her."

Julia breathed in Cullen's scent and was both soothed and aroused. She loved the feel of Cullen's arms around her, but knew Cullen was only being nice. Still, she appreciated her friendship even if she wanted more.

"I heard from Sara again this morning." Cullen stepped back, releasing Julia.

Julia's heart raced and she was immediately back in detective mode.

"What did she say? Where is she? Did she say anything that could help?"

"No, and it was from a strange number. Not her phone."

"She must have dumped her phone and bought a new one. What was the number?" Cullen showed Julia her phone, and Julia knew she needed to call the information in. "Give me just a second."

She stepped into the kitchen to make the phone call.

"This is Stansworth. I need to know the location of this phone number." She read the number off Cullen's phone. "Got it? Call me as soon as you know something."

Cullen paced while she waited for Julia to come back. She wished she could do more to help her find Sara. But Sara was careful even with Cullen. Cullen wondered if she'd been through this before. Maybe Sara Donovan wasn't even her real name. Maybe she just invented herself while running from her past. The thought made her nauseous.

Julia came back into the entryway while staring at Cullen's phone.

"What are you doing?" Cullen said.

"Just reading your texts with her. I hope you don't mind."

"Not at all. Do you see anything there that would help the investigation?"

"No, nothing. Thanks for letting me look, though. She seems really concerned about you. She's worried how you're holding up. How does that make you feel?"

"I don't know. I'm still torn, you know? I mean, I don't want to have anything to do with a murderer, but I miss us. Or at least who I thought we were. Of course, that was all based on false pretense."

"So you really don't know how to feel, do you?"

"I know I want to help you catch her. I know I want her to rot in hell. I mean, I know these things. Stupid emotions just get all jumbled sometimes."

"And that's fair. You ready to forget Sara and murder and cocaine and go play miniature golf?"

"I'm ready."

"Great. Should we take two cars or should I drive?"

"I'll drive," Cullen said. "Let's go."

"Have you ever been to Glowing Greens?" Julia asked as they headed down the back roads to Beaverton.

"Never. You?"

"I went to the one downtown once. It was a lot of fun with black lights and everything."

"Black lights?" Cullen laughed. "That should be fun. Flashbacks, though. Major flashbacks."

"No doubt."

They arrived at the course and went inside. The black lights gave it a unique atmosphere. She could see the course was adorned with 3-D decorations and she smiled thinking of the fun they'd have.

There was nobody else on the course and the kid who took their money explained they'd just opened.

"Take your time and have fun."

The course proved challenging to both Cullen and Julia. They found themselves missing what should have been easy shots. When they finished their game an hour later, Cullen's sides hurt from laughing so hard.

When they stepped outside, Cullen saw that the snow had begun to stick.

"We should get home," she said.

"Yeah. Are you okay to drive in the snow?"

"Sure thing. Just watch me."

It wasn't sticking in Bidwell, so Cullen drove them to a pub for burgers and beer.

"I can't believe I'm going to drink beer," Julia said. "First of all, I had too much to drink last night, and secondly, oh my God, my figure."

Cullen laughed again. She always seemed to be doing that when she was with Julia. It was a good thing. A very good thing.

"Your body is smokin' hot. Don't you worry about a thing," she said.

"Oh, it is, is it? It's nothing compared to yours."

"Hey now, that's no fair. You got a sneak peek at mine this morning, which was purely unintentional, I assure you."

"You didn't hear me complaining, did you?"

"Why, Julia Stansworth, are you flirting with me?" She tried to sound light and joking, but inside she was dying to hear a yes.

"Maybe." Julia was noncommittal. "At any rate, here's to good beer. Bodies be damned."

They clinked their glasses together and Cullen took a sip of her pumpkin ale. It was good, nice and crisp and so unlike the Guinness they'd been drinking the night before. She took another sip and watched Julia.

"What?" Julia said.

"We're pretty good friends, aren't we?"

"I like to think so. Why? What's up?"

Cullen took a deep breath. She was risking a friendship, but she couldn't keep her feelings to herself any longer.

"How would you feel? I mean, would you freak out? I mean... Oh hell. What would you say if I told you I'd be interested in more than just a friendship?" There. It was out. She braced herself for rejection.

"Are you sure, Cullen? You just got burned. I'd hate to be just a rebound for you."

"You wouldn't be, I promise. At least I think I promise. Sara and I really started dying even before she was arrested the first time. I so wanted to make it work because I didn't want another failed relationship on my résumé, but it was over. I didn't respect her anymore, you know?"

Julia nodded.

"I get that. I still don't know, Cullen."

"Fair enough. I get it. You don't feel the same way. I hope I didn't just screw up our friendship."

"You didn't screw anything up. And no, you don't get it. I'd like very much to date you, Cullen. I'd like to see where things go. I just want to make sure you're emotionally ready. I mean, crumbling or not, you were still in a relationship until yesterday morning."

"Was it only yesterday? It seems like so long ago."

"I know."

"So you're really interested in me? I mean, honestly?"

"Honestly. We need to go slow, though, Cullen. It's imperative to me that you're healed. I need to make sure I'm not going to be some flash in the pan to help you get over Sara."

"You're not, Julia. I promise you that. And we can go as slow as you want. I'm just thrilled you didn't shoot me down."

"How could I? I'm crazy about you, Cullen Matthews. Have been for a while now."

"Not all the way back to high school, I bet."

"You'd be surprised."

CHAPTER FOURTEEN

Julia's heart was thudding in her chest. This was like a dream come true. Cullen wanted to be with her. Her. Julia Stansworth. She wanted to pinch herself to make sure it was real. But she had to play it cool as she needed to protect her heart as well as Cullen's.

She didn't doubt that Cullen had feelings for her. Cullen was an honest person. If she said she wanted more than a friendship, then Julia believed her. But she couldn't get Sara out of her head. Cullen and Sara had been brief, but it seemed like they'd burned hot and if Cullen was still burning hot but looking for somewhere to direct that heat, Julia didn't want anything to do with that. So they'd go slow like she'd said and they'd see where they ended up.

"So does that make today our first date?" Julia asked.

"Like miniature golfing? Or here?"

"I was thinking golfing."

"Sure, we can call it that."

Julia beamed. She'd asked Cullen out for their first date. It was a great feeling.

"You look proud of yourself," Cullen said.

"I am, if you must know."

"Good." Cullen laughed. "I'm through here. Are you ready to head back to my place?"

Julia's whole body vibrated. She definitely wanted to go back to Cullen's place. She wanted to get there, rip Cullen's clothes off, and find her way to heaven. But she couldn't, wouldn't do that, not yet. She took a deep breath.

"What will we do there?"

"I'm in the mood to play poker."

"Oh, you are, are you?" Cullen had wiped the floor with Julia the first time they'd played.

"Maybe strip poker?" Cullen grinned at her.

"Cullen…"

"I'm just joking, relax. We said we'd take it slow and we will. I promise."

"Phew. Okay, let's go back to your place."

When they got to Cullen's, Cullen tossed her phone on the dining room table while she went to get the cards and poker chips. Julia sat down and waited. When Cullen's phone came alive, Julia started. She reached for the phone but pulled her hand back. It wasn't her phone. It wasn't her business, or was it?

Cullen came in ready to play.

"Your phone buzzed," Julia said.

"Oh yeah?" She looked at it and her face fell.

"What's up?"

"Sara."

"Yeah? What does she say?"

"She's just checking in."

"You should respond to her."

"Why, Julia? Why do you always want me to talk to her? She's my past. You're my present. I don't want to have anything to do with her."

"Because I want her to keep texting you. I want her to get comfortable. I want her to slip up."

"Okay, what shall I say?"

"I don't know. Keep it casual, but keep lines of communication open."

What's it like where you are? It's snowing here today.

Snowing? It's sunny and warm here.

Where are you? In Hawaii? LOL

"Nice touch," Julia said. "I like it."

"I'm trying."

Have you talked to that fuckin detective yet?

"What do I say?" Cullen asked.

"That's up to you."

She's been around. Asking lots of questions.

"Tell her about her house," Julia said.

She's so inept. She needs to give up. She'll never find me.

Julia's blood boiled. Inept? How dare she?

"You sure you want me to keep this conversation going?" Cullen asked.

"I'm sure."

Did you hear about your house?

What about it?

Someone shot it up last night.

There was no immediate response.

"Maybe she's gone now." Cullen set her phone down and picked up the cards. "I'll deal and you pass out the chips."

"Sounds good."

Cullen's phone buzzed again.

Who did it?

Whoever shot Donnie.

No shit?

Yeah. Good thing you weren't there.

No shit. I gotta go. I'll check in later.

"Speaking of her house getting shot up," Cullen said.

"Yeah?"

"When can I get my stuff?"

"I don't know, Cullen. Everything in her house is evidence right now."

"Damn." Cullen shook her head. "What was I ever thinking getting involved with her?"

"You didn't know. You had no idea." Julia paused. "Right?"

"Of course, that's right. How could you even ask?"

"Just checking. Sorry. I trust you, Cullen. Sometimes I just slip into detective mode."

"Well, leave your badge and holster at the door when you're with me, okay?"

"I'll try. I really will."

"Thank you."

"So, did I ruin the mood? Everything?"

"No, we need to get used to each other. I get that. And I was involved with one of your suspects. That's the truth, so it's got to be weird for you."

"I do trust you, though. It's important to me that you know that."

"I do."

Cullen laid her hand over Julia's. It was warm and strong, and Julia flipped her hand over so she could interlink their fingers. Her heart thudded, and she was scared that Cullen would pull away. But she didn't. She gave Julia's fingers a squeeze.

Julia's phone rang interrupting the mood.

"Stansworth," she barked.

"Detective? The locksmith got the safe open in Donovan's house."

"What did you find?"

"A ton of residue, presumably cocaine. But we found something in the very back of the safe. It's a slip of paper and we think you should see it."

"I'm on my way."

She hung up.

"Where are you going?" Cullen said.

"To Sara's house. I'll be right back. I promise."

"Can I go?"

"Sure. But stay in the car, okay?"

"You got it."

Julia drove carefully through the snow. She waved to the uniformed officers at Sara's house and went inside. She found the officer who'd called her, Officer McKinney, in Sara's room.

"Where's the paper?" she said.

"On the dresser. Don't worry, we took pictures of it before we touched it. It looks like a list of some sort, handwritten."

Julia picked up the small piece of paper. It was indeed a list. There were names, neighborhoods, and phone numbers, and Julia planned to call each one. At first glance, the only one that stuck out to her was Sherry in Mount Tabor. She'd have to check the phone number to be sure it was the same Sherry, though she had little doubt.

Then she saw the name Donnie at the Delta Iota Kappa house. That must be Montague. This list might turn out to be priceless.

"Great job, McKinney. Go ahead and bag this and take it to the evidence room. I'll look into it more tomorrow."

"Yes, ma'am."

She got back into the car.

"Anything exciting?" Cullen asked.

"I think so. Looks like she might have left a list of clients behind."

"Is that right? That's great, isn't it?"

"You'd better believe it."

Cullen was happy for Julia. She wanted to see her succeed. She knew she was a determined, hard worker, and she deserved to move up the ranks if that's what she wanted. She realized that she didn't know anything about Julia's hopes and dreams. She made a mental note to ask her as soon as they got home.

They were in the middle of a game of Texas Hold'em when Cullen remembered her question.

"So where do you see yourself in five years?" she said.

Julia laughed.

"Are you interviewing me now?"

Cullen laughed, too.

"No, nothing like that. I just realized I don't know what you aspire to. Like, do you want to be police chief someday or what?"

"Hell no! I don't want the headaches that go with that job. I just want to be the best damned detective I can be."

"Yeah? That sounds worthy."

"Thank you. What about you? What are your hopes and dreams?"

"I want my own ad agency someday."

"Really? That would be cool."

"I think so."

"What did you want to be when you were a kid?" Julia asked. "I mean, I can't imagine a young Cullen dying to run her own ad agency."

Cullen laughed again. She couldn't help it. Julia was funny which was a good thing. She needed humor in her life. Maybe she and Sara had laughed at some point in their relationship, but it didn't seem like it. They'd had a lot of sex, at least in the beginning, but toward the end cocaine had become more important to Sara than anything.

"Hello?" Julia said. "Earth to Cullen. Were you going to answer the question?"

"Sorry." Cullen blushed. She didn't need to be comparing Julia to Sara. That wasn't fair. "I wanted to be an author."

"Really? What did you want to write?"

"Mysteries."

"Do you still want to do that? I mean, is the dream still intact?"

"I don't know. Sometimes I think I should and other times I don't know if I have it in me."

"Really?" Julia said. "Why not?"

"I don't know. It just seems like so much work."

"Maybe we could write a book together."

"How so?"

"Believe me, I have plenty of fodder for mystery books. Or maybe you could write about you and Sara."

"Nah, that's too close to home for me."

They tabled the conversation and focused on cards for the next couple of hours. They were pretty much even when Cullen's stomach growled loudly.

"Sorry about that." She was embarrassed.

"You're hungry? How is that even possible?"

"I don't know."

"You want to go grab some food?"

"I'm so tired of eating out all the time. Let's go grocery shopping. We'll fill my cupboards and then I'll make something for dinner."

"That sounds good to me, except I want to make dinner. If you can wait, I make a mean lasagna."

They brainstormed together and Julia wrote out a shopping list. They got in Cullen's truck and she carefully navigated the snowy streets to the grocery store.

"I love how everything is so close here in Bidwell," Julia said.

"Yeah, it's convenient. That's for sure."

The parking lot for the store was practically empty. The cars that were in it were parked all willy-nilly since the lines were covered with snow. Cullen gently tapped her brake until she came to a stop.

She felt good wandering the store with Julia. She took her hand and squeezed it at one point. She wanted to hold it the whole way through the store, but Bidwell was a conservative town and she didn't want trouble. She could handle herself and was comfortable Julia could too, but she wanted this to be a pleasant experience without ugliness of any sort.

They got home an hour later, and Julia excused herself to the kitchen. Cullen cleaned up the cards and poker chips and set the table for dinner. The house smelled good, like garlic, which was one of her favorite smells. She went into the kitchen to see how Julia was doing.

"Do you need any help?" she asked.

"Nope, I'm good. I'm just putting it in the oven now. What do you want to do while we wait?"

Cullen could think of a million things she wanted to do with Julia, some of which involved eating. But now wasn't the time.

"Why don't I open a bottle of wine? Then I'll get a fire going and we can chill in front of it."

"That sounds wonderful."

Cullen got the fire roaring then poured them each a glass of wine. Julia was already on the couch, so she handed her glass to her and stood there contemplating where to sit. Normally, she'd sit in the recliner to avoid temptation. But now that they were dating, she could sit next to Julia, right?

Julia patted the couch next to her as if reading Cullen's mind. Cullen sat next to her and ran her arm along the back of the couch as Julia snuggled against her.

"This is nice, isn't it?" Julia said.

"Mm, very."

"This wine is very good, too. Who knew you were such a connoisseur? I have a feeling I'm really going to enjoy getting to know you better, Ms. Matthews."

"Think so, huh?"

"I do."

Cullen couldn't believe the turn of events. One minute, she was practically begging Sara to quit coke, which she now knew she had no intention of doing. The next minute, Sara killed some woman for an as yet unknown reason. And now? Well, now she was cuddling on the couch with a woman she'd been pining for since she was a sophomore, nearly thirty years ago. Life was definitely looking up.

"What are you thinking?" Julia rested her hand on Cullen's thigh, and it seared through her jeans and into her flesh. She rested her hand over it.

"Just thinking about life and all its crazy twists and turns."

"I'm glad those twists and turns brought us to where we are now."

"Amen to that."

Cullen tore her gaze away from the mesmerizing fire to look into Julia's deep blue eyes. Her lashes were long and full. She didn't need makeup, and Cullen was glad she didn't wear any. Julia's eyes sparkled in the firelight and seemed to beg Cullen.

In that moment, Cullen wanted nothing more than to taste Julia's lips. Something she'd dreamed of since she was a kid in school. Julia's lips were full and parted, and Cullen wondered just how slow Julia wanted to go. She could always ask or she could say to hell with it and just find out.

Cullen looked into Julia's eyes which seemed to darken as she stared at her. She lowered her gaze to Julia's lips again. This would be their first kiss, and she wanted it to be perfect. What could be more perfect than this moment?

She was only vaguely aware of the crackle in the fire and the smells of lasagna wafting through the house. She leaned closer to Julia who turned her head up to meet her. Cullen watched

Julia's eyes close before she closed her own and touched her lips to Julia's.

The shock wave that tore through her was unexpected. She'd anticipated it being wonderful, but her heart was beating so hard she thought it might pound its way out of her chest. Julia tasted sweet. She tasted like wine and snow and her own unique flavor. Her lips were soft and pliant, and Cullen couldn't help but kiss her harder.

She was growing lightheaded and needed more. So much more. How much was allowed though? How much was too much?

Cullen ran her tongue along Julia's lips, and Julia opened her mouth to welcome her in. Their tongues danced together for what seemed like an eternity. Cullen wanted to run her hands over Julia's body, to explore every inch of her. Instead, she wrapped her free hand around Julia's back and pulled her into her.

The feel of Julia's small, firm breasts pressed against her made her even dizzier. She leaned Julia back until she was on top of her on the couch. And still the kiss continued. Cullen was about to bring her knee up to press into Julia's center when she came to her senses. She needed to end the kiss before she did anything they weren't ready for.

She closed her mouth and sucked on Julia's lips before kissing her nose and opening her eyes. She sat up and helped Julia to a sitting position. She held her close and kissed the top of her head.

"You know how to kiss," Julia whispered.

"As do you." Cullen almost didn't recognize her own voice. It was deep and husky and full of need. "As do you."

CHAPTER FIFTEEN

Julia was shaking as she fought to catch her breath. She could have lost herself with Cullen and was so appreciative Cullen had stopped when she did. The sound of the timer cut through the lust induced fog in her brain.

"Oh, shit. Dinner's ready." She jumped off the couch and hurried to the kitchen.

Cullen sauntered in shortly after.

"What can I do?" she said.

"Where do you keep the plates?"

"Right here."

Cullen handed the plates to Julia, who served lasagna and salad to them. They carried their plates to the table and began to eat.

"So, was that okay?" Cullen said.

"What?"

"The kiss. I mean, am I allowed to kiss you?"

"Of course. You didn't hear me saying no, did you?"

"No, but I just wanted to check. You know, make sure we're okay."

"We're fine, Cullen. As a matter of fact, we're excellent."

After dinner, Cullen got the fire going again and they sat on the couch alternating kissing and watching the fire. It was a wonderful evening. One Julia didn't want to end, but soon she was yawning against her will.

"Is it time for bed?" Cullen said.

"I'm afraid so."

"Will you stay here?"

"I'd like that very much. If you'll excuse me, I'll hit the guest room now."

"Why not stay with me?"

"Cullen." Julia was frustrated that Cullen would think she'd have sex with her. Did she not hear her statement about taking things slow? Just because they'd kissed didn't mean she'd fall into bed with her. Not that she didn't want to. She just knew it wouldn't be right. Not yet. "I meant what I said about taking things slow."

"And I understand and agree. We'd just sleep. I promise."

"I don't know..."

Cullen disappeared into her bedroom and came back bearing some sweats.

"Here, we'll each wear sweats to avoid any temptation," she said.

"Fair enough. I think I'd love to sleep in your arms."

"I know I'll enjoy it."

Cullen's arms were strong and sure and felt so right wrapped around her. Julia slept better than she had in a very long time. When she awoke alone in the morning, she was disoriented then disappointed. Where was Cullen?

She stretched then got out of bed and followed the smell of coffee to the kitchen, but Cullen wasn't there either. Julia helped herself to a cup of the fresh brew then went into the dining room where she found Cullen working on her laptop.

Julia kissed Cullen good morning. It was a brief kiss that made her heart do somersaults. She had it bad, there was no doubt about that. But was it just lust or did she have feelings for Cullen? She thought she had true feelings for her but knew only time would tell.

"Whatcha working on?" Julia said.

"Just a campaign for a client. I figured since I didn't work yesterday I'd better take a look at things today."

"Ah, no rest for the wicked, eh?"

"Exactly. And what about you? Any plans to work today? It's Saturday, after all."

"Yes, it is, but murder investigations don't wait. I need to go into the office at least for a while. Did the snow stop?"

"Yeah, but it's still white outside. It's probably icy. I'd rather you not drive in it."

Julia rested her hand on Cullen's shoulder.

"I appreciate that, but I need to make an appearance. Besides, I've got work to do. I need to get ahold of those people on Sara's list. I need to learn all I can."

"Right. Well, the Ducks play at four today, so I'd like it if you were home by then."

"Home, huh?" Julia laughed. She loved Cullen's house and she loved being with Cullen. But she had her own house in the city. One that she loved as well.

"You know what I mean."

"I do. Maybe I'll stop by my house and get a change of clothes or something to keep here, if that's okay?"

"That would be great."

"Okay, I'm going to get dressed and hit the road."

"Please be careful."

"I will."

Julia white knuckled the steering wheel as she slid this way and that on the icy roads leading to the freeway. The freeway had been plowed, fortunately. Although it was littered with cars that obviously hadn't reached their destination the day before.

She made it to her house where she took a shower and changed into black jeans and a black sweater with a purple long-sleeved shirt underneath. She put on her coat and drove carefully through the streets until she reached the station.

There weren't a lot of people in due to the road conditions. She greeted the skeleton crew before going to the evidence room where she collected Sara's list and headed for her desk. The first thing she did was call the number for Sherry on the list.

The phone gave a message that the number had been disconnected or was otherwise not in service. While it wasn't absolute proof it was the dead woman's number, it was pretty damning. She called Sherry's husband.

"Hello?"

"Hello. Mr. Bergstrom? This is Detective Stansworth. I'm really sorry to bother you, but can you tell me what your wife's phone number was?"

He gave it to her.

"What's this about?" he asked.

"As you know, we've got a suspect for her murder. We're just accumulating as much evidence as we can. And I came across that phone number in the suspect's belongings."

"Nail her to the wall, Detective, please."

"I'll do my best. Thank you for your time."

"Good-bye."

She looked over the rest of the list. Donnie was there, but Sara'd admitted she knew the kid. His case was still open and growing cold and Julia needed to catch a break there. She decided to start at the top of the list and work her way down.

The first name was Molly who apparently lived in the South Hills. That was where Sara had been pulled over for DUI and where she'd been busted for possession. Was there a connection? Clearly, she'd been dealing that day, otherwise why would she have had so much coke on her? Julia needed to talk to this Molly woman to learn all she could. Not today, though. She wasn't about to drive up those roads in the ice. She'd wait until Monday, but she could call her now.

"Hello?" The voice on the other end was high-pitched, nasally, and annoying. Julia reminded herself she needed this woman's help.

"Hello? Is this Molly?"

"Who's asking, please?"

"My name is Detective Stansworth with the Portland Police Bureau. I'd like to ask you a few questions."

There was a pregnant silence on the other end.

"I'm not sure why you're calling me, Detective," Molly finally said.

"I believe you had some dealings with a murder suspect."

"A what? I'm sure you're mistaken."

"Still, I'd like to come by and question you. Would Monday morning work?"

"What time?"

"Say ten?"

"Do I have a choice?"

"We could always bring you down to the station for questioning." Julia hoped her intentional manipulativeness didn't come through in her voice.

"No, you can come here. Ten o'clock Monday. I'll be here."

"Great, thank you. Now, can I get your address, please?"

Molly gave it to her and Julia hung up the phone. She dialed the next number on the list.

Cullen laid out the ad campaigns for two clients. She felt productive and that was a great feeling. She checked her phone. It was three o'clock and Julia should be home soon. She thought so, anyway. Cullen hopped in the shower and dressed in her Duck gear.

She popped a beer and sat in front of the TV. There was still time before kickoff, so she got up and made a fire. The temperature had continued to drop all day and, while her house was nice and warm, a fire would help make it cozy.

Cullen had just sat back on the couch with ten minutes to spare when there was a knock at the door. She opened it to see Julia standing there looking breathtakingly beautiful.

"Come on in. You're just in time." Cullen kissed her on the cheek and took her hand. Julia pulled away and started for the kitchen.

"I'm going to get myself a glass of wine. You want a beer?"

"No, thanks, I'm good."

"Okay. Now get situated and I'll be right there."

True to her word, Julia was by her side in no time. Cullen draped an arm over her shoulders and tried to play it cool. It would be their first Duck game together and, while she would try her best to maintain composure, she was sure her intensity would freak Julia out.

She bounced in her seat when a good play was made and threw her head back when the Ducks made a mistake. She was so caught up in the game she barely heard Julia laughing. Cullen tore her gaze away from the screen to cast a sidelong look at her.

"What? What's so funny?"

"You. You're trying so hard not to yell and scream at the TV. It's amusing, but unnecessary. I don't mind it if you get into the game."

"Are you sure? I don't want to scare you off."

"You won't. I'm not going anywhere."

The game ended several hours later with the Ducks trouncing their opponent and Cullen was in a great mood. She kissed Julia, who kissed her back with such fervor that Cullen almost lost her head. She broke the kiss just before her stomach growled.

"Oh, shit," she said. "Dinner. You up for a steak?"

"Sounds delicious."

"I think I'll grill."

"Seriously?" Julia said. "It's still in the thirties out there."

"So bundle up. Come on out with me. You can tell me about your day."

They stood shivering as Cullen manned the grill.

"You really want to know how my day went?"

"I do."

"It was long. To start with, the drive in was the drive from hell on the icy roads."

"Oh, I'm sure. I'm glad you were careful."

"Of course. And then I set up meetings with several of the people on Sara's list."

"How'd that go over?"

"Like a fart in Sunday school. You can just imagine how thrilled people were to know they were linked to a murder suspect."

"I bet. I don't envy you, Julia. You have a hard, thankless job."

"I appreciate that, I really do."

They went inside and ate their dinner. They were doing the dishes when Cullen felt a buzz in her pocket and took out her phone.

"I just got a text from Sara."

"What's it say?"

Cullen set her phone on the counter so they could both read it and formulate a reply if Julia deemed one needed.

I heard about the snow. Are you okay?

I'm fine. Stayed in today to avoid the icy roads.

"Nice answer," Julia said. "Keep texting. Draw her out. Make her comfortable."

"She's not going to tell me where she is."

"You never know. Is this the same number as yesterday?"

"No. It's a different one."

"She must be using burner cell phones. Shit."

That was smart. I worry.

You don't need to worry. I'm doing okay. Is it still sunny where you are?

Yes. Please don't ask where I am. I won't tell you.

I understand.

"I can't think of anything else to say."

"That's okay. She'll probably disappear now."

"Yeah, probably."

But Sara texted again.

You know they'll never find me, right?

I believe you.

But if they did, would you come visit me?

"How the hell am I supposed to answer that?" Cullen asked.

"Feed her ego."

"You're kidding, right?"

"I'm dead serious."

Of course. I'd give anything to see you again.

She cocked an eyebrow at Julia before she hit send. Julia nodded, so Cullen sent it.

Oh, Cullen. I'm sorry things ended the way they did. But they had to. You understand?

Did you kill that woman?

Julia reached for Cullen's hand, but she'd already hit send.

"Cullen! I don't want you to scare her off."

"I'm sorry. Not really. I just want to know what she has to say for herself."

Of course not! I didn't kill anybody. How can you even ask such a thing?

Well, you left in quite a hurry. I can't help but wonder what you're running from.

That bitch of a detective would have framed me. I can't go to prison, Cullen.

Cullen looked at Julia.

"Now can I tell her to fuck off?"

Julia smiled.

"No way, Jose. It's just getting good."

"You're actually entertained by this, aren't you?"

"She's cocky. She thinks she's invincible. That's when they slip up. It's just a matter of time now."

No. I can't see you in prison

So I'll stay free, okay? And I'll be in touch. Good night, Cullen, and congrats on the win.

Thanks. Good night.

Cullen shoved her phone in her pocket.

"Shit. I hate talking to her."

"I know, babe, but it's important."

Cullen didn't miss the term of endearment.

"Babe?" she said.

"It just kind of slipped out. I hope it's okay."

"It's more than okay, Julia. It's wonderful."

CHAPTER SIXTEEN

Monday morning dawned too soon for Julia. She turned off her alarm and snuggled closer to Cullen, who was warm and soft in all the right places. The urge to play hooky crept into Julia's mind and she closed her eyes before remembering she had a day of interviews ahead of her.

"Just five more minutes," Cullen murmured against her neck.

"I wish. You take five more minutes. I'll go hop in the shower."

Suddenly, Cullen was wide-awake.

"I'll join you."

"A for effort, loverboi. You rest. I'll wake you when I get out."

She grabbed her clothes for the day and took her shower. When she was dressed, she walked into the bedroom to wake Cullen up, but Cullen wasn't there. Julia took her shoulder holster from the nightstand and put it on. She turned to go find Cullen and ran right in to her.

"Careful." Cullen struggled not to spill the coffee she was carrying. "Here, I thought you might need this."

"Thank you. You're the best."

Julia kissed Cullen lightly, but Cullen used her free hand to pull her close and kissed her harder. Julia's knees went weak at the intensity of the kiss, and she pulled away eventually, disappointed that work called. She placed her hand on Cullen's chest.

"You hold that thought. I've got to go."

"Okay, you be careful out there."

"Always."

Julia arrived at the station at seven thirty on the dot and logged on to her computer. She checked her schedule. Her day was booked with interviews but didn't start until ten. She entered all the information into her phone then went to talk to the team she'd assigned to Sara's house.

"Since I didn't hear from you guys again, I take it the weekend was fairly nonproductive?" She helped herself to a cup of their coffee. Keurig mint chocolate chip. Much better than what she usually drank at work.

"Nothing new to report. We're still watching the house around the clock, but there's been no more activity. We've searched every inch of that house and there's nothing, absolutely nothing, that might indicate where she might have gone."

Julia sighed.

"Well, that sucks, but good job tearing the place apart. I appreciate it. You guys can call off the twenty-four/seven guard duty there. I don't think she's coming back at this point. Any word yet on her car? Anybody report anything on that front?"

"No, ma'am, she must have changed plates."

"She must have, but with whom and where? She had to have done it before she left town, right? And no news from railroads, airports, or buses?"

"Not a word."

"She's a smart one, for a common criminal. Okay, I'm going to help myself to another cup of your coffee then head back to my desk. Thanks for the report."

How could Sara have simply slipped away? It was damned near impossible to just disappear nowadays. What with social media and the internet and modern technology. She must have missed something, but what?

All she knew was that Sara was someplace warm. At least that's what she'd told Cullen. It could have been a lie though. Dishonesty came so naturally to her. She sat at her desk and worked on paperwork until it was time to leave.

She gave herself twenty minutes to get up to the South Hills, but it only took ten, so she sat in her car for ten minutes, chomping at the bit, ready to get started. She had no information on Molly at all except that she was presumably a client of Sara's. But how good of a client was she? Did she buy for personal use or did Sara use her as a middleman? Since she was first on the list, Julia assumed Molly was at least somewhat of a dealer as well.

At precisely ten o'clock, she rang the doorbell. Dead silence. She didn't hear a dog barking, people moving around, nothing, so she rang again. This time someone answered the door. Molly was a forty-something housewife dressed in navy slacks and a fluffy pink sweater. Her brown hair was perfectly coiffed, but the pupils in her brown eyes were dilated. Was she coked up? Julia wouldn't have been surprised. Of course, it could have simply been the stress of meeting with a detective. A detective who wouldn't give any information prior to the meeting.

"Detective Stansworth," Molly said. "Won't you come in?"

"Thank you."

"Can I get you something to drink? A cup of coffee, something stronger?"

At ten in the morning? Oh, wow.

"No, thank you, I'm fine. Why don't we sit down?"

"Oh, certainly. You know, Detective, I think there must be some sort of mistake. I'm really not the kind of woman who associates with murderers."

Julia smiled reassuringly.

"I'm sure you're not. Do me a favor, though. Please look at this picture and tell me if you recognize this person."

She handed over a picture of Sara talking to Montague with Montague cropped out. Julia watched Molly closely. She saw a spark of recognition flash in her eyes before she regained her composure.

"I don't know who that is. And is she, the woman, a murderer?"

"We believe so. We believe she's killed at least twice. Anything you can tell us would help."

"I'm sorry. I don't know her."

"Look, Molly, I know you know her, so you can stop insulting my intelligence."

"No, I don't."

"Your name was found on a list in her house. She was arrested and charged with possession with intent to distribute while she was in your neighborhood. Any rookie cop could put two and two together. And I'm not a rookie cop."

Molly looked like the proverbial deer in the headlights.

"I swear. I don't know her."

"Save it. I could get a warrant and search your house because, based on her list, I have reason to believe she sold you coke to sell, not just to use. Or we can be civil and you can tell me everything you can."

A tear leaked out of Molly's eye. Nice touch, but it didn't work. Julia wasn't about to soften up. She simply leveled an even gaze at Molly.

"What do you want to know?"

"What can you tell me?"

"Yes, she was an acquaintance of mine."

Julia arched an eyebrow.

"Acquaintance? She was your coke dealer."

"Okay, so I used to indulge, but I don't anymore."

"This isn't about your habits. This is about finding a missing woman."

"She's missing?"

"She ran after we arrested her for murder."

"Sara wouldn't hurt a fly. I'm sure you're wrong about her murdering someone."

"Two someones."

Molly covered her mouth with her hand and shook her head.

"No. I'm sorry, Detective. You're looking for the wrong woman."

"You're entitled to your delusions. Did she ever mention running away to you?"

"No. I mean, she used to talk about moving to somewhere warm where there were a lot of lesbians. But never seriously and certainly not after she started dating that woman."

Julia's skin crawled. She hated to think about Sara and Cullen. She hated it even more when some random stranger brought it up.

"Right. So warmer climate and lots of lesbians. I guess that gives me something to go on."

"Is she really gone?" Molly said.

"I'm afraid so." Julia stood and handed her card to Molly. "If you think of anything else, anything at all, don't hesitate to call. Who knows? You may be the one who can prove her innocence."

"Oh, I'd like that."

"I'm sure you would. Enjoy your day, Molly. I'll see myself out."

The rest of her interviews went about the same, with no one really knowing Sara well enough to help. Molly had been the biggest help. Now Julia just needed to figure out what warm cities were known for their lesbian populations, but she had no idea where to even start.

She shot Cullen a text at five saying she'd be late. She got there at seven, exhausted, but looking forward to spending some time together. She rang the doorbell and Cullen answered in her sweats.

"Thanks for texting me. I would have been worried. Long day, huh?"

"Oh yeah."

Cullen wrapped her arms around Julia and held her tight. She wanted to make her forget her day. After a couple of minutes, she pulled back and lowered her lips to taste Julia's. Her lips, cold at first, quickly warmed up as she melted into Cullen.

Heart thudding in her chest, Cullen slid her tongue in Julia's mouth and their tongues frolicked together. Cullen ground against Julia, pressing into her and craving more contact. She was throbbing with desire and didn't give a damn about waiting.

Somewhere, through a fog, she felt Julia tapping on her shoulder. She broke the kiss and rested her forehead on Julia's.

"Damn, I kind of lost myself there."

"Yeah, you did." Julia laughed nervously. "It was a great kiss and a wonderful welcome home, but we need to be careful."

"Maybe I'm tired of being careful."

"I know it's not easy, babe. But it's important that we're sure this is right."

"I don't think I can be more sure."

"Aw, Cullen, you're so sweet."

Cullen took a deep breath and ran her fingers through her hair. Shaking, she took Julia by the hand and led her to the kitchen. She poured them each a glass of wine, but before she handed Julia hers, she took her by both hands and pulled her in for another kiss.

By the time that one ended, Cullen was ready to rip Julia's clothes off, but she didn't. She was strong. She handed Julia her wine.

"How was your day? Besides long?"

"It was great. I mean really. I learned a lot about Sara and may have even gotten a lead on where she is."

"And just where might that be?" Cullen listened intently while she nibbled on Julia's neck.

"Hm? You make it hard to concentrate, Cullen Matthews."

Cullen straightened.

"Fine, I'll stop. Come on into the living room where we can relax."

Julia slipped off her shoes and curled next to Cullen on the couch. Cullen's body was alive with need, every nerve ending Julia was pressed into sizzled with unspent desire.

She was thinking about kissing her again when Julia sat up straight.

"Did you and Sara ever talk about moving anywhere?"

"You mean like in together? Julia, we were only together about six weeks."

"True. Did she ever mention maybe thinking about moving somewhere else? Even if in just a fantasy kind of way?"

Cullen grew frustrated and fought to curb the anger at what she thought she was being accused of.

"Julia, if I knew where she was…if I had any idea…I'd tell you. I wouldn't keep any information from you, especially something that vital."

Julia rested her hand on Cullen's thigh, and Cullen forced herself not to pull away.

"I didn't mean to imply that you would. I was just curious. I learned something today that could be important."

"And what might that be?" Cullen started to defrost slightly.

"She wanted to move somewhere warm. Some place with a high population of lesbians."

"Is that right? Well, I guess that's where she is now."

"Maybe," Julia said. "Maybe. I wish she'd text you."

As if on cue, Cullen's phone buzzed in her pocket. She pulled it out and stared at it.

"Speak of the devil," she said.

"What does she have to say tonight?"

Cullen showed her the phone.

I miss you. I wish things hadn't ended how they did.

Well, at least I know now you had no intention of quitting coke.

"Cullen!" Julia said. "Be nice."

"Shit. Okay, I'll try again."

In response to Sara's silence, Cullen sent another text.

Are you seeing anyone?

LOL I just moved.

Still...

No. I'm not. Are you?

Cullen looked at Julia who shook her head.

No. Me, neither.

"Ask her if there are lots of lesbians there."

Is there a decent gay community there? Are there lots of lesbians?

She looked at Julia who was beaming.

A ton. It's like paradise here. I tell you.

That's great. I'm happy for you.

I've got to go. I'll text you tomorrow.

Good night, Sara.

Good night.

Julia patted Cullen's arm.

"You did good, babe. You did really good."

"You think she'll ever tell us where she is?"

"Not intentionally. But I'm thinking we'll get enough clues to piece it together."

"I hope you're right."

"Count on it, handsome."

She kissed Cullen then and Cullen's mind went blank. She couldn't think; she could only feel. She felt every emotion so keenly. She felt her hormones raging against their confines, and she felt her boxers dampen with the urge to make love to Julia.

When the kiss finally ended, Julia threw herself back against the couch.

"I'm famished," she said.

"I know something you could eat." Cullen grinned and wiggled her eyebrows.

"All in due time, dear heart. All in due time."

CHAPTER SEVENTEEN

Cullen woke when she heard Julia get up the following morning.

"Why do you always get up so early?" she whined.

"To beat traffic and to make sure there haven't been any new developments in either of my two favorite cases."

"Wouldn't someone have gotten in touch with you if something had come up?"

"In theory, my dear, but in reality? Who knows?"

Cullen rolled over onto her back and stared at the ceiling.

"What's on your mind?" Julia said.

"Nothing really. I was just wondering if we should split our time between our houses. Don't get me wrong. I love having you here and I love my house, but the commute is so much better from yours."

"True statement. Why don't you pack some clothes and we'll just plan on staying at my house for a few?"

"That sounds good. I'll do it."

"Great." Julia kissed her, and Cullen's nipples puckered painfully. "I'll start getting ready. I'll be out in a jiff."

Cullen tried to relax, but it was hard knowing Julia was naked in the next room. How could she be so calm, cool, and collected? Didn't she want Cullen? She said she did, but she was so strong, damn it. Cullen knew she had to be strong too. It sure as hell wasn't easy, but was anything that was worth having?

Julia came out of the bathroom, the scent of her body wash wafting in with her. Cullen breathed deeply. She smelled so good. Cullen just wanted to eat her up.

"What's with you?" Julia smiled.

"What?"

"I don't know. You have this odd look on your face. Is everything okay?"

"It's fine. I just want you and it's getting harder to not take you."

"Patience, my dear. I promise to make it worth your while."

"Oh, I don't doubt that. I don't doubt that one bit."

She pulled Julia in and kissed her.

"Okay, Cullen," Julia said. "Any more of that and I'll never go to work again. Now you behave and I'll get out of here."

"Yes, ma'am. Be careful out there."

"I will. You drive carefully to work when you finally hit the road."

"Will do," Cullen said.

"I'll see you at my house this evening."

Julia gave Cullen a sweet peck on the cheek before she left. Alone in the house, Cullen lay back down. She knew she needed to get going, but she was in pain from wanting Julia so desperately. What would it hurt to take matters into her own hands, just once?

No! She catapulted herself out of bed and took a cool shower, dressed, and took off for work. She sat in her office, powered on her computer, and checked her email. Top of the list was an email from Samantha in human resources asking to see her. Samantha and Cullen had gone on a couple of dates a few years ago before Samantha started working at Logan and Bremer. What could she possibly want to see Cullen for now?

She sent her a chat message saying she was on her way and didn't wait for a reply. Cullen arrived at Samantha's office one floor up from hers and poked her head into the office.

"You wanted to see me?"

Samantha looked up from her monitor.

"Cullen. Great, yes, please come in."

Cullen stepped inside the plush office decorated in soft blues and browns. Samantha stood and closed the door. She motioned to one of the leather chairs on the near side of her desk so Cullen sat and was surprised when Samantha took the other chair.

"What's going on? Why did you need to see me?"

"Cullen, I like you and I respect you. So I'm going to give you a heads-up before our staff meeting today."

Cullen's skin crawled and her stomach tightened. Why didn't this sound like a good thing?

"Okay, shoot. I'm all ears."

"You do great work. You're one of our best."

Why did she stop?

"And? But? What?"

"As you have no doubt noticed, the firm isn't doing real well. And because of that, we're facing massive layoffs."

Cullen thought she was going to puke.

"And this affects me? I'm going to be let go?"

Samantha drew a deep breath.

"I don't want to see you go, Cullen. I really don't. Nobody does, but we need to let people go. I wanted to talk to you about your attendance lately. Or lack thereof. You've missed a lot of work in the past month or so. I hate to say it, but that's one of the criteria we're going to be using."

"So you're letting me go?"

"No, not at the moment."

"Good. Look, I've had some personal issues I've had to deal with. But they're all resolved now. I won't be missing any more work."

"I hope not. It won't look good if you do."

"I won't."

"Excellent, that's what I needed to hear."

"So," Cullen said, "lots of layoffs, huh? This should be fun."

"It's all confidential still at this point. I could lose my job for telling you this."

"I won't say a word. You know you can trust me."

"Yes, I do know that. Keep your head down and your ass in your office and you should make it through the first round of cuts."

Cullen nodded.

"Got it. I'll be here every day."

"Thanks, Cullen."

"No, thank you."

Cullen went back to her office and closed her door. She was in a foul mood and didn't want to deal with anyone. She was close to losing her job over her absences? She had enough time off earned to be off every day for the next year practically. Why hadn't she thought to point that out to Samantha? It didn't matter. She was on their radar and that wasn't good.

Damn Sara anyway. It was her fault Cullen had been missing work. First, to be with her and then because she ran away. She wished Julia would catch her and put her away. But she also wished she didn't have to play a part. Not that she minded helping Julia; she just never wanted to speak to Sara again.

Julia's morning started the minute she hit the station. She had just settled in at her desk when her phone rang. A rock had been found at Sara's house, a large, fist-sized rock with blood on it. She drove back out to Bidwell and met her team at the house.

The rock was in a rock garden in the backyard.

"Holy hell, who thought to look here?"

"It was Cooper's idea."

"Cooper, where are you?"

"Over here, ma'am." A middle-aged man with greasy dark hair approached her. "It was driving me crazy that we never found the murder weapon. I was determined it had to be here somewhere. We were just taking down the police tape and going over the house one more time when I spotted the rock garden and I thought what better place to hide a rock than in plain sight?"

"You're a genius." She slapped him on his arm. "Sheer genius."

She picked up the overturned rock in her gloved hand and slipped it into an evidence bag.

"Did we find anything else?" she asked.

"Nothing yet," Cooper said.

"Yet? You're still looking? I thought you guys had already been over this place."

"We had, but we somehow missed a garbage can out here in the shed. It was hidden pretty well. We're going through it now."

"Hey, Detective," a uniformed woman called to her. "I think you're going to want to see this."

Julia hurried over to the shed. The officer was holding something in some tweezers.

"What have you got there?" Julia said.

"A driver's license belonging to one Sara Donovan."

Julia's heart skipped a beat. Adrenaline and coffee coursed through her making her heart race. They had Sara's driver's license. Which confirmed her suspicions that she'd created a new identity before she moved on. It would make her that much harder to find.

She bagged the license and turned to leave.

"You guys are the best. Keep up the good work."

Julia took the evidence to Mike in the lab.

"I want this rock gone over so carefully it'll make you nuts, got it? I want fingerprints, blood type, hair follicles, the works. When can you have it to me?"

"Seriously? I suppose you want it today."

"You know it. That's probably the murder weapon in the Bergstrom case and I want a definite yes by end of day."

"Yes, ma'am. I'll have the results to you before I leave."

"Thank you."

"Welcome." His terse response did nothing to cool her mood. She was getting closer to Sara. She could feel it.

She was very excited and she wanted to celebrate, so she called Cullen.

"Hey there, I'm taking you out for dinner tonight. My treat. Can you sneak out early for drinks first?"

"Sorry, hon, no can do. I'm being watched like a hawk right now and have to be here until four thirty no matter what. What are we celebrating?"

"I'm having a great day. We're so close to getting Sara, babe. So very close."

"That's great."

"You sound flat. And why are you being watched?"

"Nothing I can talk about right now. I'll explain it all when I get home."

"Fair enough. Let's meet at El Gaucho as soon as you're off. We'll have drinks and dinner and you can even have a cigar."

That got a laugh out of Cullen.

"That sounds great. I'll see you then."

"Hope your day gets better."

"Yeah. Me, too."

Julia tossed her phone on the desk and turned to her computer. She searched for warm climate cities with large lesbian populations. Portland was number four, which was interesting, but she needed to focus on the task at hand.

The top three were Ft. Lauderdale, Austin, and Atlanta. She delved into researching those three communities. All three were likely candidates. They all had universities, which was a draw for Sara. Young partiers meant cocaine sales. Just look what happened here.

Austin. She really liked Austin. It was big enough and college oriented and obviously had a large lesbian population. All draws for Sara. Next was Atlanta. It was a nice, big city with universities as well, and it was warm this time of year.

Julia tried to narrow her choices down, but couldn't. She scrolled farther down the list. Palm Springs and Santa Fe were next on the list. She supposed she couldn't rule them out either. Of course, these choices were all contingent on the fact that Sara was telling the truth. And they had no proof of that. Then again, Molly had said she'd talked about moving somewhere warm, so Julia had to trust her gut and contact the police departments of the cities.

She got her information together and sent pictures of Sara to the main police departments in all the cities she'd selected. She mentioned that Sara was a lesbian so to keep their eyes on any parts of the city she may be attracted to. Julia also pointed out her history of selling coke to college students. She finally let them know her fingerprints were in the system and to please notify her if they found anything.

That took most of her afternoon, and she was ready to head home. She was putting on her coat when her phone rang.

"Stansworth."

"Detective? It's Mike from the lab."

She sat back down.

"Mike, great. What have you got for me?"

"That rock was definitely your murder weapon. Bergstrom's DNA was all over it."

"Any fingerprints?"

"No, your suspect was probably wearing gloves. As I recall, it was cold and rainy that day."

"True, well, thanks for the information, Mike. I'll be right down to pick up the evidence. Oh, were there any other fingerprints on Sara's license?"

"A few. Mostly smudged. None that match anybody in the system."

"Great, thanks again. I'm on my way."

Julia picked up the evidence and delivered it to Marge to be filed. Feeling like she'd accomplished a lot that day, she went home and changed into some blue jeans and a thick royal blue sweater. She slipped her coat back on and drove to El Gaucho to meet Cullen.

CHAPTER EIGHTEEN

Cullen was engrossed in working on a campaign for a new client. When she finally glanced at the time, it was past time for her to leave. She logged off her computer, donned her coat, and headed for the parking garage.

Work had been good after the two meetings she'd had that day. The second meeting was the staff meeting where the official announcement had been made and morale plummeted which was to be expected. She locked herself in her office and focused. The day flew by, and it was finally time to see Julia.

The short drive to the restaurant seemed to take forever. She loved Portland and couldn't imagine living anywhere else, but she hated the traffic. It was unbearable at times. She finally arrived at the restaurant and spotted Julia at the bar and snuck up behind her.

"Whatcha drinking?" she whispered in her ear. Julia leaned back into Cullen, and Cullen's pulse quickened. She was really into Julia. There was no denying that, and while the waiting was making her crazy, she knew it was the right thing to do. She wanted to claim Julia as her own in every way possible, but they both needed to be certain where this was going. Sara had betrayed Cullen in a big way, and it was the second time that had happened to her. She needed to know in her heart and soul that she could trust Julia. Only time would tell.

Julia sat up straight.

"I'm having a margarita. Won't you join me?"

"I think I will."

Julia signaled the bartender while Cullen slipped off her coat and draped it over the back of her barstool.

"So, what are we celebrating?" Cullen asked.

Julia looked around the bar, which was empty save the two of them, but she still lowered her voice.

"We found the murder weapon."

"For that Sherry woman?"

"Exactly. She was killed by a blow to the head by a rock. And that rock was in Sara's backyard."

Cullen's stomach lurched. More proof that Sara had been a murderer as well as a drug dealer. She knew it in her heart, but it still hurt that all the proof was piling up to show that Cullen never really knew Sara to begin with.

"That's great," she said. "Now to find the murdering bitch."

"Ah, yes. I worked on that, too. Assuming she's telling you the truth about where she moved, and why wouldn't she, I've sent her information to several warm cities with decent lesbian populations. I had a good time researching that, let me tell you, and when all this is over, I have some cities I want to visit that I'd never considered before."

Cullen laughed.

"Yeah? Like where?"

"Oh, there are several. Primarily Austin and Ft. Lauderdale, and I suppose Atlanta wouldn't be bad, either. I don't know."

"So you researched lesbian meccas at work today, huh? I think I want your job, minus all the death and criminals and stuff."

Julia laughed and leaned into Cullen.

"Yeah, minus all that. So what about your job? What happened today?"

Cullen exhaled and rolled her eyes.

"Today sucked. There's no way around it. There are going to be massive layoffs at the firm and that's never good to hear."

"They won't let you go, will they? You've been there forever and I'm sure you do good work."

"True, but I've missed a lot of work lately, and that's making them look at me harder than they normally would."

"How do you know that?" Julia said.

"I dated the head of human resources a few years back."

"You dated a coworker? Cullen, that's not smart."

"Oh, no. She wasn't with the firm at the time. Anyway, as a courtesy she called me into her office and told me she was all for keeping me, but that my attendance or lack thereof had me square in the crosshairs of some."

"That's not good."

"No, and it's not like I don't have the time to burn. But apparently I've burned too much recently, so no leaving early or staying home to nurse a hangover for me in the near future."

"Fair enough. That reminds me though. Do you get Friday off?"

"Friday?"

"Yeah, Thursday is Thanksgiving, remember?"

"Oh wow, with everything going on, I completely forgot. Yes. I get Friday off. Do you?"

"We'll see."

"What are you doing for Thanksgiving?" Cullen asked. "Are you going over to your folks' place?"

Julia shook her head.

"My parents disowned me when I came out. My siblings usually go over there for the day, so I'll just hang. What about you? I suppose you'll be at your parents' house?"

"I should. Or we could spend the day together."

"Cullen, you should be with your parents. Do you have any brothers or sisters?"

"Nope, I'm it. I'd rather spend the day with you. I'll go see them Friday while you're working."

Julia smiled and nodded.

"That sounds good to me."

They got a table and enjoyed their celebratory dinner. When it was over, Cullen followed Julia back to her house. Once safely in for the night, they hit the leftover Guinness.

"I'm so proud of you, Julia," Cullen said.

"Yeah? Thank you, but what for?"

"For all your hard work to arrest Sara."

"Have you heard from her today?"

"Nope."

"Maybe you should text her."

Cullen hated that idea. She hated having any contact with Sara, but how could she let Julia know that? She knew Julia was only trying to do her job.

"I don't know her number. I think she uses a different phone every time she texts. Besides, I really don't like talking to her. In fact, it makes me sick."

Julia laid her head on Cullen's shoulder and placed her hand on her lap.

"I get that, babe, I really do. But we need to keep lines of communication open. We're close to catching her. I know we are. We just need to hope she slips up and at least tells us where she is."

"She's not going to do that."

"You don't know that."

"One thing I do know is that she's a conniving bitch who only cares about herself. She's not going to take any chances."

"Wow, that's a lot of hostility. Maybe we need to talk about your relationship more."

"Why?" Cullen said.

"All that anger. Clearly, you feel betrayed. That's natural, but I'm wondering if maybe you... I don't know. That's just a lot of anger toward someone you don't care about."

Cullen couldn't believe her ears. She pulled away and turned to face Julia.

"Are you implying I still have feelings for her? Because let me assure you, the only feeling I have for her is disgust."

"Please don't be angry. I didn't mean to upset you. I just want to make sure you're ready to move on."

"So you doubt me? What if I start to wonder if you're only using me to find her?"

"You know that's not true," Julia said softly.

"Oh, do I?"

"Is this our first fight? Because I'm not enjoying it and I'm sorry I said anything."

"No, I'm sorry. You have to be able to talk to me about anything. I shouldn't have jumped down your throat."

"So, we're okay?"

Cullen scooted next to her again and wrapped her arm around her shoulders.

"We're more than okay, Julia. Trust me."

Julia wanted to believe Cullen. She knew Cullen had been burned a couple of times already and had trust issues, so Julia needed to tread lightly. But Cullen was so upset with Sara. And that made sense, but Julia still couldn't help but wonder what other emotion lay underneath that anger.

She took a deep breath and decided to do her best to salvage their evening.

"Kiss me, Cullen?"

"Gladly."

Julia watched Cullen's eyes as her gaze shifted from Julia's eyes to her lips. She looked down at Cullen's lips, full and parted. Her heart raced as she readied herself for the onslaught of feelings that were about to wash over her.

Sure enough, Cullen moved her mouth over Julia's and Julia's whole body sizzled with electricity. Her hormones raged, and moisture pooled between her legs, but there was more than a simple carnal reaction.

Underneath everything was a contradictory sense of calm, of feeling like she was right where she needed to be. She felt like she'd finally come home. Like being with Cullen was where she belonged.

When she felt Cullen's tongue dart into her mouth, she moaned. She longed to feel that tongue all over her body. Her breasts ached for her touch, and she throbbed in places long untouched.

Julia lost herself in the kiss, in the feeling of Cullen's demands on her mouth. She wrapped her arms around her neck and pulled her closer. They continued to make out for a long time, and Julia felt a sense of emptiness when Cullen pulled away.

"That was some kiss," she said when she finally found her voice.

"Indeed, I want another one."

"You may have it."

"No, not now." Cullen pulled her slacks away from her crotch and repositioned herself on the couch. "If I kiss you again I don't know that I'll be able to stop."

"Fair enough. Would you like another beer?"

"Sure, I'll get them. I need to walk around for a bit."

Julia was grateful she didn't have to get up. She didn't know if she could trust her legs. Her whole body still hummed, and she wondered how long she'd be able to stay strong.

Cullen was back and handed her a beer, then tossed her phone in Julia's lap.

"What's this?" Julia set her beer on the coffee table and picked up Cullen's phone.

"A text from she who must not be named."

Julia laughed.

"Very funny." She picked up the phone and read it.

Just another day in paradise. How was your day?

"Damn, I wish she'd tell us where paradise was," Julia said.

"I'll ask. Why not?"

"You think she'll tell you?"

"I don't know."

Paradise, huh? Where are you, Hawaii?

Not Hawaii. I wish! Maybe that'll be my next move.

Why won't you tell me where you are?

What if that nosy bitch searches your phone? I'm not about to let her know where I am.

Why would she search my phone? Do you think she's still looking for you?

"You're doing great, Cullen. I love it."

"Thanks. As much as I want her to just go away, I really want to help you catch her."

How should I know if she's looking for me? You tell me.

How would I know?

For all I know, you're dating the scumbag now.

"How can you read this without getting pissed?" Cullen asked.

"Why would I get pissed?"

"She's not very nice about you."

"No, but I couldn't care less. I don't need her to like me—obviously."

"True."

It'll be a while before I date again. I'm not really into being burned.

I'm sorry it ended how it did, Cullen. We could have gone the distance.

"Could have gone the distance?" Cullen was incredulous. "She was dishonest with me from day one. How in the hell does she think we would have lasted?"

"Calm down, babe. Don't let her get to you. Take a deep breath and respond to her."

Maybe so. We'll never know now, will we?

Unfortunately. Okay, I need to go. I'll check in later. Take care and stay warm.

"Well, that was uninformative," Cullen said.

"I don't know. I'm thinking she might have helped us. She referred to where she lives as paradise so maybe she's not in Hawaii, but maybe she's in a tropical environment. I'll call Ft. Lauderdale tomorrow. I'm leaning toward there."

"I hope you're right. I hope she's there and they catch her."

"Me, too. Now turn around."

"What? Huh?"

"Turn your back to me so I can rub some of that tension out of your shoulders."

She massaged Cullen's tight muscles, reveling in touching her body. Even this kind of touch was heaven to Julia. She wanted to run her hands all over Cullen, to elicit moans of desire and screams of passion, but she had to be content with simply rubbing her shoulders for the time being.

"That feels amazing, baby. Thank you so much."

"You really shouldn't let her get to you."

"I know. But I don't like the way she talks about you and I don't like the idea that she thinks I'd be happy to spend my life with a druggie who deals and kills people."

"True, I get that. Now relax. You're getting tense again."

Cullen allowed Julia to ease her tension for a few more minutes before she turned around and kissed her again. Julia lay back on the couch and soon Cullen was lying on top of her. Julia instinctively wrapped her legs around Cullen's waist, and Cullen proved to be the strong one as she pulled away and sat up.

"Don't do that." She smiled down at Julia. "I don't know if I'll be able to resist next time. I felt the heat radiating from your jeans and almost ripped them off you."

"I'm sorry, I wasn't thinking."

"It's okay, come on. It's getting late. We should go to bed."

"Is it safe? I mean, maybe we should wait a little bit. You know, cool off some."

"We'll be okay. Scout's honor."

Cullen looked so cute holding her hand up like a boy scout that she almost kissed her again. No, she could do this. If Cullen could resist her, she could resist Cullen. Or she'd die trying.

CHAPTER NINETEEN

Julia left Cullen sleeping the next morning. She was excited about the possible new developments and couldn't wait to get to the station. As soon as she arrived, she checked the time. It was six thirty, so it would be nine thirty in Ft. Lauderdale. She called police headquarters there.

"Ft. Lauderdale Police. This is Officer Roane. How may I help you?"

"Good morning, Officer. I'm Detective Julia Stansworth from the Portland Police Bureau in Portland, Oregon. I have reason to believe a wanted criminal is in Ft. Lauderdale. Who do I need to speak to?"

"Hold on one moment, Detective. I'll transfer you to one of our detectives."

Julia cooled her jets while she waited an eternity for someone to pick up.

"Detective Sumner," the masculine voice on the other end finally said. "How may I help you?"

"Good morning, Detective. I'm looking for a woman in connection with a couple of murders here in Portland, Oregon, and I have reason to believe she's in your city."

"Is that right? Were you the one who sent over the information yesterday?"

"Yes. I sent that information to several cities, but information has come up leading me to believe she's in Ft. Lauderdale."

"We don't like her type here. We have enough issues of our own without out-of-towners screwing around down here."

"I'm sure," Julia said. "I'm glad you got the information I sent over. We found her driver's license here, so I'm convinced she has another ID. I wish I could tell you what name she's going by, but I can't. All I can do is please ask that you spread the word and keep your eyes open for anyone who looks like her. We really need to put her away."

"Understood. Can you give me anything to go on? I'm looking at your report. She's attractive, but so are half the lesbians down here. Blond and blue eyed? Again, could be anyone walking the streets here."

"I doubt she's blond anymore, though I don't know that for sure. Maybe a brunette with blue eyes would stand out?"

A mirthless laugh came from the other end.

"Look, Detective, we've all got problems. I'll distribute the information you sent over and tell everyone to be on the lookout, but I can't make any promises."

"All I can ask is that you guys do your best, and be aware that we want her if you happen to pick her up for anything. I don't care if her tags are expired. I don't care if you catch her jaywalking. We need her sent back and the sooner, the better."

"As I said, we'll do what we can. We're stretched pretty thin down here as it is and our busy season is coming up."

"I hear you. Never a dull moment, huh?"

"You said it. Thanks for the call, Detective. We'll keep our eyes peeled."

"Thank you, Detective. Thank you very much."

It took every ounce of self-control on Julia's part not to slam the receiver back into place. If someone called her and told her a new murderer was on the loose in Portland, she'd do everything she could to find the bastard. Oh, well.

She pulled up the pictures from the hospital again. As usual, the hooded figure taunted her. She knew it was Sara, but how to prove it? She was staring so hard at the picture that she jumped when her phone buzzed on her desk. It was a text from Cullen.

You were gone early this morning. I missed you.

Sorry. Wanted to get an early start.

We're off work at two today for the holiday. Can you sneak out early?

I should be able to. I'll let you know.

We could go get Turkey Day food.

Damn it. What part of she'd get back to her was Cullen not understanding? She told herself to calm down. She was in a foul mood, but there was no reason to take it out on her.

That sounds good. Let's have it at your place. I want to get away from the city.

Fair enough. Have a good day.

You, too.

She sat back in her chair and linked her fingers behind her head. The picture on the screen was making a fool of her. She knew it and didn't appreciate it.

"Hey, Julia. You busy?"

She turned to see Randi Hopkins standing behind her. Randi was a forensic examiner and they'd worked on many cases together. She was a short, stocky butch who really knew her shit. She'd asked Julia out more than once, though, so she always made Julia a little uncomfortable. She spun her chair around to face her.

"Good morning, Randi. What can I do for you?"

"Actually, it's more a question of what I can do for you. I know you're working on a challenging case, and I was just wondering if there's anything I can do to help."

Julia let her breath out between her teeth.

"I wish. Barring finding my suspect, I don't think anyone can really help me."

"Well, I can't do that." Her gaze cut to the picture on the screen. "Is that her?"

"I don't know. I want to think so, but there's no way to tell."

"Of course there is."

"How?"

"Do you have another picture of her?" Randi asked.

"A couple. Why?"

"Let me match them. Let me work my magic. Are they all in the database?"

"Yep, under the name Sara Donovan. You really think you can get anything out of this?" Julia arched her thumb at the monitor.

"I won't know if I don't try."

"Well, thank you."

"My pleasure. I'll get back to you when I know something."

Randi walked off and Julia realized she was holding her breath. She wanted Randi to find a match so bad it hurt. But then she realized that even if Randi determined it was Sara, it still didn't prove she was the murderer. So she was in the hospital. She could say she was visiting Montague, though that was shit and Julia knew it. Still, she needed more. She needed to be able to nail Sara for this murder beyond a shadow of a doubt.

Cullen wrapped up her workday and her spirits were high as she anticipated a four-day weekend with Julia. Maybe they'd be able to take their relationship to the next step. She was ready. God knew, she was ready.

She sent Julia a quick text.

I'm heading home. Hope you can meet me soon.

She hit send, slipped her phone in her pocket, and put on her heavy coat. Snow was in the forecast again. It hardly ever snowed in Portland and here it was supposed to snow for the second time in November. She was pondering that when her pocket buzzed. She pulled out her phone to see a text from Julia.

On my way. I'll meet you at your place.

Cullen couldn't wipe the smile off her face. This weekend was going to be epic.

Traffic was a nightmare. Everyone and their grandmother must have gotten off early that day. She crawled down I-5 and got home an hour later. Julia was already in her driveway. She must be frozen half to death, and Cullen felt horrible as she pulled in next to her.

But Julia smiled and waved, and they got out of their vehicles together. Julia reached in and grabbed her laptop and Cullen's spirits fell.

"Are you working this weekend?"

"Maybe. Probably. I don't know. I'm trying not to go into work. My goal is to spend the next few days with you."

"I like that goal." Cullen pulled Julia to her and kissed her. "I like that goal a lot."

They went inside and Julia disappeared into the bedroom. She came back minus her blazer and sweater and sporting a Portland State Vikings hoodie.

"You look comfy."

"I am. Now, let's make a list so we can go grocery shopping before all the food is gone."

"Sounds good."

Julia opened the Notes app on her phone.

"Okay, so, turkey, stuffing, cranberry jelly, what else?"

Cullen laughed.

"You buy dressing? You don't make it?"

"Have you ever had Stove Top stuffing? It's to die for. I live for the holidays so I can have it and I won't compromise there. What's traditional for you?"

"Mashed potatoes and green bean casserole and champagne and orange juice."

"Is that right?"

"Heck yeah. Gotta have mimosas for breakfast."

"Oh. And Baileys for our coffee?

"But of course."

"Excellent. Okay. Now for dessert. I make a mean apple pie, but I'm betting you're all over the pumpkin variety."

"Actually, I'm not a fan of pumpkin," Cullen said. "I usually make blackberry."

"Fine. We'll have two pies. Before we go shopping, have you talked to your folks?"

"I have and they're fine with me coming over Friday. So if you do have to work, it's okay."

"Great. Let's hit the store."

Julia pushed the cart and Cullen kept her hand on the small of her back. The shelves had been picked over, but they found what they needed.

"We still need to go to the frozen food aisle," Cullen said.

"What for?"

"Pie crust."

"You don't make your own?" Julia looked shocked.

"Nope." Cullen grinned. "Never."

They finished their shopping and went home to put their groceries away. That done, they each grabbed a beer and sat in the living room.

"I'm getting hungry," Julia said. "We have all that food and nothing to eat."

"You want to go out?"

"No way. I want to stay in. Sure, it's only just started snowing, but who knows how hard it'll be snowing in a little while. Let's order food. I'm in the mood for Mexican."

Cullen's mind drifted back to the Mexican restaurant she and Sara had frequented. She thought of the time Sara suggested she try coke. It had made Cullen so angry, and yet she'd stuck with her. Was she that desperate for a relationship?

What about now? Did she care about Julia? Truly care about her or was she just scared to be alone? She didn't like the way her thoughts were going, so she brought herself back to the question at hand.

"We have a good Mexican restaurant here. Take a look at the menu and I'll place an order."

She handed Julia her phone, then watched Julia while she looked at the menu. Cullen thought she really liked her. She'd crushed on her for her whole sophomore year, but that had been a long time ago. Was she into the woman she had become, or was she just chasing the ghost of her high school crush? She had a lot of questions and very few answers. Damn Sara for making her doubt herself. She'd fucked Cullen in the brain in a big way. Cullen needed to put Sara out of her mind once and for all. As if on cue, her phone buzzed. Julia handed it to her.

"Here you go."

"Gee, thanks."

I see it's snowing again. It's seventy degrees and sunny here. Lucky you.

I can't chat but wanted to let you know I'm thinking of you.

Thanks. Take care.

"Here, hand me your phone," Julia said.

She did a quick search in Safari.

"What are you doing?" Cullen asked.

"Shit. It's eighty degrees in Ft. Lauderdale."

"I don't get it."

"She said it was seventy degrees, so she's not in Ft. Lauderdale."

"She could be lying about the weather. For all we know, she's still in Portland."

"I doubt that."

"Can we forget about her for a while? Can we just order dinner, please?"

"Sure, dinner sounds good. But I can't forget about her, Cullen. I won't be able to until I've seen her locked up."

"I get that, I really do, and I'm happy to help. I just don't like to feel like that's why you're with me. So I can help you lock her up."

"Cullen, seriously, is that what you think?"

"No, maybe," She ran her fingers through her hair. "I don't know."

"Okay, well, order dinner and then we'll talk."

Cullen placed the order then turned to face Julia on the couch.

"I'm sorry. I don't know what came over me."

"It's okay. You've been burned. You're gun-shy. You have trust issues. It all makes sense. I hope you'll learn to trust me, I really do, and I'm patient. I'll wait as long as it takes for you to put your ghosts behind you and accept me and my feelings for you."

"I appreciate that," Cullen said. "And I do trust you. It's just that sometimes my past rears its ugly head and I freak. I need to trust you and I need to trust my feelings for you."

Julia's eyebrows shot up.

"You don't trust your own feelings?"

Cullen shrugged.

"Everything gets convoluted sometimes and I wonder if it's this you I'm into or the you I had a crush on all those years ago."

Julia stood. She turned and faced Cullen.

"Cullen, you need to figure that out."

Cullen reached up, took her hand, and gently pulled her back onto the couch.

"I know in my heart that I care for you. It's just sometimes my brain starts asking questions. Like I'm trying to self-sabotage to avoid another failed relationship. Does that make sense?"

"I suppose it does. And while I don't like to hear it, it's important that you always talk to me about what you're feeling and questioning. Please?"

"I promise. And it's important that you let me know once Sara is caught if you still want to be with me."

"Oh, Cullen, I'm sure I will, but I get it. I have to earn your trust and I will. That's my promise to you."

"Good." Cullen felt a little better. She smiled at Julia.

"Now kiss me, you fool."

Cullen kissed her. And kissed her again and again. And kept kissing her until the doorbell interrupted them.

CHAPTER TWENTY

Julia savored every bite of her dinner and forced her thoughts and Cullen's doubts from her mind. When they were through eating, though, she was tempted to bring up the whole subject again. Instead, she washed their plates and got them each a beer.

"You want to watch a movie?" Cullen said.

"Sure."

"Can we talk some more first?"

"If you want." Julia wanted to hear more about what Cullen was thinking and feeling, regardless of how painful it might me.

"I think we should take our relationship to the next level."

"What do you mean?"

"Julia, it's obvious that we want each other. We're both consenting adults. I don't see why we can't make love."

Julia chose her words carefully. She knew she had to be firm even though the idea of being naked with Cullen awakened parts of her that had been dormant far too long. But she also didn't want to be a flash in the pan. She needed to know they were both ready for a commitment before she would go any further.

"There are several reasons why I can't agree to that," she said. "The first is because I'm hip deep in a case that keeps me distracted. When we're finally in a place where we know it's right and I can give one hundred percent, then I'll say okay."

"There'll always be a case. You're a fuckin' detective." Cullen's word came out short and crisp. Julia looked in her eyes and saw anger and hurt there.

"Not like this one, Cullen. This one's different and you know it."

"How? What makes these murders different from the other ones you've handled?"

"It's personal. It shouldn't be, but it is. I care about you, Cullen, and Sara hurt you. I want to make her pay."

"If you truly cared about me, you'd let me prove my affection for you."

"You do prove it. We don't need to fall into bed. Besides, it's too soon."

"Too soon my ass. When will it not be too soon?"

"It's been a week, Cullen. A week since Sara left you. One week. I'm not going to be your rebound. I've told you that."

"Maybe you should leave then. Maybe you shouldn't bother spending the night tonight."

The words hit Julia like a punch in the gut.

"You don't mean that. You're upset. You're not thinking clearly. You don't want me out driving in the snow in the dark. I know you don't."

"No, I really don't," Cullen said quietly. "It's just so hard because I want you so desperately."

"I want you, too, but I also want this to go somewhere. I don't want to be another notch in your bedpost."

"I don't keep notches in my bedpost. That's not my style."

"You know what I mean, though," Julia said. "I don't want to be just another bedmate. I want to know we're in it for the long haul."

"I'm crazy about you, Julia."

"And I'm crazy about you, too, but that doesn't change the fact that it's too soon. When I give myself to you I plan to give myself to you completely. I want it to be for forever. Please let me have that."

"Fair enough. Well, if I can't have you, let's talk about something else, like what movie do you want to watch?"

"*The Breakfast Club*."

"Are you serious?" Cullen laughed which eased Julia's tension.

"I am. It's my all-time favorite movie."

"That surprises me. I expected you to like cop movies or something."

"I am a cop. I live that shit. I don't need to watch it while I'm relaxing. Anyway, so now you know my favorite movie, what's yours?"

"Hm."

"What?" Julia said.

"I'm thinking. There are so many good ones out there, but my favorite is probably *Rocky Horror Picture Show*."

"What?" Julia burst out laughing. "You like *Rocky Horror*? I never would have guessed. So, tell me, Cullen Matthews, when we finally get to bed, are you going to let your freak flag fly?"

It was Cullen's turn to laugh.

"What? Just because I like a sweet transvestite I have to have a freak flag?"

Julia was laughing so hard her stomach hurt.

"I don't know. You tell me."

"Only time will tell."

"Fair enough. So do you dress up and go to the shows? You strike me as more conservative than that."

"I may have dressed as Brad on more than one occasion."

"Really?"

"What's wrong with that?"

"Nothing, babe. Not a damned thing. I like learning more about you. There's obviously much more to you than meets the eye."

"I'm deep. No doubt about that."

Julia grew serious. She looked deep into Cullen's eyes.

"Yes, you are and I love that about you."

Cullen leaned in and kissed her, and Julia forgot all about *The Breakfast Club* and *Rocky Horror* and almost forgot about waiting. Almost. Damn, but she needed Cullen. Yes, she was involved in a case that was tearing her apart, and yes, she needed to keep cool and wait and see how she and Cullen would play out. But, damn! When Cullen kissed her, she forgot all that and started thinking with an organ besides her brain, and that organ longed to feel Cullen deep inside. It wanted to be stroked with her fingers and tongue until it couldn't take any more.

But Julia was an adult. She was a mature adult with many moving parts and those parts above her waist knew it wasn't time yet. If only she didn't think she'd self-combust without Cullen's touch whenever they kissed.

When they finally came up for air, over an hour had passed.

"We should get some sleep," Julia said.

"Mm. I'm not tired." She leaned into Julia again.

Julia pushed Cullen away.

"Now, now, Cullen. Come on. I'll sleep in the guest room if I have to."

"No, I'll be good. I'll keep my hands to myself."

The next morning, Julia woke to a world of white. The snow had continued overnight and was still falling. Several inches were on the ground, and the pine trees in Cullen's backyard were covered. Her yard looked like a Christmas card. It was beautiful.

Julia made a pot of coffee and took it outside to sit on the deck and watch the snow fall. It was cold but so quiet and peaceful out there. She finished one cup and, chilled through and through, went back inside.

She poured another cup and opened her laptop. She hadn't checked her email since she'd left work the day before. She was sure there would be nothing important in there. If something important had come up, someone would have called.

Cullen came down the hall and saw Julia sitting at the dining room table with a smile on her face.

"What's that smile for?" Cullen said. "You look amazing. You have the best smile. Don't lose it, okay?"

"Nothing's going to wipe this smile off my face," Julia said.

"Why's that?"

"I got a definite match."

"What are you talking about?" Cullen walked over behind Julia to look at her laptop. Julia closed it.

"Nothing personal," she said. "But you can't be looking at confidential emails."

"Got it. I'll go get a cup of coffee, then you can tell me about the match."

Julia followed her into the kitchen.

"I have proof that Sara was in the hospital at the time of Montague's death."

"You do?" Cullen smiled back at Julia. "That's fantastic."

"And I'm pretty sure I can put her in his room."

"Wait, I thought you just said she was there."

"She was at the hospital, not necessarily in his room."

"Still, that's a start. Congrats, baby."

She kissed Julia briefly. She wanted more, craved more, but she knew if she kissed her any longer, she'd drag her back to bed, and neither of them was ready for that, regardless of the hormones that raged through her.

"Yes, it is," Julia said. "Now, come on. Let's take our coffee outside. It's gorgeous out back."

"Have you had coffee already?"

"I have."

"With Baileys?"

"Oh, no. I forgot about the Baileys."

Cullen poured Julia another cup then made a second pot. She figured they'd need it. She joined Julia in the backyard and held her hand while they watched the snow fall. Everything felt right in her world. All Cullen's worries and doubts vanished, and she was left thinking how happy she was. And how lucky she was to have Julia in her life.

"Okay," Cullen finally said. "I can't feel my extremities. Let's go inside. I'll get a fire going."

"That would be wonderful."

Cullen got a roaring fire started while Julia poured them each more coffee with Baileys.

"When should we put the turkey in?" she asked when Julia handed her the coffee.

"Not for a while yet. It's not that big. There's only two of us."

"True. Do you mind if I turn on some football?"

Julia laughed, which was music to Cullen's ears.

"Football is fine. I'll watch with you until I get too hungry. Then I'll make breakfast and we can switch to mimosas."

"Yum. At this rate, I'll be passed out for dinner."

"Nonsense."

They cuddled together on the couch and Cullen wrapped her arm around Julia and pulled her close. She loved the feel of Julia against her and reveled in the feeling of her firm breasts pressed into her side.

Fortunately, there was a pass interference that wasn't called at that moment, causing her to scream at the TV and channel her thoughts in a safer direction.

Julia laughed again.

"Oh, my. I guess I know who you're rooting for."

"Anyone but the Cowboys, always."

"I'll remember that. Who's your pro team?"

"The Seahawks, though I much prefer college to the pros."

"Got it."

They sat somewhat quietly watching the game. Cullen screamed at the television on occasion, eliciting laughter from Julia. Cullen also got up several times to keep the fire going. She was enjoying her morning very much. She wanted more days like that.

"I'm hungry. I'm going to make breakfast," Julia said.

"What's for breakfast?"

"You'll see. You just relax."

Cullen watched the game, missing Julia's presence. She didn't have to miss her long, though, as Julia was soon back in the room.

"Breakfast is on the table. Can you tear yourself away from the game long enough to eat?"

"No problem."

They finished breakfast and two mimosas each. Cullen did the dishes and then she was feeling no pain.

"We should lie down." She took Julia in her arms.

"We should, should we?"

"Yep. I think it's time for a booze snooze."

"Oh, that sounds nice actually. Let's do that."

They lay down and Julia backed up against Cullen, which was the norm. Cullen was keenly aware of Julia's ass pressed into her and she almost pulled away. It was so tempting to grind into her.

She kissed Julia's neck and moved her sweatshirt out of the way so she could kiss her shoulders. Julia moaned and squealed in delight as Cullen nibbled and sucked on her, and Julia finally pulled away.

"Cullen Matthews. You're going to leave a mark."

"Who's going to see it?"

"No one, but I'll know. We're not teenagers anymore."

"Fine. Roll over then and let me kiss you properly."

"Negative, we're taking a nap, remember?"

Cullen felt like a little kid who'd just been told she couldn't have dessert. She almost pouted but kept herself together. She closed her eyes and was soon lost in dreamland.

She woke an hour later. Julia was still snoring softly, so she got out of bed and went to the living room to stoke the fire and add some logs. Once it was going strong, she checked the score of the game. Dallas was losing. Yes, indeed. It was a good day.

She helped herself to another mimosa and had just settled back on the couch when Julia came in. She stretched, lifting her hands high over her head and pulling her hoodie up with them. Cullen caught sight of her belly button and wanted to run her tongue all over it.

"What?" Julia said.

"What what?"

"You looked like you wanted to devour me."

"Guilty as charged."

"Well, save your appetite. I'm going to get started on dinner."

"Can I help?"

"Not yet. Let me get things going, then you can work on the green bean casserole and your pie."

Cullen followed Julia into the kitchen.

"I won't get in your way. I just want to be near you."

Julia rewarded that comment with a kiss that grew and expanded and soon took over Cullen's being. She placed her hands on Julia's ass and ground into her pelvis. Julia let her do this for a few moments before ending the kiss.

"Now, now, don't you get carried away," she said.

"Sorry."

"No, you're not."

"You're right."

They worked in shifts to get dinner ready, and soon it was time to eat. Cullen thoroughly enjoyed their little feast as she sat looking at the leftovers that were strewn about the table.

"That was the best Thanksgiving dinner ever," she said.

"It did turn out pretty good, didn't it?"

"Yes, it did, and the company was outstanding."

"Aw, thank you. I concur one hundred percent."

When Cullen felt she could move without bursting a seam, she suggested they get the dishes done and the leftovers put away. Once again, they worked together in the kitchen, and Cullen marveled at how easy everything was with Julia.

They took their wine out back to watch the snow that had begun to fall again.

"So, do you think you'll be able to get away without going in tomorrow?" Cullen said.

"I don't know, babe. I hope I don't. I'll see if the forensic examiner will be in. If so, I want to talk with her. If not, I'll stay here."

Cullen squeezed her hand and said a little prayer to whatever powers might be listening that the forensic woman wouldn't be in. She wanted another day like this with Julia, and another and another. She really couldn't imagine not wanting to spend every day for the rest of her life with her.

CHAPTER TWENTY-ONE

Julia woke early Friday morning and checked her email. Randi had sent her a reply saying she'd be out of the office that day but that she'd see her on Monday if she had any questions. That was a relief. She climbed back into bed and, listening to Cullen's steady breathing, was soon asleep herself.

She was groggy when she woke later to the feel of Cullen's hand caressing her hip while she nibbled on her neck. She didn't stay groggy for long. She came fully awake and rolled over to face Cullen. Aroused and not thinking, she kissed Cullen and wrapped her leg around her, pressing their bodies together.

The feel of Cullen's long, lean legs against hers sent her reeling, but the feel of her pelvis pressed into Julia's almost sent her over the edge. She pulled her closer, needing more contact.

"Hey, baby?" Cullen said. "Julia?"

"Hm?"

"We need to stop."

"Why?"

Cullen propped herself up on an elbow and looked down at her. Her face was flushed and her dark eyes shone.

"Are you serious?"

Julia's mind cleared, and she took a shaky breath to calm her hyper aroused nerve endings. She pulled her leg off Cullen and rolled over onto her back.

"I'm sorry. I wasn't fully awake. I was working off feelings instead of thinking things through."

"Damn. I thought you were finally ready."

"No, not yet. Time, Cullen. We need to give it time. Come on, let's get some coffee and get started on our day."

"What are we going to do today? The Duck game isn't on until two thirty."

"I don't know. What time is it?"

"Nine."

"Dang, we slept in. Let's get coffee. That's priority numero uno."

They bundled up and sat out on the deck admiring the white landscape. The snow had stopped but hadn't melted. It was beautiful out there.

"I love snow as long as I don't have to go anywhere in it," Julia said.

"And now it's all ice, which is even worse."

"True. Is it supposed to snow anymore?"

"Let me check." Cullen slid her phone out of her pocket. "No. Rain by this afternoon."

"Bummer."

"It was fun while it lasted."

She slid her phone into the pocket of her hoodie and Julia heard it buzz.

"Is that her?" She leaned forward, excitement coursing through her veins.

"Let me check." Cullen looked at her phone. "Yep."

Julia got up and read the text over Cullen's shoulder.

How was your Turkey Day?

Nice. How did you spend your day?

Thanksgiving dinner for one. But it was yummy.

"What should I say now?" Cullen asked.

"Ask her if she's making friends, that kind of thing."

Haven't you made any new friends yet? Contacts? People you could hang out with?

LOL It's been a week, Cullen. Not quite, actually. I'm working on meeting people.

Yeah, you need to set up your clientele.

"Easy, Cullen. Don't sound bitter."

"Why not? I am."

Everything will come together. I'm sure of it.

Good. I wish only the best for you.

"Better?" Cullen said.

"Much."

Sara didn't respond so Cullen put her phone away.

"And now my day sucks. I hate hearing from her."

"I get that, but it helps. Every little bit helps. And soon she'll be locked up with no access to a cell phone."

"God, I hope you're right."

"I am."

"Speaking of that, do you have to go to work today?"

"Nope. I've got the day off to spend with you."

"That's great." She didn't sound excited.

"What's up?"

"I forgot. I need to go see my folks today."

"And I can't go with?"

"Don't you think it's a little soon to play meet the parents?" Cullen said.

Julia felt like she'd been slapped. Was Cullen embarrassed to be dating a cop? Was she not good enough for her parents? Sure, she'd forgotten that Cullen was going to spend some time with them, but since she didn't have to work, why couldn't she tag along?

"If you say so." She tried to keep her voice even. "Is there a reason you don't want them to meet me?"

"I have no problem with you meeting them."

"Could have fooled me." She didn't try to keep the edge out of her voice.

"I just wondered. Since, you know, we're not sleeping together yet, is it a little soon, after a week, to meet my parents."

"You can go to their place. I'll stay here." She wanted to add not to expect her to be there when Cullen got home, but she didn't.

"No, you can come. I just wanted to make sure you're ready."

"That's not how it sounded. It sounded like you don't want them to meet me, and that's fine. It's just that I deserve to know why."

Cullen took her hand.

"I'd love for them to meet you, Julia. I'm sure they'll remember you and will absolutely love you."

"What time should we be there?"

"Nothing was set in stone. We should probably go sooner rather than later, though. I really do want to be home to watch the game."

"I'll make breakfast. Why don't you call them?"

"Okay."

Julia's thoughts jumbled together while she worked in the kitchen. Meeting Cullen's parents was a huge step. She admitted that and it had been her idea to take things slow. So why had Cullen's reticence aggravated her so? She really didn't care about meeting her parents. She just wanted to be with Cullen, and if that meant spending a few hours with them, then so be it. Maybe she should go to work. That would make everything easier. She made up her mind. She'd get a few hours in while Cullen went to her parents' house.

She sensed rather than felt Cullen's presence in the kitchen and turned to face her.

"I've been thinking," she said.

"I want to hear your thoughts, but first let me tell you my folks remember you and are dying to see you again."

"For real?"

"For real. Now, what were you thinking?"

"It's not important. Let's eat. Breakfast is ready."

❖

Cullen let the shower pummel her as she fought to overcome her nerves. Her parents had met a lot of women over the years, but this was big. She couldn't put her finger on why she knew Julia was the one for her, but she was sure she was. Maybe that was why. Whatever the reason, she needed to get over it. She hadn't seen her parents in a while. Not since she and Sara had gotten together. Thank God they'd never met her.

She finished up and dried and dressed then went out to find Julia on her laptop.

"Whatcha working on?"

"Looking at reports. Trying to decide how much I have and whether it's enough to convict Sara for the Montague murder."

Cullen worried at how hard Julia worked. She walked up behind her and rubbed her tight shoulders. She didn't miss that Julia slammed her laptop shut.

"Let it go for today, baby. Let's go relax and hang with my folks."

"Sounds good."

Cullen's parents lived in a large, rambling, ranch style house in the northwest quadrant of the city. As they approached the door, Cullen took Julia's hand.

"How are you doing?" she asked.

Julia squeezed her hand reassuringly. The butterflies in Cullen's stomach were fluttering at Mach speed, but the squeeze helped and she took a deep breath before knocking on the door.

Her mom opened the door and pulled Cullen, who towered over her, into a hug. Her mom looked good at seventy-two. Her silver hair was perfectly coiffed and her arms were strong as they held her.

"So good to see you, Cullen." She stepped back. "And you must be Julia."

"Hello, Mrs. Matthews." Julia extended her hand which Cullen's mom shook enthusiastically.

"I remember you from all those high school games. You were something else."

Cullen noticed the pink on Julia's cheeks and smiled.

"Thank you. That was a long time ago."

"Where are my manners? Please come in."

Cullen stepped aside to let Julia enter before her. She rested her hand on the small of her back before following her in.

"Cullen's dad is in the family room watching football." She rolled her eyes. "Tell me, Julia, do you watch football?"

"Not very often, I'll admit."

"Oh, wonderful. I just knew we were going to get along."

Cullen laughed.

"Nothing wrong with football."

"Are you sure you can't stay and watch the game with your father this afternoon?"

"I don't think so."

"Maybe, though?"

"I'll give you a definite maybe," Cullen said. She really wanted to watch the game in the privacy of her own home where she could yell and scream and cuss at the TV if she wanted. She might be an adult now, but she wouldn't be caught dead swearing in front of her parents.

"Why don't you go join your dad?" Julia said. "I'll help your mom in the kitchen."

"Everything's under control in the kitchen," Cullen's mom said. "But let's go introduce you to Bob, and then you and I'll visit while they waste away in front of the boob tube."

"That sounds good."

Cullen followed the two of them down the step and into the family room.

"Bob," her mom said, "I want you to meet Julia."

Her dad got out of his recliner gracefully and shook hands with Julia.

"Well, if it isn't the star of the team. So good to see you again, Julia. It's nice to see Cullen returning to her roots."

It was Cullen's turn to blush. Her dad patted her shoulder.

"Welcome to our house," her dad continued. "Can we get you anything?"

"You and Cullen relax and watch your games. I'll take care of Julia."

Cullen felt bad leaving Julia alone, but her dad was watching the Alabama game. If they lost, Oregon would be in the playoffs so this was important. She couldn't miss it.

At halftime, she went to the kitchen to get her dad and herself a beer. She passed by the table in the corner of the room and glanced down.

"Mom! What are you doing?" It was clear she was showing Julia Cullen's baby pictures.

"What?" Julia smiled up at her. "You've always been adorable."

"It's wonderful that you think that," Cullen's mom said. "I think I'll enjoy having you around."

"I'm glad she meets with your approval," Cullen said sarcastically.

"Is your game over already?" her mom asked.

"It's halftime."

"I'll put out some snacks then."

"I'll help," Julia said.

"Nonsense. You sit tight. I'll be right back."

"How are you doing?" Cullen whispered in Julia's ear.

"I'm doing great. I love your mom. How are you doing?"

"Not bad. We can stay for another hour or so, but then I'm going to want to head home."

"Fair enough, today's for you."

Julia smiled up at her and Cullen's heart melted. Damn, but she was crazy about Julia. She just wished she could show her how much.

"What are you thinking?" Julia said.

"Nothing we can discuss at my parents' house."

"Ah. Got it."

Julia winked at her and Cullen almost kissed her. She decided to be strong, though. While she'd never made any bones about being gay, she didn't think she needed to make out with Julia on her first trip to their home.

"Get some food," Julia said. "And I'll see you in an hour or so."

Cullen took the beers to the family room then went back to the dining room where she filled two plates full of deviled eggs, salami and cheese, and veggies and dip. She handed a plate to her dad and sat down just in time for the second half kickoff.

The third quarter ended, and Alabama was down by a touchdown. Cullen was excited and wanted to watch the rest of the game, but decided she'd just check the score when she got home.

"Okay, Dad, it's time for me to head out. It was good seeing you."

"Cullen. Don't stay away so long next time, okay?"

"You got it."

She walked back to the kitchen to find Julia and her mom poring over her sports pictures.

"Seriously, Mom?" Cullen said.

"Seriously," Julia answered. "I'm thoroughly enjoying myself. But you've got our coats so I'm guessing it's time to leave?"

"Yeah, we need to get home."

"Okay."

"Thank you so much for bringing Julia over today," her mom said. "It was so nice visiting with her."

"We'll come over more often, I promise."

"Come over next Sunday for dinner, say four o'clock? Please?"

"I'd love that," Julia said.

"Sounds good to me," Cullen said.

She hugged her mom good-bye and stood aside while Julia hugged her.

"You take good care of my Cullen," her mom said.

"You have my word."

"Good. You drive safely, Cullen."

"Will do. See you next week."

On the drive back home, Cullen took Julia's hand and held it on her thigh.

"I hope my mom didn't bore you to tears."

"Not at all. She was very pleasant. She loves you so very much."

"This is true. She seemed quite fond of you, as well."

"Good. I really enjoyed meeting her and I can't wait for next Sunday."

"Do you miss your parents?" Cullen said softly.

"All the time. I mean, I try to be pissed and indignant and all, but it's hard to take that my parents don't love me anymore."

"Have you ever thought about reaching out to them?"

Julia shook her head.

"That's not going to happen. I don't need that sort of rejection in my life again."

"I'm sorry, Julia. They don't know what they're missing."

"Thank you, Cullen. I appreciate that."

CHAPTER TWENTY-TWO

Sunday evening, Julia and Cullen packed their bags and drove to Julia's house. Cullen had had such a wonderful time spending four days with Julia and didn't want to see it come to an end. But they both had to work the next day so decided to stay at Julia's for a few nights.

They had dinner out then picked up some beer and headed home. Cullen tried not to think about everything that was going down at the office. She didn't want to contemplate layoffs and budget cuts, but that was reality. She knew it paled in comparison to what Julia faced every day, but still, it was her reality and it wasn't pleasant.

She was thinking it was about time to go to bed when her phone buzzed. She hadn't heard from Sara in a few days and wasn't complaining. Still, she knew what she had to do.

"You just tensed up," Julia said. "What's going on?"

"My pocket just buzzed and I'm sure it's Sara."

"Good."

"Why? I've been enjoying not hearing from her."

"We need to narrow down where she is. Try to find out more from her."

Cullen took her phone out and showed the text to Julia.

How was your weekend?

Nice. How was yours?

Have you heard from that bitch lately? Is she still trying to frame me?

Cullen glanced at Julia before answering. Julia wasn't framing Sara. She had proof that she'd murdered those people.

"What should I say?" she asked Julia.

"Tell her you haven't seen me."

"Seriously?"

"Yes."

I haven't seen her. Why? Are you thinking about moving back?

"Oh, good question, Cullen. You're a natural at interrogation." Cullen laughed dryly.

"Gee, thanks."

Hell no. I love where I am and there are no paranoid cops looking for me.

Well, that's good, I guess. Is it still warm there?

It was in the high sixties today. I'll take it.

Are there colleges there? Can you ply your wares?

No comment. But don't you worry. I'll be fine. I'll talk to you later.

"Shit. I think I blew it."

"No worries. She can't confirm anything over text, but she didn't deny it either. So it's safe to say that wherever she is, she's dealing."

"Why can't she just get a regular job?" Cullen mused aloud.

"That's not how criminals work, babe."

"I suppose that's true."

Julia started playing on her phone.

"What are you doing?" Cullen asked.

"Checking temperatures in my target cities."

"Okay and what are you finding out?"

"Atlanta seems like our best bet now. I'll call them in the morning."

"I thought you liked Ft. Lauderdale."

"It looks like it was warmer there today."

"You know, you're working under the assumption that a drug dealer and murderer is telling the truth."

Julia nodded slowly.

"Right. I'm aware. But I don't think she'd have any reason to lie to you. She doesn't know I'm sitting right next to you."

"Maybe. Or maybe she does."

"How? Unless she's outside peeking in my window right now."

"I don't know." Cullen was uneasy. "Maybe she has friends watching us."

"I doubt that. I think she cut all her ties to Portland when she left. I think she changed her name and started brand new in a new location, like Atlanta."

"Do you think Sara Donovan was even her real name?"

"Truth?"

"Truth." Though Cullen wasn't sure she wanted to hear it.

"No. I think she reinvents herself in every new city."

Cullen nodded.

"I guess that makes sense. Damn, don't I feel like a fool? I didn't even know her real name yet there I was planning on a future with her."

Julia placed her hand over Cullen's.

"Babe, don't beat yourself up. She's a professional and maybe she was really hoping to go the distance with you. We'll never know. I mean, you can ask her, but will you believe her answer?"

"No, I don't suppose I would."

"I didn't think so."

They went to bed and Cullen wasn't feeling any better Monday morning. Being duped so completely by Sara weighed heavily on her mind. That, and not knowing what she was walking into at work did nothing to ward off the Monday blues.

"You're awfully quiet this morning, babe," Julia said over their second cup of coffee. "Anything you want to talk about?"

"Not really. I mean, I don't know. I'm still bummed about the whole Sara situation, plus I don't know if I'll have a job at the end of the day. I guess I'm just down in the dumps right now."

"Well, I can't help with the job situation, but I'm happy to be a sounding board on the Sara front. That is, if you're comfortable talking to me about it."

"I'm comfortable talking to you about anything. I just wish Sara and that whole situation didn't upset me."

"She hurt you, Cullen. You can't deny that, and that takes time to heal. If you need more space, just say the word. I can back off and give it to you."

Cullen panicked at the thought.

"No, please don't! I don't want you going anywhere. But I do see why we're moving slowly. I need to get my head on right before I can be the partner I want to be."

"Do you think seeing a counselor would help?"

"I don't think I need my head shrunk."

"Don't think of it as a bad thing. She'd just be a neutral party you could talk to."

"How much could I tell her?" Cullen was warming up to the idea.

"Anything, everything. It would all be confidential."

"Maybe I'll look into it."

"I think you should, but not right now. We're going to be late as it is."

"Yeah, we should get going."

Cullen powered through the first couple of hours at work alternating between a couple of accounts that had deadlines looming. She was doing good work, and when she finally took a minute to breathe, her mind went back to the discussion she and Julia had had that morning.

She searched for lesbian counselors in the greater Portland area and was surprised to find one in an office building right down the street. She closed her office door and called them, and when she hung up she had an appointment for after work that day.

She felt conflicted. On one hand, yes, it would be good to talk to someone unrelated to the cases and her relationship. On the other, did she really need to see a mental health professional? What if they found out at work? Would she be kissing her job good-bye?

Not convinced she was doing the right thing, she opted to keep her appointment. She'd just check it out and see how it went. She sent Julia a text letting her know she'd be late getting home that evening and settled back to work.

When four thirty rolled around, Cullen logged off her computer, grabbed her coat, and headed down the street. She found the building without any problem and took the elevator to the seventh floor.

She walked into the suite and felt a little more comfortable. She didn't know what she'd been expecting. Something clinical and cold perhaps? But the muted waiting room was pleasant and well-appointed, and soft strands of music wafted through the speakers in the ceiling. She felt better as she approached the receptionist who smiled brightly at her.

"How can I help you?"

"My name is Cullen Matthews. I have an appointment with Leslie McNabb."

"Great. I'll need a photo ID and an insurance card, please."

Cullen's gut tightened. Would this visit affect her insurance rates?

"Can't I just pay out of pocket?" she asked.

"You can, but at two hundred and fifty dollars a visit, most people have us bill their insurance."

Cullen pulled her information out of her wallet and handed it to the receptionist who made copies of them. She clicked away at her computer.

"It looks like your co-pay will be forty dollars."

Cullen handed over her debit card and when the transaction was complete, the receptionist handed her a clipboard.

"Go ahead and fill these out and Leslie will be out to get you shortly."

Cullen read through the reams of paperwork. Had she ever been in counseling before? Was she suicidal? Did she have a mental health diagnosis? She stood to return the paperwork and cancel her appointment when a short brunette dressed in a calf length gray skirt and black sweater opened the door.

"Cullen?" She smiled at her.

"Look," Cullen said. "I don't think I need to be here."

"I'll tell you what. Why not come on back and talk with me for a few. Then, if that's still your decision, you can leave."

Cullen wavered then followed Leslie down a hallway to a carpeted office with abstract art on the walls. There was a large brown leather couch along one wall and a desk by the door.

Leslie closed the door and sat at the desk, spinning the chair so she faced Cullen.

"Go ahead and have a seat." She motioned to the couch.

Cullen sat on the edge of it, determined not to get too comfortable.

"What brings you here today? Surely there was a reason you made the appointment."

Cullen held up the clipboard.

"None of this applies to me. I don't have a history of mental illness or anything like that. I think I'm wasting both our time."

"Why don't you let me be the judge of that?" Leslie's voice was soft and comforting. "Here, hand me the clipboard. We'll deal with it later if we need to."

Cullen gladly handed it over and rested her empty hands on her knees.

"So, why did you make the appointment, Cullen? Which, by the way, is a great name."

"Thank you. I just need someone to talk to. Someone with no vested interest in what I'm going through or where I've been."

"Sounds like you're in the right place. I know nothing about you and I promise not to pass judgment, so why don't you tell me what you're going through."

Against her better judgment, Cullen found herself spilling her guts about everything from her relationship with Sara to Sara's involvement with the law, to Julia's investigation, to Cullen's relationship with Julia.

"Oh, my," Leslie said when Cullen had told her story. "You've got a lot of issues to resolve it sounds like. Not the least of which being reconciling your feelings over Sara so you can move on with Julia."

"Exactly." Cullen forgot her unease and leaned back on the couch. "I need someone to help me see things clearly, I guess."

"I can do that. If you want me to, I mean."

"Can you? Can you really help me?"

"I like to think I can help you help yourself."

Cullen breathed a sigh of relief.

"That would be wonderful."

"Now, first things first," Leslie said. "I can only help you if you're completely honest with me. Remember this is all confidential. No one outside of this room will know anything you don't choose to tell them."

Cullen nodded her understanding.

"Good. Now that we've cleared that up, let's start with some basics. When you think about Sara, what do you feel?"

"Feel?"

"Yes, about her. Not the situation, just about her. Tell me your feelings where she's concerned."

"I'm hurt, I'm angry, I'm disgusted."

"Anything else?"

"I don't know."

"Fair enough," Leslie said. "Let's take those one at a time. Let's start with the hurt."

"I shouldn't feel hurt anymore. I think that's one of my issues. Yes, she burned me and dumped me and used me, but I've moved on. I'm with Julia and I'm happy with her. So why do I still feel hurt when I think of Sara?"

"Let's dig a little deeper. Do you have any positive emotions when you think of her?"

"No."

"That was a quick answer. I want you to really think about it."

Cullen thought for a while.

"I really don't think I do. There's no room for that."

"When you think of happier times, before she was arrested, what do you feel?"

"Sadness really. Like, we were so happy. Why'd everything have to go to hell in a handbasket? But then I feel guilty because I shouldn't miss those days because I have a new girlfriend now."

Leslie smiled warmly at her.

"Ah, yes, so you're conflicted. That's where the turmoil all comes from. I'm going to say something you're not going to want to hear. Are you ready?"

Cullen tensed.

"I guess."

"I'm sure Julia is a wonderful person, but could you maybe not date her right now? You should take time to get your head and heart together before you move on, and I can help with that."

Cullen shook her head vehemently.

"I can't not see her. She's like a dream come true. Besides, we're taking things slowly to give me time."

"How slowly? How often do you see her?"

"Every day."

Leslie nodded slowly.

"That's not very slow. Are you sleeping together?"

"No. I mean, yes. I mean, we sleep in the same bed, but we're not having sex."

"Well, that's a good start. But I don't know if sharing a bed with her is a good thing. I think you should back things up a bit."

"I can't do that."

"And I can't make you. I can only offer suggestions."

"I understand. I just really like being around Julia."

"How does she feel about you?" Leslie asked.

"What do you mean? She likes me a lot."

"Enough to wait for you?"

Cullen shook her head again.

"I'm not going to ask her to wait for me. I don't want to wait. I want to move forward, not backward. That's why I'm here."

"I understand, but I think you may need to back up a bit to move forward. I think you'll both be better off in the long run. Not to mention you'll have a stronger relationship. Tell me about your fears. Are you afraid of losing her?"

"Not really, but…maybe. I've liked her since I was a kid. She's like a dream come true."

Leslie nodded.

"I understand that, too."

"So you really think we need some time apart?"

"I'm not asking you to split up with her, Cullen. I'm just saying slow down. I think it will benefit you both. And now, our time is up. I'd like to see you again Thursday if you're still interested."

"That's probably a good idea. I think you can help me. Not that I'm going to break up with Julia, mind you."

"Again, I'm not asking you to break up with her. Just slow things down. Talk, text, spend free time together. Date. But don't act like you're living together. You're not ready for that, Cullen, and acting like you are isn't going to help you heal."

"Thanks for your insight. I appreciate it. I'll make an appointment for Thursday."

CHAPTER TWENTY-THREE

Julia was getting nervous when she finally heard Cullen pull into her driveway. Cullen had told her she'd be a little late getting home but hadn't said how late. Julia figured she'd be home by five thirty, but now it was pushing six thirty and she was just getting there.

Relief washed over her as she greeted Cullen at the door. She threw her arms around her and held her tight. She felt Cullen's arms tighten around her waist and could finally relax.

"Where have you been?" Julia said.

Cullen stepped inside and closed the door behind her.

"I had a therapy session."

"You what? I thought you weren't into that."

"I did some thinking about what you said and thought what the hell? They were able to get me in after work today, so I went. I go back Thursday."

"You go back? So you liked it? That's fantastic. Have a seat. Tell me all about it. But hold for just a moment while I pour some wine."

She felt lighter than air as she went to the kitchen. She was so thankful that Cullen had taken that first step. She was sure it would help her and by extension, them, move forward.

"So tell me about your therapist. What did you talk about? Tell me, well, tell me anything you're comfortable telling me."

"Well, my therapist's name is Leslie and she's a lesbian, so that's a plus."

"Great. That's a major positive right there. Did you guys talk about Sara?"

"Of course and you."

"Okay. Well, you don't have to tell me anything you don't want to. You know that. I respect confidentiality."

Cullen took a sip of wine and sat back against the couch with her eyes closed.

"I don't know," she said finally.

"What don't you know? You're going back, so it must have been good."

"I think she can help me. I believe that."

"Excellent, so, why the hesitation?" Julia said.

"She thinks we need to slow down."

"Us? Like you and me? How much slower can we go?" Julia laughed nervously.

"Like she doesn't think we should spend nights together. She thinks we should see each other and text and talk and stuff, but not practically live together."

"Did you explain to her that when we sleep together that all we do is sleep?"

"I did."

"Okay." Julia place her hand over Cullen's. "And what do you think? What are you feeling? Talk to me."

"I don't know. I mean, it makes sense, but I don't like the idea of going backward. I also don't like not being with you all the time. I don't want to lose you."

"Not spending every waking hour together doesn't mean you're going to lose me." She squeezed Cullen's hand. "And if you think it'll help you in the long run, then I'm up for it."

"Really? Seriously, you don't hate me for asking it of you?"

"Not at all, and if Leslie thinks that's best, then I think we should listen to her. I want you to feel great, Cullen. I want you to be able to come to me free of Sara so we can move forward and work on us."

"That's what I want, too."

"So it's settled."

"I want to spend the night tonight, though. I'll pack up my stuff in the morning and drive back to Bidwell after work."

"Okay. That sounds good."

"This won't be easy," Cullen said.

"No. No, it won't, but it's important."

"Yeah, I guess it is." She took another sip of wine. "How was your day?"

"It was good. I learned that Sara was right outside Montague's room minutes before he flatlined so I think I've got enough evidence to get Sara for his murder as well. Now if we could just find her."

"I wish you would find her. I think maybe seeing her locked up will really help me close the book on that chapter of my life."

"I think you're right, and believe me, I'm doing everything in my power to do just that."

"I know you are."

They ordered pizza and sipped their wine until Cullen's eyes were drooping.

"Poor baby, you're tired."

"I had a busy day."

"And a very emotional one, I'm sure. Come on, let's get you to bed."

They lay in bed together and Julia finally heard Cullen's breathing even out and knew she was asleep. She disentangled herself from Cullen and slipped out of bed, poured herself another glass of wine and curled up on the couch.

Her mind was racing and wouldn't let her sleep. Not even close. She was so curious what Cullen and Leslie had talked about and she wondered how honest Cullen had been. She had to trust Cullen to be perfectly honest in order to get anything out of her sessions, but what was the complete truth?

Did Cullen still harbor feelings for Sara as Julia suspected, and how deep were they? Had Julia pushed Cullen too hard and moved too fast? The questions whirled around in her head until she was finished with the wine and was no more settled than she had been. But she needed sleep so climbed back into bed.

Trust. It was all about trust, and that was something Julia was short on. It came with her line of work. She needed to trust that Cullen would work with Leslie to move forward. She had no choice. She certainly wasn't going to walk away. Not now that she'd found Cullen. She just needed to be patient and trust the process. Two things she had no idea how to do.

The following morning, Julia did not want to get out of bed. She turned off her alarm and struggled to keep her eyes open. When Cullen reached out and pulled Julia against her, she snuggled close and almost allowed herself to fall back asleep.

The thought of how close she was to nailing Sara popped into her head, and suddenly she was wide-awake. She had things to do, leads to follow up on. She slid out of bed and poured a cup of coffee. She carried it and one for Cullen into the bedroom before she hit the shower.

It would be weird not having Cullen there that night, but it would be nice to be able to get ready in her own room in the mornings rather than having to dry and dress in the bathroom to avoid any temptation on either of their parts.

When she came out of the bathroom dressed and ready for her day, Cullen was sitting up in bed sipping her coffee.

"I'm going to head out now," Julia said as she kissed Cullen good-bye. "Have a great day and call me tonight?"

"You know I will."

"Thanks, babe. This won't be easy, but I'm sure we're doing the right thing."

"I know, but it still sucks."

"Have a good day, babe."

She let herself out into the cold morning air.

Cullen got up, packed her clothes, showered, and headed for the office. She was feeling down about not spending every available moment with Julia, but she didn't want to be codependent either.

That was a big word she'd learned that morning while waiting for Julia to get out of the shower. She got to work, fired up her computer, and settled in for the day. She was working away a little after lunch when her phone buzzed. Hoping to see a message from

Julia, she was disappointed when she saw an unknown number. Sara, shit.

Haven't talked to you in a few days. What's new?

If you must know, I'm in therapy thanks to your mindfuck, she wanted to say but refrained.

Not much. Work, work, work. What's new with you?

Still settling down. Getting the lay of the land. That sort of thing.

Good. I'm glad you're getting situated.

You need to tell that bitch to back off. She's cramping my style.

Huh? Who? How?

You know who. Some cop was giving me the once-over like he was suspicious of me.

What were you doing?

Nothing suspicious. I was clothes shopping.

I'm sorry that happened to you.

Yeah, me, too. I've got to go, but tell her to leave me the fuck alone.

Cullen texted Julia immediately.

Some cop was giving Sara a hard time, so you're on the right track with your cities.

Excellent. Thanks for letting me know.

My pleasure.

Cullen settled back in to work and was lost in a campaign when she heard the ping of her email. It was from her manager. He wanted to see her. She replied that she was on her way and headed down the hall to his office.

Her stomach was in knots. Was this it? Was she going to be let go? Would he do that? Or would human resources? What the hell did he want from her?

She knocked on his door.

"Matthews? Come on in. Go ahead and close the door behind you."

The knots in her stomach tightened, but she closed the door and sat down, careful to keep her face impassive.

"As you know," he began, "We're doing a lot of layoffs around here."

"Yes, sir, that's what we were told. Just how many is a lot, if I may ask?"

"A lot. That's all you need to know. As a result of that, I called you in to see me."

Cullen went numb all over. She didn't want to start over at a new firm. She loved where she worked. She'd spent almost half her life there and couldn't imagine trying to find another job. This place was like family. She managed to nod but didn't trust her voice to speak.

"Layoffs are hard on everybody, Matthews. Let me preface what I'm about to say with that statement. They're no fun no matter how you look at it. So why are you here you're probably asking yourself right now. Am I right?"

She nodded again.

"We're letting twenty-five people go today."

Shit. Shit, shit, shit. Stay cool. Don't lose it. Not here, not now.

"Unfortunately, that leaves a lot of accounts homeless, and we need to divvy up those accounts among those of us that remain. I know you work hard, Matthews, and I hate to dump more on you, but I've got ten accounts that I'm handing over to you right now. I expect them to be treated with the same respect and creativity as your other accounts. In other words, it's not the account's fault they're now homeless. These accounts are in various stages of development. Some have just come on board, some have campaign deadlines looming. You're good, as I said, so I'm sure you can handle the added work. Prove me right, Matthews. Prove me right."

It took a moment for the cloud of impending doom to lift from Cullen's brain. She wasn't being let go. She had more work to do. That was a good thing, right?

"Yes, sir," she said. "I won't let you down. I'll get right on those."

"I'll email you the list of accounts so you can pull them up in the system and familiarize yourself with them. You'll have that list when you get back to your office."

Cullen stood.

"Yes, sir. Thank you."

She was still lightheaded as she walked to her office. She'd been so terrified, so certain she was being canned. Relief washed over her as she collapsed in her chair and buried her head in her hands.

She pulled up the list and went through them. Two of them had deadlines looming so she checked what had been put together so far and decided she could work with it. She threw herself into the campaigns and didn't look up until her stomach growled. She checked the clock. It was six already and she hadn't eaten all day.

She was going to text Julia to see if she wanted to meet for dinner somewhere. There were already two texts from her, the second one, asking where she was, sounded worried.

Sorry. I lost myself in work today. I'm just leaving the office now. Dinner?

She didn't have to wait long for a reply.

Sure. Where?

El Gaucho?

Are we celebrating anything?

Yeah, I still have a job.

I'll be there in fifteen.

Cullen fought through downtown traffic and arrived at El Gaucho twenty minutes later and found Julia at the bar.

"Hey, beautiful," Cullen said.

"Hey yourself." Julia stood and hugged her tight. "I was worried about you."

"Sorry. I didn't hear your texts come in."

"That's fair. You were at work, after all."

"Indeed I was."

"And you still have a job? For sure?" Julia said.

"I was just given ten clients from people who'd been let go. So I'd say I'm pretty secure at the moment."

"That's great, but do you have time to take on that many clients? What about your usual work?"

"It'll take a while to get my timing down. It'll mean a lot of late nights for me, but that's okay since I don't really look forward to going home now."

"Believe me, I hear that. Shall we eat?"

They got a table and Cullen relaxed with a glass of wine, some good food, and Julia's presence.

"You're like a drug," she said.

"How's that?"

"I can't get enough of you and it's painful not to be with you."

"I feel the same way, Cullen, but we're doing the right thing."

"Yeah. I know."

Dinner was soon over and they were standing in the pouring rain in the parking lot.

"We should make this quick, so we don't catch pneumonia," Julia said.

"Okay, I'll kiss you good-bye and you can be on your way."

"I'll text you in the morning."

"Please do."

"Good night, Cullen."

"Good night, Julia."

Cullen felt like a drowned rat, but she watched until she couldn't see Julia's taillights any longer, then got in her truck and drove home to her empty house.

CHAPTER TWENTY-FOUR

Wednesday night found Cullen at work until seven. She was exhausted at the end of the day so messaged Julia that she was just going to go home and go to bed. She missed her something fierce though. It had been painful on such a deep level not to see her for a day. Cullen vowed never to let that happen again.

Thursday, she logged off at four thirty on the dot and walked down to Leslie's. She was excited about seeing her, believing she'd help her get her feelings squared away and she needed that so desperately. She wanted to spend every moment she could with Julia, and living apart wasn't fun. It was, however, only their second week together, and when she thought of it that way, she realized they'd really rushed into things.

Leslie opened the door to the back hallway wearing black slacks and a cream-colored sweater. She greeted Cullen with a smile and Cullen followed her to her office.

"How are you today?" Leslie asked.

"I'm okay overall I guess."

Leslie arched a perfectly shaped eyebrow.

"Overall? Only okay? What's going on? Talk to me."

Cullen leaned back on the couch.

"I don't know really. I'm just working too hard, and not seeing Julia every day is killing me."

"Oh, so you took my advice?"

"We did. It made sense, but it's not easy."

"You're still so new. I want you to be able to enjoy that newness, that excitement. The living for each phone call, every text. I didn't say you couldn't see each other every day though. Whose choice was that?"

"I worked late last night and I was fried, so just wanted to drive home and crash. So we didn't meet for dinner or anything and I missed her."

"Well, that's no good. I'm sure you did. Will you see her tonight?"

"Yeah, we're meeting for dinner after this."

"Good. So, what else is going on? Why are you working so late?"

"They laid off a bunch of people at the office," Cullen said. "I got a lot of the distributed leftovers."

"Hm. Not fun and not good with everything else you've got going on. Have you heard from, what was her name?"

"Sara?"

"Yes, Sara."

"Not for a couple of days, which is a good thing. She pissed me off last time she texted me. Oh, sorry. Am I allowed to swear?"

Leslie smiled at her.

"That's fine. Just no f-bombs please."

"I can live with that."

"Tell me how she upset you."

"She said horrible things about Julia. I hate when she does that. She calls her names and cusses her out."

"Do you think she knows about the two of you?"

"I don't know. I wondered that myself," Cullen said.

"What does Julia think?"

"Julia thinks she cut all ties with Portland when she left so she shouldn't have any spies here reporting to her."

Leslie nodded.

"That makes sense. So what does she have to say about Julia?"

"Just that she's got the cops looking for her wherever she lives now."

"Paranoid much?" Leslie said.

"Right?"

"Are her texts still helping Julia?"

"Sort of, kind of, I guess. I don't really know. I just know I want her locked up so I won't have to hear from her again."

"So, let's talk about your feelings for Sara."

"Ugh, do we have to?"

"I think we do," Leslie said. "I think we need to talk about them and address them and help you move past them."

"I don't still care about her. I don't know how I can make that any clearer."

"But I'm sure you're still mourning the loss of your relationship. That's only natural."

"Is that what I'm doing?" Cullen said.

"I think it is. You may resent Sara for what she did to you and to everyone she came in contact with. You may hate her for running out on you, but it's the relationship that's over. One you'd put your heart and soul into and that's got to sting still."

"We were only together like six weeks or so. So how much of a relationship did we actually have?"

"Don't negate your feelings, Cullen. You need to feel your feels, that's the only way you'll be able to move on."

"Isn't there a fast forward button or something? Where I can just forget about Sara and the relationship that wasn't and move on with my life?"

Leslie laughed.

"If only it were that easy, and if it were I'd be out of a job."

Cullen smiled.

"Yeah, I suppose that's true."

"Tell me about the early days with Sara. What attracted you to her in the first place? How did you get together?"

Cullen ran her hands through her hair. She didn't want to think about those days, much less talk about them. She looked at Leslie who looked like she wasn't going to let Cullen get away without answering.

"We used to go to the same Chinese restaurant and would see each other waiting for our to-go orders. This went on for months.

One evening I decided to eat my dinner there, and she came over and asked if she could join me, and we never looked back."

"What about her attracted you that night? Was she pretty, smart, funny?"

"All of those things. She was so together. She struck me as a professional woman and I enjoyed talking to her. We went out dancing after that and then back to my place. The rest, as they say, is history. And now, I've come to find out, the restaurant we met at is closed. It's under investigation for drug trafficking."

"Do you think she was involved in that?" Leslie said.

"I don't know. Probably. I have no reason to believe she wasn't."

"Tell me about your relationship. In the beginning, before you knew she was a drug dealer."

"Not much to tell. We got along great. We always had fun, but like you said about Julia and me, it was new, fresh, exciting so of course we had fun."

"Did you ever have any doubts? Anything like that?" Leslie said.

"I don't know, maybe. She quit coming to bed with me, and I thought she was just tired of me. Turns out she was a cokehead. She stayed up all night snorting coke."

"I'm sorry, Cullen."

"Thanks."

"Okay, we need to find a way to help you get over her."

"I am."

"Fine, we need to help you through the stages of grief."

"What stage am I at?"

"Anger. That's the third stage, so you're moving in the right direction."

"Good for me."

"Do you exercise, Cullen?"

"I used to. I don't have time anymore."

"Make some time. I want you to work out or just walk. But I want you to do something physical that can clear your head."

"Seriously?"

"I'm dead serious. Okay, time's up for today. I'll see you Monday. Have a good weekend and make some time for yourself."

"Yes, ma'am. I will."

Julia sat at their table in Santeria. She was hungry and excited to hear how Cullen's appointment had gone. She missed her the night before but understood that work was a priority. She just hated to think of her working too hard. She needed to take care of herself, but she was sure her therapist would have told her that so Julia would keep her mouth shut.

Her heart did a somersault when she saw Cullen walk through the front door. She looked haggard, but still had that cocky stride that Julia loved. Julia stood and kissed her cheek.

"So good to see you," she said.

"Likewise. I'm glad I'm not working until midnight tonight." She laughed.

"Tell me you didn't work more after we got off the phone last night."

"I didn't. I crashed. Hard. It felt good to sleep like the dead."

"That's great. So, how was your appointment?"

"It was good. Turns out I'm not hung up on Sara after all, so you can rest assured."

"Cullen I don't think you're still hung up on her per se. I just think you have feelings about her you need to work through."

"It turns out I'm mourning the loss of the relationship," Cullen said.

"Okay, that makes sense. I mean, I can see that. So we just have to play a waiting game?"

"Pretty much. I'm making progress already through the grief process and I'm going to start exercising again. Leslie said that would help."

"Right on. That's great, babe."

Dinner passed too quickly and Julia wasn't ready to say good night.

"Want to come over to my place for a nightcap?" she asked.

"No, thanks. I mean, I appreciate the offer, but I should get home."

"I miss you, Cullen. I miss kissing you for hours on end. Are you sure you won't come over?"

"Let's go make out in your car for a while. Then I really need to head home."

Julia loved the way Cullen kissed her. When their mouths were together, Julia forgot everything else in the world. Nothing mattered except the feelings Cullen elicited. When Cullen finally broke the last kiss, Julia wanted to cry.

"Are you sure you have to go?" she whispered.

"Positive. If we kiss anymore, I'll end up at your place and I won't stop at kissing. Tell me good night and I'll see you after work tomorrow."

"Okay."

Julia kissed her one more time then watched Cullen leave her car and walk to her truck. Her hormones were on overdrive and she was shaking all over. She took a deep breath and started her car. She drove home still aroused and very lonely.

She woke before her alarm the next morning, but she'd hardly slept at all. She was too keyed up. She needed Cullen so completely. She didn't want to wait anymore, logic be damned. She wanted Cullen to make love to her and she wanted to please Cullen. She wanted to please her in such a way that she completely forgot about Sara and the way she'd hurt her.

But she knew that wasn't going to happen and it shouldn't. She knew that in her head, but her body certainly had other ideas. She took a shower, drank her coffee, and even made herself breakfast.

When she could put it off no longer, she drove to the station for another day she was sure would lead to frustration over Sara's cases. She went over every last detail a few more times, making sure her cases were airtight. She just had to find her. How the hell was she going to do that?

At noon, she walked up the street to a deli and grabbed a sandwich and another cup of coffee. She was sitting there scrolling through her phone when it rang.

"Stansworth here."

"Detective Stansworth? This is Detective Harrington from Zone Five Police Department in Atlanta."

Julia's heart leaped to her throat. She hoped this was the break she'd been waiting for, but she had to play it cool.

"Detective Harrington, how can I help you?"

"Actually, it's more like how I can help you."

"Is that right?" Her heart stopped.

"Yes, ma'am. I'm in the Midtown division. We just picked up a woman by the name of Jolie Mariota. She was caught on the campus of Georgia State with enough coke on her to kill a horse."

"Really? And this benefits me?"

"Yes, ma'am. Her fingerprints matched the woman you've been looking for. A Sara Donovan?"

Julia exhaled heavily. She couldn't believe it. Sara would be coming back to stand trial for two murders and the coke charges which were inconsequential as far as she was concerned.

"That's fantastic news," she said. "When can I come get her?"

"She's been booked, so she's yours whenever you want her. What do you need from me?"

"Oh, Detective, you've done more than enough. I don't know how I can thank you. I'll try to book a flight so I get there tonight."

"Sounds good. We can have dinner and chat about the cases."

"It'll probably be too late by then."

"So I'll have a snack." He laughed.

"Okay, well, it'll be my treat. I'll see you in a few hours."

"I'll email you directions to my office."

"Thank you."

She hung up the phone and practically ran back to the office. She checked in with the powers that be, marked herself out of the office for the rest of the day, and headed to the airport where she barely got a flight. While waiting for takeoff, she texted Cullen.

On my way to Atlanta. Don't know when I'll be back. I miss you already.

Atlanta? Does this have anything to do with Sara?

It has everything to do with her. Okay, I need to turn off my phone now.

Be safe, baby.

I will. I'll call you tonight.

CHAPTER TWENTY-FIVE

Hartsfield-Jackson Airport was bustling when Julia got off the plane. It was ten o'clock there, but she was still on Pacific Coast time. She worried about Detective Harrington, though. It really was late for dinner, but she was starving, so she'd at least see if he still wanted to meet.

She hailed a cab and gave the directions for the Zone Five police station. The cabby gave her an odd look, but drove her there without a word. When she arrived, she showed her badge to the officer at the front desk.

"I'm Detective Stansworth from Portland Police Bureau. I'm here to meet Detective Harrington."

"Have a seat. I'll let him know you're here."

A few moments later, a tall, beefy man came through a door and approached Julia.

"Detective," he said. "So good to meet you."

"I'm so happy to be here. You have no idea."

He smiled at her.

"I think I have a pretty damned good idea. So, dinner or would you like to see the prisoner?"

"As much as I'd love to see her, I trust that she's who I'm looking for. Let's go get food and I'll see her in the morning. Does she know I'm coming?"

"I haven't said a word."

She smiled a slow grin.

"Oh, that's going to make it that much sweeter."

"That's what I was thinking, too."

Julia enjoyed her dinner with Harrington and he was nice enough to drop her at her hotel after. She knew she needed her sleep, but she was too excited, so instead she called Cullen.

"Hey, baby," Cullen answered.

"Hi, gorgeous. How are you?"

"I'm great. So you're in Atlanta, huh? For how long?"

"I'll be flying back tomorrow. We got her, Cullen. She's ours."

"That's so fantastic."

"I think so, too. I can't wait to see her face when I walk into the interrogation room tomorrow."

"Oh, so you haven't seen her yet?"

"Nope," Julia said. "Not yet. I figured I'd save that little treat for the morning."

"Where have you been? It's got to be late there."

"It is. I went to dinner with the detective who arrested her. He was a nice guy and I'm eternally grateful to him."

"I'm sure you are."

"What are you doing?"

"Getting ready for bed, which you should be doing, too."

"Yeah, yeah, yeah," Julia said. "I know."

"So tell me good night and I'll see you tomorrow."

"Good night, Cullen, I miss you."

"I miss you too, baby. So very much."

"I'll see you tomorrow."

"Take care and be safe."

"Always."

Julia was up early the next morning despite the late hour she went to sleep. She was excited and ready to get Sara and take her back to Portland. She couldn't wait to make sure she spent the rest of her life behind bars. Everything was ready. She felt the cases were airtight. It was time.

She arrived at the station and met with Harrington.

"Are you ready for this?" he asked.

"I am."

"Okay. I'll call ahead and make sure she's in an interview room. Then we can drive over and you can see her."

"Excellent. She's not going to be happy to see me and I can not wait."

Harrington laughed.

"I do love that attitude. I'm sure she's going to freak."

"Did she ask why she couldn't post bail?"

"We told her we had reasons for wanting to retain her. She may have figured it out." He shrugged. "Who knows?"

"Okay. Well, make your phone call so we can go."

They drove over to the jail and Julia took a deep breath. She needed to be calm, cool, and collected. She couldn't bubble over like a schoolgirl. She had to be on her game.

"You ready?" Harrington said.

"I am."

Harrington walked into the room first.

"Why am I still here?" Sara said. "I hope you're here to release me."

Julia walked in and Sara's face blanched. Her mouth dropped open and her eyes widened. Julia fought not to break into a wide smile.

"Ms. Donovan," she said.

"What are you doing here?"

"I'm here to take you back to Portland. You're coming back to stand trial for the murders of Sherry Bergstrom and Donald Montague. Not to mention your arrest for possession with intent to distribute. I hope you enjoyed your night behind bars last night because you're going to be behind them for the rest of your life." She turned to Harrington. "Did you get us booked on a plane?"

"I did. Let's get out of here."

Guards were waiting for them when they landed in Portland. They escorted Sara to a waiting van, but Julia opted to take a taxi back to the station rather than accompanying them to the jail.

She finished up the transfer paperwork then headed out. She was ready to meet with the DA on Monday. They had an appointment at nine and Julia was beyond ready to get the ball rolling.

Julia sat in her car and called Cullen.

"Hey, baby," Cullen said. "Where are you?"

"I'm back and I'm heading home. But then I thought I'd rather come to your place. Would that be okay?"

"Hell, yes. That would be awesome. We can go grab some lunch then come back here and make out."

Julia felt her face heat as well as other body parts. A make out session with Cullen was just what the doctor ordered.

"I'll drive as fast as I can," she said.

Cullen laughed.

"Drive carefully. I want you here in one piece."

"Yes, ma'am, I'll see you in a few."

Cullen picked up the dirty clothes on her bedroom floor and threw away the cartons that last night's dinner had arrived in. She brushed her teeth, slipped into some jeans, and was ready for Julia.

She heard the knock a few minutes later and opened the door to see a radiant looking Julia standing there. She took her by the hand and pulled her inside.

"You look amazing. Traveling across the country and back in one day certainly agrees with you."

Julia laughed and leaned into Cullen.

"Why, thank you. That's good to know."

Cullen closed the distance between them and took Julia's lips with hers. They were soft and yielding and tasted like fall. Such a wonderful combination. Cullen held tighter to keep from falling over. She was lightheaded as all the blood in her system had headed south. She was soon swollen with desire and knew she'd have to end the kiss soon.

She didn't get the chance as Julia softly closed her lips and backed away.

"Damn, Cullen. If that's the way I get greeted when I return, remind me to go away more often."

"Silly girl. I'll greet you like that if I just saw you five minutes ago. I love kissing you."

"Mm, I love it, too. Not to be a wet rag, but I haven't eaten today. Let's go get some food."

"Give me a minute so my legs can work right. They're a little shaky at the moment."

"Got it. Let's go sit on the couch for a minute then."

"No, I'll just want to kiss you again if we do that. Let's head out."

"I want something with substance," Julia said. "What do you want?"

"You."

"Very funny, to eat."

Cullen glanced over at Julia and arched her eyebrow. She gave her a most lascivious grin. Julia laughed and swatted her arm.

"Okay, okay. I want pizza. Let's go get pizza."

"Sounds good."

"We could have had it delivered," Cullen said.

"I didn't want to wait that long."

"You are just scared I'd ravish you if we stayed in the house."

"Maybe." Julia laughed. "Maybe indeed."

They ordered their pizza and found a table.

"So, tell me," Cullen said. "What was her reaction when she saw you?"

"It was awesome. The color drained from her face and she stared at me like her worst nightmare had come true. She recovered quickly though, and then she was pissed and I mean royally."

"That's great. I'm glad it went well. And now she's cooling her heels in the jail downtown?"

"Yes, she is. I meet with the prosecutor Monday to go over the cases. Should be a slam dunk."

"I hope so."

They finished their lunch and started back to Cullen's place.

"Why don't we stop for some beer?" Julia said.

"But you'll have to drive home tonight."

"I can stay in the guest room."

"Do you think that's such a good idea?" Cullen pictured Leslie and knew she wouldn't be happy with that arrangement.

"Sure, I'll be in the other room so no temptation. And that way I can wake up here and we can spend the day together tomorrow."

Cullen still wasn't convinced, but she had pulled into the store parking lot.

"I don't know, Julia. I'm not sure what Leslie would say."

"Then she doesn't have to know. Seriously, though, if you'd rather I not then just say the word. I don't want to interfere with the good work you're doing to move forward."

Cullen parked her truck and sat there thinking. She was making good progress even in the few short days she'd been working on it. Still, the idea of all day today and tomorrow with Julia? She wasn't strong enough to say no. It wasn't like they were sharing a bed every night.

"Cullen?" Julia said. "Say something."

Cullen smiled at her.

"Let's go get some beer. I think your plan sounds great."

They each grabbed a beer and Cullen sat on the couch to watch her Ducks game. Julia remained standing.

"What's up?" Cullen said.

"I think I'd like to put on some sweats if that's okay."

"Sure, you want me to get them for you?"

"No, thanks. You settle in for the game. I'll be right back."

Julia looked amazing in Cullen's sweats, and Cullen's heart raced at the sight of her. When Julia curled up next to her on the couch, she thought she would combust from the heat surging through her veins.

Forgetting about the game for a moment, she pulled Julia against her and nibbled on her neck and earlobe. Julia squirmed against her, pressing her breasts into her chest. Cullen kissed up her neck until she reached her chin. She sucked on it and ran her tongue over the soft skin.

"You're making me crazy," Julia said.

"Mm, I know the feeling."

She kissed her full on the mouth then. Julia met her kiss with an open mouth and Cullen felt her shiver when their tongues met. Urged on, she leaned into Julia, forcing her down onto her back. She climbed on top of her and ran her fingers through her silky blond hair.

She brought her hand down to cup her jaw and reveled again at how smooth her skin was. She was losing herself in the kiss and dragged her hand down Julia's arm until her hand came to rest on one of her small, firm breasts.

White-hot chills coursed through her, settling between her legs. Julia moaned into her mouth and Cullen needed more. She felt the pressure of Julia's arms against her chest. She came to her senses and quickly sat up.

"I'm sorry," she said. "I'm so sorry."

"I'm not complaining," Julia said. "Not one bit. I just knew one of us had to break it off, and I had a feeling it wasn't going to be you this time."

"You're right." Cullen took a deep breath to calm her shaking limbs and racing heart. Damn, but that had felt good. Julia's breast in her hand felt so right. She was glad Julia stopped her before she slid her hand under her hoodie because that was next on her agenda.

"Have a drink of beer," Julia said. "That'll cool you off."

Cullen picked up her beer with a trembling hand.

"I hope I'll be strong enough not to jump your bones tonight," Cullen said.

"You won't jump me. We both know that's not okay. Besides, I'll be in the other room. I'll lock my door if you need me to."

"That won't be necessary. I can be strong. I know I can."

"Why don't you settle down and watch your game? You can sit in the recliner if you need to."

"No, I'll be okay. Come here and watch with me."

She draped her arm around Julia and held her close. All was right in her world.

CHAPTER TWENTY-SIX

Julia stretched when she awoke the next morning and tried to get her bearings. Oh yeah, she was in Cullen's guest room. She lay back and played over the night before. The Ducks had won, which pleased Cullen no end. The beer had flowed and they'd both been feeling good.

Her mind drifted back to earlier in the evening and their mini make out session on the couch. Damn, her whole body came alive when she reflected on the way Cullen's hand had felt on her breast. Her mind had short-circuited briefly. She'd wanted more, craved more, and almost gave in. She'd come to her senses just in time. She needed Cullen and soon.

She stretched again and made herself get out of bed lest she be tempted to take matters into her own hands. She didn't need to do that, tempting though it was. She was saving that for Cullen, whenever that may be.

Cullen was nowhere to be found when Julia wandered through the house. Coffee was made, though, so she knew she was awake. She looked out at the driveway. Cullen's truck was there so where was Cullen?

She helped herself to a cup of coffee and sat at the dining room table to drink it. She was halfway through when Cullen came in from the garage. She was a sweaty mess and every nerve ending in Julia sparked. She'd never wanted her as much.

"Ah, I wondered where you were," she said.

"I've been trying to work out every day. You know, Leslie suggested exercise, and I do love lifting weights and using my punching bag."

"What a great way to take out your aggressions, too, right?"

"Indeed. I've thought about putting a picture of Sara on the punching bag, but didn't bother."

Julia laughed uncertainly. It was funny, sure. But it also meant Cullen had deep-seated feelings for her. Even if those feelings were hatred and disgust, Julia longed for the day when Cullen would feel a twinge of those rather than being consumed by them.

"I'm glad you didn't. You want to join me for a cup of coffee?"

"If you don't mind, I think I'll drink some water then hit the shower. Is that okay with you?"

"That's fine, but come here and kiss me first."

"But I'm all sweaty and disgusting."

"You're hotter than hell. Please, kiss me."

Cullen laughed, then acquiesced. Julia grew lightheaded when their lips met. She wanted to pull Cullen closer and prolong the kiss but knew Cullen wasn't feeling as sexy as she looked.

Cullen came out after her shower wearing black sweatpants and an Oregon Ducks hoodie.

"You and your Ducks," Julia said.

"Go Ducks."

"I'm hungry. Is there anything here to eat?"

"I'm afraid not, but there's a deli over by the grocery store that makes a mean breakfast. Shall we?"

"Let me get dressed and brush my teeth and hair. I'll be ready in a sec."

She emerged feeling better and kissed Cullen soundly.

"What was that for?" Cullen asked.

"Does a girl need a reason to kiss her boi?"

Cullen grinned.

"No. I don't suppose she does."

After breakfast, they drove into the city and bowled for a few hours. Cullen wiped the floor with Julia, but Julia didn't mind. She thoroughly enjoyed her time with Cullen, and watching Cullen's form as she bowled made her heart race and her hormones rage. She wished to God it was time to sleep together. She was beyond ready. The waiting was killing her.

After bowling, they went to a dark bar and had a couple of beers.

"You know," Julia broached the subject she'd been dreading. "You may be called upon to testify at the trial."

Cullen choked on her beer.

"Me? Why?"

"Character witness. It would do Sara a world of good to be seen in a relationship with someone as successful and together and law abiding as yourself."

"A lot of good that did her. She still was a common criminal."

Julia reached across the table and took Cullen's hand.

"Yes, she was and I'm sorry all that happened to you, but I want you to be prepared."

"Okay. Well, what do I say? I've never been to court. That's not my thing."

"And I get that. All you can do is answer as honestly as you can. I can't stress that enough."

"Won't I be under oath? Of course I'll be honest."

"That doesn't mean much to some people," Julia said.

"It does to me. I'm not about to lie under oath."

"Good. I would expect nothing less from you."

They finished their beer and Cullen stood.

"Come on, let's get out of here. Suddenly my mood has soured."

"I'm sorry. I didn't mean to put a damper on the day."

"I'll get over it. Let's go buy some beer and head back to my place."

"Okay."

They got back to Cullen's house and Cullen was still quiet.

"Cullen, babe, talk to me. I'm sorry I ruined the day. I just thought you should know. You know, mentally prepare yourself. Tell me what you're feeling."

"I don't know. What if my testimony springs her? What if it puts her away? That's a lot of responsibility."

They sat on the couch and Julia turned to face her.

"There's going to be a lot of damning evidence, Cullen. She's not going to get off. Besides, I thought you wanted her put away."

"I do. I just don't want to be the one who does it."

"No," Julia said. "That's my job and the prosecutor's. We'll make sure she's locked up. You just tell the whole truth regardless of who asks you what, okay?"

"Okay, I guess."

Julia turned so she could snuggle against Cullen, who draped her arm across her shoulders and pulled her close.

"What would I do without you?" Cullen said.

"I hope you never have to find out."

"Do you mean that? I mean, honestly?"

Julia looked into Cullen's eyes.

"Of course I do. I'm in this for the long haul, Matthews, so you'd just better get used to it."

She watched Cullen's eyes darken as they looked into hers. She saw her glance down at Julia's lips as she licked her own. Julia knew what was coming. She braced herself for it, for the onslaught of emotions and hormonal responses. But still she wasn't ready. When their lips met, her heart galloped like a runaway horse. She thought it would burst out of her chest.

Cullen applied more pressure to her lips and Julia opened her mouth and welcomed her in. Their tongues romped together and each stroke of Cullen's tongue along her caused her lower lips to swell more. She was a swollen, wet, hormonal mess and she never wanted the kiss to end.

Cullen must have been feeling it too as she was soon lying on top of Julia. She brought her knee up and pressed into Julia's center. Without thinking, Julia ground into her. It felt so good and if she did it for just a little longer, she knew she'd find relief. Cullen came to her senses before Julia and sat up.

"I'm sorry," she said.

"Cullen, you don't have to apologize. We're two consenting adults here. This isn't all on you."

"I know. I just want you so badly, but I don't want to make a mistake, and it's no fair for me to keep teasing you like I do. You're only human."

"I am, but I'm feeling everything you are, babe."

"Are you?" Cullen said. "Are you really? How can you be sure?"

"Tell me what you're thinking. Tell me what you're feeling. Then I'll tell you if I'm with you or not."

Cullen ran her hand through her hair. She hated talking about her feelings. Wasn't it obvious how she felt about Julia? But then, maybe it wasn't. Maybe it looked like she was only after her for one thing. She took a deep breath and exhaled slowly. Julia was waiting for her to say something.

"I like you, Julia. Like, really like you, but I'm scared. I don't want this to be another short-lived disaster in my life."

"Okay. That's a good start, I'm with you so far," Julia said.

"And I want you. God knows I want to taste and touch every inch of you. It's so hard not to give in and just say fuck it and please you. But I can't. I'm not ready. I don't think either of us is."

"Again, I'm with you one hundred percent."

"And then I do something stupid like touch your boob or press my knee into you. I could feel how hot and wet you were and wanted to be inside you so desperately."

"And that's where I want you. I want you so deep inside me I don't know where you end and I begin. But you're right, it's not time. We both need to be sure this is right before we do that."

"But it feels so right, so fucking right. I don't know how it could ever get more right, you know? And then I do those stupid things when I get carried away and I worry you're going to seek release from someone who's not afraid to give it to you."

Julia smiled at her and her heart grew.

"We'll know when the time is right, Cullen. When you can talk about Sara without clenching every muscle in your body. We'll know. And in the meantime, you can relax. I'm not going anywhere, and I'm certainly not looking for a quickie from anyone. You're the only one I want."

"Are you sure, though? It's got to get old to have me take you down that path and then draw you back."

"It doesn't get old because I know why you do it. It's important that we wait. But it's also important we keep the lines of communication open. That way we both know where we are in relation to the other."

"True. It's just so hard for me to talk about my feelings," Cullen said.

"Well, I hope it'll get easier, because I like to hear how you feel. Words are important to me. Actions speak louder, of course, but words are crucial."

"I'll try to remember that."

"Good and now that we've moved forward, I'm hungry and should think about heading home. Let's go get dinner then I'll be on my way."

Cullen kissed her, a deep, passionate kiss that promised so much in the not too distant future.

"Okay, let's go."

They drove separate cars to the restaurant, and Cullen already missed Julia. She knew she'd be busy in the coming days preparing for the trial and everything. But she hoped they'd still have time together every day. It was critical for Cullen. She needed her time with Julia.

After dinner, they climbed into Julia's car and made out for a half hour or so.

"I'm bummed you have to go," Cullen said. "I mean, I get it and all, but I miss you already. This has been a great weekend."

"Mm, it really has. I love spending time with you, babe."

"I can't get enough of you."

"Well, you hold that thought. I'll see you tomorrow after work, right?"

"For sure. We'll do dinner?"

"Yep, we'll order Chinese. Sound good?"

"Sounds wonderful."

"Okay," Julia said. "I should go and you need to get out of my car since you've succeeded in fogging up my windows."

"I'd say I'm sorry…"

"I know better." Julia laughed. "You're not even slightly sorry."

"Okay, I'll get going. Good night, baby."

"Good night, babe."

"Drive carefully."

"Always."

Cullen arrived back at her house and felt antsy. She had a ton of pent up energy and no way to expend it. She knew how she wanted to, but Julia wasn't there, and even if she was, it wasn't going to happen.

She stripped down to her boxers and undershirt and attacked her home gym again. She felt exhausted and exhilarated when she was through so she took another shower and went to bed.

As soon as she lay down, her mind kicked into overdrive. She couldn't turn it off. She thought about Julia and their relationship. About how it felt so right but how her past, including Sara, made her drag her feet.

And then she thought about Sara and the fucking trial. She didn't want to see her, but now knew she would. What would that be like? Would Sara think she was trying to help her? If she got off, would she pursue Cullen again?

That would mean barking up the wrong tree. That train has left the station. All Cullen wanted now was Julia. She rolled over and forced herself to think of all the fun they'd had over the weekend and finally fell asleep.

CHAPTER TWENTY-SEVEN

Julia's meeting with the DA went very well, and the ball started rolling toward the trial. Sara's case would go in front of a grand jury later in the week, hopefully Thursday, and then the real trial would start. Julia was excited and proud. She'd solved two murders, and the woman who'd committed them would spend the rest of her life in prison.

She wanted to scream it from the rooftops, but instead walked back to the station to see what else had come up. A dead body had been found under the Burnside Bridge. It was a homeless man, but he'd been stabbed, so Julia was asked to go look into it.

The case would probably never be solved, which didn't make Julia feel good, but it was something to do to take her mind off Sara. She arrived at the scene and found a young man in his mid twenties lying on his back. The front of his shirt, which had been cut away, was covered in blood, as were his hands.

"Is all this blood his?" she asked the CSI team.

"Probably, but we won't know until we have Mike run some tests."

"Fair enough. What else can you tell me?"

"Not much. What you see is what you get. Caucasian male stabbed just under the sternum. Likely he bled out. It's doubtful the murder weapon killed him instantly. Again, we'll know more after the autopsy."

"Great, thanks for the info. Please keep me posted. Does the vic have a name?"

"Dustin O'Hara, age twenty-six, address in Beaverton. No telling how long he'd been on the streets."

"He's too young," Julia said.

"No doubt. A preliminary report shows a laundry list of mental illnesses."

"Poor kid."

She excused herself and approached a group of uniformed officers.

"What have you found out?"

"Nobody saw anything. Nobody has ever seen the kid before. The usual."

"Keep asking. Someone saw something. I want a report on my desk by morning."

"Yes, ma'am."

She went back to her desk and sat quietly researching Dustin O'Hara. The kid was a mess and now he was dead. Normally, they didn't waste a lot of resources on homeless victims. They did their best, but those crimes were hardly ever solvable. But there was something about the young man that spoke to her though and she wanted his murderer brought to justice.

Julia heard a ping and checked her email. It was from CSI. They'd found the murder weapon. Excellent. They'd catch the killer and it would mean another murder solved. Julia could almost see the pay raise coming, almost. It probably wouldn't come, but she knew she deserved it. Solving murders wasn't easy, but she was on a roll and she deserved more money.

Her stomach rumbled, and she realized she hadn't eaten yet that day. She checked the clock and it was already four. That was a good enough time to leave. Cullen would see Leslie that day so she'd be over a little later, but Julia could pick up some wine and beer and meet Cullen at her house.

She arrived at her house and poured herself a glass of wine. She took it into the bathroom where she took a shower to wash off the grime of the day. She always felt dirty after visiting a crime scene. She rinsed off then allowed herself some time to soak in the tub.

Julia felt amazingly relaxed between the wine and the bath. She put on sweats and called in an order for dinner. She had just poured another glass of wine when she heard Cullen pull into the driveway.

She greeted her with a kiss before stepping aside to let her in.

"How was your day? How was Leslie?"

"Ugh." Cullen took the beer Julia offered and collapsed onto the couch. "My day was brutal, but Leslie was good."

"Oh, no." Julia sat next to her. "What was wrong with your day?"

"I had lunch with a client today. It was a case I took over due to layoffs. The client hated it. I mean, he hated the campaign I worked up for him. It wasn't at all what he wanted."

"Oh, babe, I'm so sorry. What did you do?"

"What could I do? I started from scratch with him. I interviewed him like he was a new client off the street and dug deep to find out what he was looking for. He was right. I totally missed the mark, but the notes on his account had been sparse at best. Ugh. Oh well, I started a new campaign for him which he insists I need to be ready to share with him Friday. Friday, Julia. That's not very long to put together an ad campaign."

"No, it's not. So you'll be busy this week."

"Right. I probably won't see again you until Friday night."

Disappointment flooded over Julia. She didn't want to wait that long to see Cullen again. But work got in the way. God knows she knew that. Sure, she had time to spend with Cullen now, but if another big case showed up, things would be different. She had to be supportive and not sulk and pout like she wanted to.

"The customer's always right. Isn't that what they say? You do what you need to do, babe. I'll still be here."

Cullen kissed her. It was a soft, chaste kiss, but it sent her heart racing.

"Thanks, Julia. You're the best." She took a swig of beer. "So, tell me, how was your day?"

Julia couldn't hold back the smile.

"I met with the DA today. Sara's case will be presented to the grand jury before the week is over. After that, we'll move ahead with the trial."

"Yay you. That's great."

"Yep, and then I caught another murder case. A kid, homeless, but we got the murder weapon so I'm hoping we'll find his murderer soon."

"I hope so, too."

Dinner arrived and they ate in comfortable silence. Julia was inhaling her food and barely taking time to breathe, much less talk and Cullen seemed lost in her own thoughts.

After dinner they sat at the table with their drinks.

"Did you want to tell me how things went with Leslie?" Julia said.

"She thinks I'm healing well. She's seeing progress, which is a good thing. She tried to warn me about depression, but it seems I'm already there—less sleep, less appetite. So I'm making my way through my grief and that's a good thing."

"Oh, Cullen, I'm sorry you're depressed."

"I didn't really realize I was. I mean, it's taken an act of God to get me to do any work, but I just thought I was burned out you know? From burning the candle at both ends? But apparently lack of motivation is also a symptom of depression. So, I'll get through this and then I'll be at the acceptance stage and I should be good to go. I don't know that I'll get there for a while, but you never know."

"Right, I get that."

"And now, my dear, it's time for me to go. I've got a long few days ahead of me. Kiss me like you mean it."

Julia was happy to oblige. She leaned in so her body melded with Cullen's as they kissed good-bye. The feel of Cullen's tight body pressed against her made her dizzy with need. Her head felt like it would float away while her briefs grew damper with each passing minute.

Cullen finally decided they'd kissed long enough. She was throbbing and knew she was about to cross the line again, so she slowly closed her mouth and hugged Julia close. The feel of her soft body against Cullen had her wishing they could fall into bed right then.

Soon, she told herself. Very soon now. She just needed to power through this last stage of grief and they'd be home free. She couldn't wait. She released Julia and took a step back.

"Okay, sweetheart, I'll see you Friday night. Let's plan on doing something fun."

"Sounds good. Call me when you get home."

"Will do."

The next few days flew by. Cullen got to work at seven each morning to work on the campaign and worked on her laptop each night until close to midnight. She was afraid she'd fall asleep driving to work Thursday morning. She was exhausted, but the campaign was almost complete and ready to present.

Her work was interrupted midmorning by a text from Julia.

Grand jury says she can stand trial. Woot!

That's great. Congrats.

Thanks. She should be going to court soon.

Excellent news.

Okay, babe. Don't work too hard.

See you tomorrow.

She worked hard the rest of the day and felt the campaign was finished when she left to go see Leslie. She could feel a spring in her step as she followed Leslie back to her office.

"You look happy," Leslie said. "What's going on? Talk to me."

"Lots of good things. The client I told you about Monday? Well, I think his campaign is done. I'll present him with it tomorrow. I'm exhausted, which means I need my sleep, which I think is a good sign. And the grand jury found enough evidence for Sara to stand trial. So life is good right now, Leslie, real good."

"That's fantastic. That's what I like to hear. Except that you're exhausted. Are you still not sleeping?"

"No, but that's because I've been working on the campaign. I'm sure I'll be able to sleep tonight."

"Good. I hope so. So, let's talk about this trial. You mentioned Monday that you may be called on to testify and you were terrified. How are you feeling now?"

"I don't know. Not really scared anymore, more determined, I'd say. I don't relish the idea of spending a day or more in a courthouse. That's more Julia's thing, you know? But if that's what I have to do to put Sara away for good, then so be it."

"Excellent attitude," Leslie said. "That's what I want to hear. Now, Sara going to prison for the rest of her life. How does that make you feel?"

"I don't know, to be honest. Um, I think I'll be happy, but then it's almost like it's a television show I'm watching. Like, I want the bad guy to be put away. I don't know if I can explain it, but it's hard to feel like this is my ex we're talking about. It's like it's some stranger who did bad things and should be punished. Does that make any sense?"

Leslie nodded.

"I just hope you're not disassociating yourself to protect yourself. If you're really not emotionally vested anymore, well, that's fantastic."

"I don't know what I'm doing really. I just know that I'll do my part whatever that is."

"Good for you, Cullen."

"So does this mean I'm healed? Can I sleep with Julia?" She smiled.

Leslie laughed.

"I don't know about that. How much time have you spent together this week?"

"Like none. I haven't seen her since Monday, though I'm hoping we can get together tonight for dinner."

"That would be nice, but don't go too far yet, Cullen. I want to make sure you're out of the woods with Sara."

Cullen sighed loudly.

"Yes, ma'am."

When her session was over, Cullen sat in her truck and texted Julia.

Dinner tonight?

I just ordered a pizza. Come join me?

I'm on my way.

She arrived just as the pizza delivery guy was leaving. She knocked on the door and took Julia in her arms when she got in the house.

"How's my beautiful girl tonight?" she said.

"I'm great." Julia laughed. "How's my boi and to what do I owe this pleasure?"

"I finished the campaign. I'll meet with the client tomorrow, but it's about as good as I can get it."

"That's fantastic news. Congratulations. Come on in and celebrate with me."

"Not so fast, my dear."

Cullen kissed Julia with no pretense of chastity. She kissed her hard and ran her tongue along her lips. She ran her tongue along Julia's and felt her need at her core. Soon. Very soon. She broke the kiss.

Julia leaned against her.

"Am I supposed to walk now?"

Cullen laughed.

"Come on, I'll help you."

Julia remained leaning against Cullen as they walked to the dining room. She felt amazing and once again, Cullen couldn't wait to feel their naked bodies pressed together.

"I'm glad you had a good day," Julia said. "I had a great day, too."

"I know, cheers." She held her bottle up to Julia's wineglass. "So when's the trial?"

"We don't know yet, but it'll be soon. No reason for Sara to take up space at the jail when she belongs in prison."

Cullen nodded.

"That makes sense."

After dinner, they sat together on the couch.

"Will you come over to my place tomorrow night?" Cullen said.

"I'd love that."

"Great. I should probably get going."

"As someone very dear to me once said, kiss me like you mean it."

Cullen's blood roared in her ears as she kissed Julia with all the pent up passion flowing through her. She leaned her back and climbed on top of her, not quite losing control, but coming close.

She finally ended the kiss.

"Time for me to head home, unfortunately. I'll see you tomorrow?"

"As soon as I can get there."

"Excellent."

CHAPTER TWENTY-EIGHT

Cullen's presentation went well the next morning. The client loved what she'd done with his ideas.

"I wish you'd been assigned to us from the start," he said. "I hope you'll be our main ad contact from here on out."

"I'm sure I will be." Cullen handed him her card. "And you can always request me."

"Will do. It's been a pleasure, Cullen. Really. You're a genius."

"Thank you. I'm glad you like it."

She was walking on air as she went back to her office. She couldn't wipe the smile off her face. Sure, it had been a pain in the ass, but in the end, the client was happy and that made her happy.

Unfortunately, all the work she'd put into that one client had put her behind on other projects so she settled in and worked through lunch to get caught up. She was so engrossed in one campaign that she jumped when her cell phone rang.

Thinking it must be Julia, she answered with a smile.

"Hello?"

"Cullen?" That was not Julia's voice. But a man.

"Yes. Who's this?"

"This is Robert Allen. We met a few weeks ago?"

She felt a cold lead weight settle in the pit of her stomach.

"Yes, I remember you," she said coolly. "What can I do for you?"

"As you may or may not know, Sara was arrested elsewhere and brought back here to stand trial on some trumped up charges."

"I'd heard something about that."

"Well, I'm going to call you as a witness in the trial."

Shit! It was really happening. God, how she'd hoped that Julia had been mistaken.

"I see."

"Look, I'm sure it sounds scary, but I assure you it'll be easy. I'll just ask you some questions about your relationship with her. You know, how happy you two were and that kind of thing. I'd like to go over the questions with you. Can you meet me Monday at ten?"

"I don't know..."

"It's important, Cullen. I'm going to call you whether you're prepared or not. I suggest you be at my office at ten."

She exhaled loudly.

"Fine, I'll be there."

"Good. I know you want to help Sara. You're doing the right thing. I'll see you Monday. Have a great weekend."

She slid her phone in her pocket then pulled up the company email. She sent an email to Samantha asking her to call her as soon as she was available. At three o'clock, Samantha called.

"Can I come to your office?" Cullen said.

"Is it important?"

"Very."

"Then sure, come on up."

Cullen's stomach was in knots. She had to miss more work. One, to meet with Robert and two, for the fucking trial. Samantha was not going to be amused. She stood when Cullen knocked on her door.

"Cullen, come in. Have a seat. What's going on?"

This time, instead of coming around to sit with Cullen, Samantha sat in her desk chair.

"I don't know where to begin," Cullen said.

"Are you quitting?"

"No, nothing like that."

Samantha's face relaxed.

"Okay, so, what's up?"

"I'm not even sure where to start. I guess the best thing I can say is a friend of mine got in trouble."

"Friend? Were you involved with her? Never mind. You don't have to answer that. Hell, I can't ask that, so just disregard that, okay? And what kind of trouble?"

"Yes, we were involved, and she's in trouble with the law."

Samantha raised an eyebrow.

"That doesn't sound like your type."

"You have no idea. Anyway, I've been called as a witness for her trial."

"That doesn't sound like fun."

"No," Cullen said. "I don't anticipate it will be. At any rate, I'm meeting with her lawyer Monday at ten. I'll come in early to make up the time, but I wanted you to know I'm not flaking, and I don't know about the trial. Like when it'll be or how long I'll have to be out for it."

"I understand." Her tone was like ice.

"Samantha, look, if I could get out of this, I would."

"I'm sure you would. Just keep me posted and I'll try to keep the wolves at bay, okay?"

Cullen stood.

"Okay and thank you."

She went to her desk, good mood completely gone, and did very little until four thirty. She left her building and stopped by a liquor store on the way home. She bought Malibu rum and Coke. She was going to drink hard that night. She hoped Julia would be okay with it.

Cullen ordered Italian food for dinner and was just plating the lasagna when Julia arrived.

"Hey, beautiful." Cullen took her in her arms. "Man, is it good to see you."

"It's wonderful to be here. What smells so good?"

"I ordered us dinner. I hope you don't mind."

"Not at all." She motioned to her overnight bag. "Just let me put this in the bedroom and we can eat."

She was back out in no time and they sat down to dinner.

"How was your day?" Julia said. "How did your presentation go?"

"The presentation went very well. The client loved the campaign I put together for him."

"That's fantastic. So, why are you not bouncing off walls in excitement?"

"Sara's lawyer called me today," Cullen said.

"Oh, babe, I'm so sorry."

"Yeah, I'm meeting with him Monday morning."

"We knew this was going to happen," Julia said.

"I know we talked about it, but I was still hoping it wouldn't happen. I just hope I don't say the wrong thing."

"What do you mean? I've told you, babe, all you have to do is tell the truth. Even if you paint Sara as a fun loving, wonderful girlfriend, we'll be able to show she's still a cold-blooded murderer. You just relax, okay?"

"I'll try. Ugh. And Samantha wasn't happy about me missing more work."

"Samantha? Oh, the ex that you work with?" Julia said.

"She's not my ex. We just dated a few times. Nothing serious."

"Okay. Well, let's focus on your excellent campaign and how well you're doing with therapy, shall we?" Julia said.

"Ah, yes, and how close we are to sleeping together."

Julia laughed. She had to. If she didn't she would cry. Her need for Cullen was all-consuming. She was lucky she had the job she did or she'd think of nothing else, she was sure of that. She wanted nothing more than to play pillow princess for hours and experience all the pleasure she was sure Cullen could provide.

And then, after resting and recuperating, she wanted to meticulously explore Cullen's body. She longed to learn what really got her motor running, what sent her teetering on the edge of oblivion, and what got her to topple over the edge and soar to new heights.

But it wasn't time yet and she knew it. They both knew it, but damn, it was getting harder to wait.

"Say something." Cullen brought her back to reality. "Say anything."

"Sorry, you sent me off into fantasyland with that last statement."

Cullen laughed a deep rumbly laugh that caused a chain reaction of desire rolling through her veins.

"Sorry to do that, but next time take me along."

"Take you along?"

"To fantasyland. Talk to me, baby. What's going to happen when we finally split the sheets?"

"Oh, no," Julia said. "I'm not about to put that into words. It may take us there sooner than we're ready. So, for now, you keep your fantasies in your head and I'll keep mine in mine. And then, when we're ready, we'll share those fantasies and make them come true."

"That sounds reasonable," Cullen said. "But will you at least tell me what you're like in bed?"

"What do you want me to say?"

"Are you a tiger or a pussycat?"

Julia felt the blush start at her chest and work its way up her cheeks until her scalp was even on fire.

"I can hold my own."

"Okay, not sure exactly how to take that, but I guess I'll let it slide for now," Cullen said.

"What about you? Although I've no doubt you're a tiger."

"Oh, yeah, aggressive and hungry for more. That's me."

"Aggressive but gentle?" Julia said.

"If that's how you want it. I'm versatile and flexible. So whatever you want you get. Now just tell me what you want."

Cullen had gotten up and walked around the table. She rested her hands on Julia's shoulders. She rubbed them lightly before sliding her hands forward and rubbing Julia's chest, stopping just as her fingertips hit the swells of her breasts.

"Cullen." Julia leaned back and closed her eyes.

"Yes?" Cullen eased her fingertips lower, and Julia felt herself swell at the contact. She needed Cullen's fingertips lower still. One brush across her nipples would send her soaring, she was sure of it.

Julia placed her hands over Cullen's.

"You need to stop."

"If you insist."

"I'm afraid I must. Damn, woman, I love the way you touch me."

"I love touching you." Cullen's voice was husky with need. "It makes me think of touching the rest of you, of how soft and warm you'll be."

Julia twisted in her chair and pulled Cullen down. Their mouths came together and tongues explored. Julia couldn't fight the thoughts that Cullen's tongue was strong while soft and she wanted to feel that tongue inside her.

She broke off the kiss and sat breathing heavily in her chair. Her head spun and blood thumped, and she wanted to cry at the painful frustration of it all. Still, she knew that the anticipation was only building up to what certainly would be fantastic sex. She was sure Cullen wouldn't disappoint.

"We should find something to do," Cullen said. "Want to play poker?"

"Sure." Julia finally found her voice. "That would be fun."

Again, they were evenly matched in the card game with Cullen having a slight edge. Julia finally looked at her phone. It was one o'clock in the morning.

"We should go to bed, er, sleep."

Cullen laughed.

"True, it's late. Come on, babe."

Cullen held tight to Julia's hand as she walked her to the guest room. They stopped at the doorway and Julia slipped her arms around Cullen's neck. She rested her elbows on her broad shoulders and looked into her eyes, begging Cullen to kiss her.

Julia's world tilted off its axis when their lips met. Her knees went weak and she held on to Cullen so she wouldn't fall. And still the kiss went on. It intensified, it became gentle, it grew persistent again.

She wantonly pressed her breasts into Cullen's, knowing full well she was playing with fire, but not giving a damn. She was aroused to the point that she was ready to say fuck it and get naked right then and there.

She felt Cullen's hands cup her ass and when Cullen ground into her, she almost lost it. One touch, just one little touch, and she'd feel so much better.

Julia was surprised when Cullen ended the kiss. She stood dumbfounded. The drumming between her legs drove her to try to pull Cullen in for another kiss, but Cullen stood stiff.

"That's enough for tonight," Cullen said. "You have sweet dreams, baby."

She kissed Julia's forehead, and Julia watched her walk down the hall to her room. Julia lay in bed with her legs crossed, applying pressure to her red-hot center. Nothing worked to calm her down, and she slid her hand under the waistband of her sweats.

She was wet, so very wet. Her head still pounded from the blood rushing through her. She dipped a finger inside.

No, I can't do that. I'll wait for Cullen. No matter how long it takes.

CHAPTER TWENTY-NINE

Monday morning rolled around, and Cullen woke to an empty house. Julia's absence was pronounced, and she hated it. She couldn't stand not waking up to Julia and having coffee together and just being with her. She longed for the time that they'd wake in the same bed and she'd be able to start her day by making love to Julia until she couldn't take any more.

She went out to the garage and worked out, then came in, showered, filled a travel mug, and headed in to the office.

She got there just after seven and had the place to herself. She turned on some music and got started wrapping up one of the two campaigns that were due that week. She was surprised when her music turned off. She looked up to see Samantha standing there.

Shock and dread warred within her. What was Samantha doing there? And why now when she only had a few minutes before she had to leave to meet Robert?

"What can I do for you?" Cullen struggled to keep her voice even.

"I just wanted to thank you for making up the time you'll be missing. And to check if you know when you'll be at trial yet."

"I don't know that, and I told you I'd make up the time I'm missing today."

"I know you did, but I'm still thankful. I'm your biggest champion, Cullen, as I'm sure you can imagine. And I felt like our last meeting didn't go very well."

She closed the door and sat down. Cullen glanced at the clock. Shit. She needed to go in the next fifteen minutes or so and she didn't want to be late. She wanted to get there and get it over with.

"You weren't happy," Cullen said. "But as I said, it can't be helped."

"Well, I just want you to know I support what you're doing. Testifying on behalf of someone takes cojones. If you need some time off to recuperate from the stress, just let me know, okay?"

Confused but grateful, Cullen sat silently for a moment.

"Thank you, but I don't think that would be necessary."

"Okay, but the offer stands."

"I thought my attendance was being closely watched," Cullen said. "I mean, I appreciate what you're saying, but wouldn't there still be a risk I'd be let go?"

Samantha smiled sweetly.

"I'm saying I've got your back and, as head of HR, I've got a lot of pull. So you just do what you need to to take care of yourself."

"Thanks. I appreciate that. Now, if there's nothing else, I really should get going."

"Oh, yes, okay. Good luck."

"Thanks."

Cullen followed Samantha down the hall to the elevators. She had no idea why Samantha was being so nice to her, but she was glad she was. Maybe Cullen would take some time off when the trial was over. Maybe she and Julia could get away for a day or two to celebrate, assuming Sara was convicted.

She arrived at Robert's office just before ten. She was tired from working three hours already, she was perplexed at Samantha's impromptu visit, and she really wasn't in the mood to deal with Robert or say nice things about Sara. Yet here she was.

Robert came out to take her back to his office. He was wearing a black suit with a charcoal tie over a white shirt and looked impeccable as always. Did nothing ruffle this guy?

"Cullen, thank you for coming. Let's go into the conference room, shall we?"

"Sure."

"Would you like some coffee? Tea? Water? You need to relax. You look like a rubber band wound too tight. Trust me, everything is going to be fine."

Cullen wasn't sure how to respond to that last statement.

"I'll have some coffee, please."

"Coming right up. How do you take it?"

"Lots of cream, no sugar."

"Excellent." He smiled at her and he picked up the phone and told the person on the other end what she wanted. He hung up and motioned for Cullen to sit. She did and he sat across from her.

"I saw Sara this morning," he said. "She doesn't look good. She says jail is wearing on her. Cullen, we need to get her out of there. And just think, once she's released, the two of you can pick up where you left off. We just have to establish her innocence, and I think you're going to help paint a picture of what she's really like instead of the ugly images the prosecution is going to try to smear her as."

Cullen kept her mouth shut. Sara was a murderer. She couldn't get off. There was no way. But she couldn't say that in front of Robert.

"So first things first, Cullen, and I need you to be honest. If she gets out, will you be there waiting for her?"

Cullen's stomach burned. Hell, no, she wanted to say, but played it cool.

"Honestly? I don't think so."

Robert raised his eyebrows.

"Why not?"

Cullen chose her next words carefully.

"She's never going to change, Robert. She loves her cocaine more than she ever cared about me."

Robert looked relieved at her answer.

"Besides," Cullen blurted. "She ran. Why would an innocent person run?"

"To avoid being framed. She knew that detective...I can't think of her name right now...that she would stop at nothing to pin those crimes on Sara. So she ran away to avoid going to prison. And now that detective," he said it like it was a bad word, "is in the driver's seat. We need to make sure Sara gets a fair trial. That's where you come in."

Cullen clasped her hands on the table. Her knuckles went white. She didn't want to help Sara or Robert.

"I don't know if I can do what you're asking me to do," she said.

They paused their conversation as Cullen's coffee was delivered.

"All you have to do is answer my questions," Robert said when they were alone again. "Just be honest. I'll ask you about when you first got together. I'll ask about her demeanor and behavior and that sort of thing. You just have to be honest and talk about the beginning of your relationship. Do you think you can do that?"

Cullen nodded.

"Good. Now, after I ask you questions, the prosecutor will ask you some. Just focus on the good times you had, okay? You never saw her sell drugs, did you?"

"No."

"And can you imagine her killing someone?"

"No."

"Great." He flashed his pearly whites at her. "You're going to be fine. Just remember to stay calm and focus on the good times. I'll warn you right now Sara doesn't look good so you'll want to brace yourself for that. It won't be easy for you to see your girlfriend bedraggled."

Cullen's attitude shifted. Suddenly, she wanted to testify. Not to help Sara, but to hurt her. She wanted to hurt her like she'd been hurt. To betray her in front of everyone but rather than point out Sara wasn't her girlfriend, she just nodded.

"The important thing to remember is to tell the truth," Robert said. "Always tell the truth, okay? Do you have any questions?"

"When will the trial take place?"

"We're pushing for it to happen sooner rather than later. The sooner we get her to trial, the sooner she's free."

"Okay, thanks."

"Thank you. I appreciate you taking the time to come down here and meet with me. We'll see you at the trial."

"I'll be there."

"I'll let you know when it is."

"Thank you."

Julia was at her desk going over the O'Hara case when her phone rang.

"Detective Stansworth."

"Detective, it's Mike. I think you should come down to the lab."

"On my way."

Shit. It better not be bad news. She was close to closing out three murders at the moment and she didn't need anything to fuck that up.

"What's up, Mike?" She found him looking into a microscope. "Tell me you're not going to blow a hole in my O'Hara case."

Mike straightened and turned to face her, smiling.

"Au contraire. I just started going over the evidence from items brought it from the House of Good Fortune drug case. Remember that restaurant in Bidwell that was busted for drug trafficking?"

"I remember that. What's that got to do with me?"

"Well, take a look."

Julia bent to look into the microscope.

"What am I looking at?"

"On the left is the gun we found and traced back to the owner of the restaurant."

"And on the right?"

"The bullets that were shot into Montague and at Donovan's house."

"They're a match." She stood up and smiled at him. "So that restaurant was involved in the dealings that killed that college kid."

"Looks like it to me."

"So that's where Donovan must have gotten her drugs."

"That would be my bet."

"And they shot up her house to warn her to keep quiet."

"Bingo again."

"I could hug you, Mike."

"Please don't."

"I won't." She grinned.

Julia hurried upstairs to get her coat and called the jail to have Sara brought to an interview room. By the time she got there, Robert Allen had arrived and was in the room with her.

Sara looked like crap. She had bags under her eyes, and her face was pale and swollen. She looked like she hadn't slept in days and Julia knew it would only be rougher in prison. She felt no sympathy for her. She'd made her bed, now let her lie in it.

"What is this about, Detective?" Allen said.

"New evidence has told us who your supplier was," Julia said. "Now we just need you to confirm it, testify against them, and we'll try to get you a lighter sentence."

She saw a look pass between them. What was it? It almost looked like Allen sent her a warning look of some sort.

"I'm not a rat," Sara said.

"We've got the evidence against them, for Christ's sake, woman. They tried to kill you. Doesn't that call for some action on your part?"

Sara looked to Allen again, and she saw Allen barely shake his head.

"You can't prove that."

"Ah," Julia said, "but we can. Look, we're going to nail them. It would just be quicker and easier if you helped us."

"Go fuck yourself."

Julia rose.

"Suit yourself."

She motioned for the guard to take Sara back to her cell. Allen walked with her to the parking lot.

"She's not a snitch," Allen said.

"She's a murderer and she's going to do life without parole. You'd think the opportunity to maybe get out sometime would be enough incentive. But you seemed pretty dead set against it. What are you hiding, Mr. Allen?"

"Watch yourself, Detective."

Julia had no intention of watching herself. She could only surmise that Allen was defending the owners of the House of Good Fortune as well, and she was sure they were the ones who paid him to defend Montague. Were they paying him to defend Sara or did they leave her blowing in the wind?

She didn't care, not really. It was none of her business. She didn't give a rat's ass who paid for whom at this point. All she knew was that Allen had a reputation as one hell of a defense attorney and she wanted to be sure her case could stand up to him

At four o'clock, she called it a day and texted Cullen.

Are you coming over after Leslie's?

You know it.

Excellent. Can't wait to see you.

Me, too.

She drove home and poured herself a glass of wine and climbed into the tub. She leaned back, closed her eyes, and reveled in the feel of the hot, scented water caressing her skin. She closed her eyes and woke to the sound of her phone ringing. It was the DA.

"Hello?" She sounded groggy so cleared her throat and tried again. "Detective Stansworth here."

"Detective, just got word we go to trial Wednesday. Will you be ready?"

"I sure will."

"I want you there every day of the trial. I don't know when we'll call on you to testify."

"I understand. I'll be there."

"Excellent. See you then."

Julia tossed the phone back on the floor and rinsed off before slipping on sweats. It was cold and getting colder. Her house was comfortable but could be warmer. Maybe she'd make a fire.

She heard Cullen pull up and opened the door when she was on the front step.

"Come on in, handsome," she said.

"You smell divine."

"Thank you."

Cullen stepped inside and nuzzled Julia's neck.

"I love that smell."

"Thank you again. It's lavender vanilla. It soothes me."

"It does anything but soothe me." Cullen ran her tongue over the base of Julia's neck.

"Easy, tiger. Come in. Come in now."

Julia closed the door, but the late afternoon chill had already crept in and Cullen rubbed her hands.

"We need a fire," she said.

"I was thinking the same thing."

"Will you grab me a glass of wine while I get one going?"

"Of course," Julia said.

She came back to the living room to find a blazing fire.

"Nicely done," she said.

"Thanks."

"No, thank you." Julia handed her a glass of wine. "How was Leslie?"

"Good. We talked about the trial a lot."

"Oh, that's right. You met with Allen today. How'd that go?"

"I'm excited about testifying," Cullen said.

"You are? That's a switch."

"I guess I didn't realize the prosecutor would also be questioning me. So even if I paint a rosy picture from Robert's questions, I may be able to paint a more accurate one by answering theirs."

"That's true," Julia said. "So, you're not worried about the pressure anymore?"

"Not really. All I can do is tell the truth. You guys have enough to convict her with or without my testimony."

Julia leaned in and kissed Cullen.

"What was that for?"

"For being you. Because you're wonderful and I want you to know I know that."

CHAPTER THIRTY

Julia spent Wednesday at the courthouse watching jury selection. They'd found a good group of jurors, those who hadn't read the news of the murders. Julia was surprised, as always, how many people simply didn't follow the news.

It took all day, but they finally found fourteen people both sides agreed on. So the jury was set and they had two alternates. They were ready to start presenting evidence the next day. Julia was certain it would be a quick trial. She knew they had enough evidence to nail Sara's coffin shut. Of course, she didn't know what Allen had up his sleeve, but she couldn't worry about that. The prosecutor was the assistant DA and she was good. She wanted to be DA some day and her record showed that. She had a propensity to win.

Julia felt relaxed as she walked out to her car. Day one was often not that easy. Day two would be harder, but she was ready. She texted Cullen.

Want to meet for dinner or come to my place?

I'll stop by your place. I'm heading out now.

What do you want for dinner?

Chinese. Go ahead and order for me.

Will do. See you soon.

Julia slid her phone in her pocket and drove to a store to stock up on beer. She wasn't in the mood for wine. Then she drove home and ordered dinner. She got off the couch to go change when she heard Cullen pull up.

She opened the door for Cullen, took her hand, and placed something in it. Cullen opened her hand and looked at it.

"A key?" Cullen said.

"Yes, there's no reason for you to knock when you come over. That's ridiculous. Now you can just let yourself in."

"Thanks, baby."

She kissed her hard on her mouth, and Julia almost forgot about the cold rain blowing on her. She broke the kiss.

"Come on in. We can kiss on the couch. But it's freezing out here."

Cullen laughed and followed her in.

"Would you like me to get a fire going?" she said.

"Sure, but first I want you to fan the flames burning in me. Kiss me again, Cullen."

They sat on the couch and Cullen kissed Julia again. This time, Julia relaxed into it. She leaned back until she was lying on the couch and pulled Cullen on top of her. They were still kissing when her doorbell rang.

"Shit." Cullen sat up then stood. "Are you expecting someone?"

"Yeah." Julia laughed. "Dinner."

"Oh, yeah, I'll get it."

While Cullen went to the door, Julia sat up and tried to catch her breath. When she could trust her legs again, she followed Cullen into the dining room.

"How was the trial today?" Cullen said. "Anything exciting happen?"

"We chose jurors. Nothing too exciting."

"Ah."

Cullen's phone rang then. Julia glanced down and saw Allen's name.

"Shit," Cullen said. She switched it to speaker then said, "Hello?"

"Cullen, it's Robert Allen. How are you?"

"Good. What's up?"

"Sara's trial should start in earnest tomorrow. Since I don't think the prosecution has much to present, I'd like you to be at the courthouse all day tomorrow just in case I get to call you."

"Okay. I'll be there."

"Great, thanks."

She disconnected.

"He doesn't think we have much to present?" Julia was incredulous. "He's seen what we have. He knows what's coming. Either he's delusional or stupid."

"He doesn't know I know that," Cullen said.

"True. Okay, let's eat."

After dinner, they sat together on the couch again and silently drank their beers until Julia spoke.

"You know, we have to act like we don't know each other at the courthouse."

"Huh? We do? Oh, yeah, I guess that makes sense. That's going to be hard."

"I know, but we can't have anything muddling the case."

"I understand."

"Good. I'm sorry you're going to have to waste your day at the courthouse tomorrow."

"Me, too. Oh, that reminds me, I have to email Samantha."

Julia waited, and when she was through, took her phone from her and set it on the coffee table. She placed their beers by it and lay back on the couch. She tugged on Cullen's lapel.

"Come here. Let's get back down to business."

They made out until Julia was ready to rip Cullen's clothes off her. She was on fire and Cullen was the only one who could put that fire out. Cullen seemed to sense where Julia was because she stopped kissing her and stood.

"I should get going."

"Now?"

"Yes, baby, now. I need to get home. You sleep well and I'll see you at the courthouse."

"Remember, you don't know me."

"I'm aware. Though Sara knows otherwise."

"True. Still, I don't want to take any chances."

"You got it. I'll see you here after the trial then."

"Okay. That sounds wonderful. Good night."

"Good night."

The courtroom was fairly empty as the trial got underway the next day. Julia had worn a black pantsuit with a royal blue shirt under it. She knew she looked professional and personable all at once, and that was important. She didn't want anyone to doubt her credentials, but she also didn't want to seem too standoffish. She needed the jury to be able to relate to her.

At nine o'clock, just before the judge came in, Cullen walked through the door looking dapper in a gray suit with a kelly green shirt. Julia was sure her eyes were shining like emeralds, but she couldn't stare. Especially since Cullen was a witness for the defense. Cullen took her seat in the hallway of the courthouse and didn't look at Julia. Good for her.

The assistant DA called Julia to the stand, and they went through all the evidence she'd found. It took a few hours to explain everything as simply as she could. The prosecutor led her through everything just as they'd practiced and then it was time for Allen to question her.

"Do you really think you were the best detective for this case?" Allen didn't even stand.

"Yes."

"But isn't it true you were sleeping with the defendant's girlfriend while you were investigating her?"

"No."

"May I remind you you're under oath?"

"I'll swear again if I need to. I knew the defendant's girlfriend from high school. We had a few beers and reminisced. I've never slept with her."

"Ever?" Allen said.

"Never." Julia's gaze never wavered.

"But you were interested in her, right? Is it possible you planted evidence to send Ms. Donovan away so you could have a clear shot at her girlfriend?"

"I would never do that. I ran the investigation, but my team of officers worked hard to find the evidence and the lab worked hard to prove it was involved in the case. It was a team effort, so I couldn't have skewed it if I'd wanted."

Allen looked like he might say more.

"No further questions."

It was only then that Julia chanced a glance at the jurors. Their faces were unreadable.

Cullen watched Julia come out of the proceedings. What had gone on in there? Julia looked liked she'd been put through the ringer. Had Robert done that to her? And if Robert could make Julia look like that, Cullen could just imagine what he could do to her.

Julia went into the restroom and it took every ounce of self-control not to follow her. When she emerged, she marched right back into the courtroom. She didn't even cast a glance at Cullen. Good for her. She reinforced Cullen's own need to be strong.

People started emerging from the courtroom. Cullen checked her watch. It was already four. Wow, the day had flown by. Julia came out and stood with a group of people off to the side. Without looking Julia's way, Cullen let herself out of the courtroom and drove to Julia's house.

She let herself in using her new key and helped herself to a beer. She looked around for something stronger and spotted a bottle of amber liquid. One whiff told her it was whiskey and she put the beer away. She needed a stiff drink.

Julia came home about a half hour later and she was not in a good mood.

"Hey, sweetheart." Cullen went to kiss her, but Julia turned her head away and Cullen planted a peck on her cheek.

"I think you should leave," Julia said.

"What? Why?"

"Look, it may be like closing the barn door after the horse got out, but I still think we shouldn't be seen together until after the trial is over. I don't want anything screwing this up for us."

"Shit. Well, okay, if you're sure. I'll leave. Can I still call or text?"

"Nope, no contact for now."

"Damn. Okay. You know what's best."

Cullen drove back to her house where she mixed a Malibu and Coke. It tasted good and went down easy. With nothing else to do and a ton of pent up energy inside, she stripped to her underwear and went out to her gym.

Her garage was bitter cold, but soon she was warmed up and raring to go. She pushed herself hard, and when it was time to take on her punching bag, it was Robert's face she saw, not Sara's.

She woke up the next morning sore after two workouts the day before. She skipped her workout that morning, showered, and got ready for another day in court. She wore a navy suit with a white shirt under it. She contemplated a tie but opted against it. She needed to look respectable, not uber butch. Not that she could hide that fact if she wanted to. She just didn't need to flaunt it.

That day, Cullen was called to the stand. She fought the bile that rose inside. She was nervous so she took a deep breath. She just had to tell the truth.

When she walked in, Sara turned around in her seat and flashed a broad smile at her. The smile didn't reach her eyes, though, and Cullen didn't miss that. She nodded at her and smiled a small smile.

Sara looked like shit. She looked exhausted, and her hair, which had been dyed black, was starting to grow out and her roots looked messy. Her eyes were sunk back in her head, and she looked like she was living a nightmare. She deserved it, though. That's what happened when you killed people.

Cullen was sworn in and sat on the witness stand.

"Good morning, Ms. Matthews," Robert began.

"Good morning."

"Will you please tell the court what your relationship is with my client?"

"She was my girlfriend."

"Was?" Robert's eyebrows shot up. "Have you officially broken up?"

"I'd say so."

"Okay. Details. Tell me how you met."

Cullen went into the story of meeting at the House of Good Fortune. She then told them how they went dancing after dinner and never looked back.

"Did you sleep with Ms. Donovan that first night?"

"Yes."

"And did she spend the night or did she leave?"

"She stayed over."

"Did she seem like she was on drugs?" Robert asked.

"Not to me."

"What was her personality like? What attracted you to her?"

"Well, she was beautiful, but she was also incredibly intelligent and funny."

"Could you imagine her killing somebody?"

"No."

The questioning went on along those lines with Robert trying to get Cullen to paint a picture of a saint.

"One more thing," Robert said. "When Ms. Donovan started being investigated, did you start seeing someone else?"

"No, I was determined to stick with her. We'd even talked about getting her help to quit cocaine."

"Thank you."

The prosecutor stood and walked until she was mere feet in front of Cullen.

"Ms. Matthews, you say you were determined to stand by her yet you no longer consider yourself her girlfriend. What happened?"

"She left town."

"But isn't it true she kept in touch with you?"

"Yes. But—"

"So, maybe in her eyes she's still your girlfriend? Have you visited her since she's been in jail?"

"No."

"Why not?"

"She ran. Why would she run if she was innocent?"

Out of the corner of her eye, Cullen saw Sara put her head down and saw Robert pat her on her back.

"Thank you, Ms. Matthews. I have no further questions."

Cullen sat and watched as the prosecutor called more people who had helped with the investigation, including a guy from the lab named Michael Branson. His testimony included pictures of the dead bodies of both Sherry Bergstrom and Donnie, which was tough to take, but Cullen simply glanced away from the big screen. She didn't need to stare at the bodies, but she listened to Branson drone on. When his testimony was over, Robert cross-examined him. He had nothing to say that was important, Cullen didn't think. He seemed to be grasping for straws.

But he did make one point. Couldn't someone have planted that rock in Sara's yard? Branson said he had no way of knowing how that rock got in the yard. He only knew it was the murder weapon.

The judge declared that that had been enough for one day and dismissed them.

CHAPTER THIRTY-ONE

Julia sat through the rest of the trial feeling more confident with each new witness. Allen's witnesses were weak at best and she knew they'd won. At two thirty Friday afternoon, the judge dismissed the jurors with instructions.

Julia sat talking to the prosecutor before she planned to go home and face a quiet, lonely weekend without Cullen. She had just said good night to the assistant DA when it was announced that the jurors had reached their decision.

Her heart fluttered and she took her place behind the prosecutor's table. She was ready. In fact, she couldn't wait.

The jurors didn't disappoint. Sara was found guilty on all charges and would likely be sentenced to life without parole. That would be up to the judge, but Sara had been found guilty of killing two people. The chances of her getting out were slim and none.

The prosecutor hugged Julia and Julia wanted to sing. She took out her phone and texted Cullen.

I'm coming over. Be there soon.

Are you sure that's smart?

Positive.

I'm just leaving my office now.

I'll wait in my car.

There's a spare key under the gnome in the rose garden. Let yourself in.

Will do. See you soon.

Julia wanted to gun it down I-5, but instead sat impatiently in traffic. It was stop-and-go, mostly stop. When she finally got to Bidwell, she made a pit stop to buy wine and champagne then headed straight to Cullen's.

It was cold and dark, but she found the spare key and let herself in. Cullen's house was warmer than outside, but there was still a chill in the air. Julia started a fire and had just managed to get it burning when Cullen walked in.

"Hey, babe." Julia threw her arms around Cullen.

"Well, hello. But I thought we couldn't see each other." She rested her hands on Julia's hips.

"It's over, Cullen. She was found guilty on all counts."

"Yeah?" She watched a bright smile spread over Cullen's face. "That's great. That's fantastic news."

"I know, right?" Cullen kissed her. It was brief, but Julia's heart soared. "Come on in. I bought some champagne to celebrate."

"Oh yum, let's have some."

Julia poured two glasses and they toasted to Sara's sentencing, to Julia's fantastic job, and to their future.

"And speaking of our future." Julia took Cullen's hand and led her down the hall to Cullen's bedroom. "Do you think it's time? Are you ready? Have we waited long enough?"

"Have you waited enough?" Cullen said. "Have I proven that I'm here for you and only you?"

"I know this, Cullen. I know it in my heart."

She set her glass on the nightstand and took Cullen's from her. She placed Cullen's hands on her hips and placed her hands on Cullen's muscular shoulders.

"You feel so good," Julia said. "So strong and sturdy."

"I'll always be strong for you, Julia. I'll be your mighty oak. Lean on me whenever you need to."

"I'm going to lean on you right now."

She did just that, pressing the length of her body into Cullen's while Cullen lowered her mouth to claim Julia. The kiss was frantic, hurried, and intense. Knowing what was to come, Julia didn't fight the rush of feelings that cascaded over her. Desire and passion washed over her, leaving her breathless and craving more.

Julia soon grew weak in the knees and lowered herself onto the bed. Cullen never broke the kiss as she sat with her. Cullen's hands were on Julia's ass, pulling her closer and Julia climbed into her lap, straddling her, grinding into her.

Cullen stroked Julia's thighs and Julia tensed, bracing herself for what she was sure was next. But Cullen stopped and ran her hands up and down Julia's arms. She moved them to her back and stroked it while she held Julia tight against her.

Julia felt Cullen's small breasts against hers and almost lost her mind. She wanted to be naked with Cullen. She was beyond ready. They'd waited so long.

Then Cullen's hands were on Julia's face, cupping her jaw and caressing her cheek, and each touch sent sparks flying. She ran her hands through Cullen's hair, along her back and down her arms before linking them behind her neck again.

Cullen lay back and Julia pulled on top of her. She braced herself with one hand on either side of Cullen's head and propped herself up to look at her. Her body was alive with desire and her pants felt too tight as her seam rubbed her. Her breasts strained against her bra, begging to be set free from their confines.

"You're beautiful," Cullen whispered.

"I need you, Cullen."

Cullen raised her head and kissed Julia again. She tangled her fingers in her hair and held their mouths together. She ran her hands down her back again and over her arms. Julia was ready to beg for more when Cullen brushed her thumbs over her breasts.

The contact was slight, but it was there, and Julia moaned into Cullen's mouth. She pulled away slightly.

"More," she murmured against her lips. "More, please."

Cullen slid her hand around and cupped Julia's breast. She kneaded it softly, each squeeze sending Julia closer to spiraling out of control. When Cullen brushed her nipple, Julia drew in a sharp intake of breath.

"Oh God, yes, Cullen. That's it. Please."

Cullen slipped her hand under Julia's blouse and teased her nipple through her bra. Julia fought to maintain composure. When

Cullen slid her hand under her bra and pinched her nipple, Julia shivered as an orgasm tore through her. Cullen stopped what she was doing and looked into Julia's eyes.

"Are you okay?"

"I'm better than okay. I'm just so ready for you. I'm sorry. I didn't mean to come so soon."

Cullen grinned at her then unbuttoned her blouse and eased it off her shoulders. She unhooked her bra and sat gazing at her breasts. Julia's arousal heightened at the way Cullen looked like she was about to devour her. When Cullen took a nipple in her mouth, Julia arched into her.

"Oh, God, yes. Oh dear God, Cullen. I'm going to come again."

Cullen stopped what she was doing.

"What? Why'd you stop?"

"Not yet. I want the next one to blow your mind."

"But…"

Cullen silenced her with a kiss. Julia's nipples ached. They longed to feel Cullen's mouth on them again, but so did the rest of her. She needed Cullen in every way. Cullen eased Julia off of her and pulled down her sweats. She peeled off her briefs and sat taking in every inch of her.

Rather than be embarrassed, Julia found herself growing wetter under Cullen's scrutiny. She spread her legs wider.

"Please, Cullen. I'm in agony. Please grant me release."

Cullen lowered her head and tasted Julia. Slowly and deliberately, she ran her tongue over her. Julia felt like exploding at every lick, but Cullen never stayed in one place too long. Just when Julia thought an orgasm was about to come, Cullen moved again.

"Please, stop teasing me."

Cullen buried her tongue deep inside her. She drew it out and sucked her lips. Julia struggled for control. She was a breath away. If only Cullen would let her come.

And then she felt Cullen's strong, powerful tongue on her and her whole body tensed. Cullen reached up and tweaked her nipples while she flicked her tongue over her clit. Julia's world coalesced into a minute microcosm. And that tiny space only consisted of the feelings Cullen was creating.

Her center ached and throbbed, and still Cullen pleased her. And then, with one stroke of her tongue, Julia's world exploded into a million tiny pieces. She screamed unintelligibly as the orgasm she'd been craving ripped her apart. Her body turned to Jell-O as she floated back from oblivion.

Cullen's ego swelled. She was so proud of herself for getting Julia there. Julia's whole body was flushed and she was breathing heavily. But Cullen wasn't through. She slid her fingers inside Julia's wetness and reveled in the feel of her. She was warm and tight and enveloped her fingers like a glove. By stroking and licking, Cullen coaxed another climax out of Julia. And then another and another.

Julia was so easy to please. Cullen never wanted to stop. Julia tapped her shoulder.

"That's enough for now, loverboi."

Cullen was bummed.

"Are you sure?"

Julia was delicious and Cullen never wanted to move from between her legs.

"I'm sure. Come here and kiss me."

Cullen moved up Julia's body and kissed her soundly.

"You're delicious," she said.

"As I'm sure you will be. Just give me a second to come to my senses."

Cullen had waited this long. What was a few more minutes? She was throbbing and her own thighs were slick with excitement. It didn't take long before Julia was ready.

She reached over to the nightstand and dribbled some champagne onto Cullen's breasts. She licked the rivulets that ran down them before sucking her nipples. Hard. The cool liquid and warm breath combined to make Cullen crazy. She rose off the bed at the contact, then held Julia's head in place until she felt Julia fighting to get free.

Julia kissed down Cullen's body until she came to rest between her legs.

"Someone's ready for me."

"I have been for a long time now."

"Good answer."

Julia slowly and deliberately licked every inch of Cullen. Just when Cullen thought she'd settle into one spot, she moved again, driving her mad, but she knew the wait would be worth it. There was no doubt in her mind.

Cullen was filled completely when Julia entered her. She felt a oneness she'd never felt before at their joining. And then Julia sucked on her clit and Cullen could hold off no longer. She closed her eyes tight as the pressure inside increased. She lost all semblance of control when, with one swipe of her tongue, Julia catapulted her into orbit. Her whole body exploded and she watched the lights burst inside her eyelids as she rode the crashing wave of the orgasm.

Julia continued to make love to her and, to Cullen's surprise, she came again. It was less powerful, but equally satisfying. She pulled Julia up and took her in her arms. Julia snuggled against her and rested her head on Cullen's shoulder.

"That's never happened to me before," Cullen said.

"What's that?"

"I've never come twice before."

"Seriously? And how many women have you been with?"

Cullen laughed.

"Ha, very funny. Enough to think I was a one climax kind of woman."

Julia lazily traced Cullen's nipples.

"You're gorgeous, Cullen. This was more than I could even fantasize about."

Cullen glanced down at her.

"Yeah, and did you fantasize a lot?"

"Of course."

"Tell me."

"No."

"Fine." Cullen smiled then grew serious. "So tell me. Promise me. We're in this for the long haul, yes?"

"Oh, yeah. I give you my word."

"I'm going to hold you to it, you know."

"You won't have to. I'm not going anywhere Cullen."

"Good."

"And you? You're ready to put Sara and all the others behind you and be with me only from now on, right?"

"From now until forever, Julia."

"You know, the champagne was good, but I like this way of celebrating more."

"Mm, as do I. Are you ready to celebrate some more?"

"I'll never say no to you, Cullen."

"Promise?"

"I swear."

Cullen took a deep breath. She knew it was too soon, but was it really? She had feelings for Julia that she'd never had before. Yes, there had been other women and other relationships, but Julia was different. Dare she speak those words yet?

"What are you thinking?" Julia asked.

"There's something I want to tell you, but I don't want to freak you out."

"What is it? You're into whips and chains? You need me to dress up like a schoolgirl? Talk to me, babe."

Cullen was laughing too hard to speak. She got control of herself and took another deep breath.

"No, nothing like that."

"Then what?"

"Promise not to freak?"

"I'll do my best," Julia said.

"I think I love you."

"You think or you know?"

"I know, okay? I love you, Julia."

"You know what?"

"What?"

"I love you too."

About the Author

MJ Williamz was raised on California's central coast, which she left at age seventeen to pursue an education. She graduated from Chico State, and it was in Chico that she rediscovered her love of writing. It wasn't until she moved to Portland, however, that her writing really took off, with the publication of her first short story in 2003.

MJ is the author of eighteen books, including three Goldie Award winners. She has also had over thirty short stories published, most of them erotica with a few romances and a few horrors thrown in for good measure. She lives in Houston with her wife, fellow author Laydin Michaels, and their fur babies. You can find her on Facebook or reach her at mjwilliamz@aol.com

Books Available from Bold Strokes Books

Beautiful Dreamer by Melissa Brayden. With love on the line, can Devyn Winters find it in her heart to stay in the small town of Dreamer's Bay, the one place she swore she'd never remain? (978-1-63555-305-5)

Create a Life to Love by Erin Zak. When sixteen-year-old Beth shows up at her birth mother's door, three lives will change forever. (978-1-63555-425-0)

Deadeye by Meredith Doench. Stranded while hunting the serial predator Deadeye, Special Agent Luce Hansen fights for survival while her lover, forensic pathologist Harper Bennett, hunts for clues to Hansen's disappearance along the killer's trail. (978-1-63555-253-9)

Death Takes a Bow by David S. Pederson. Alan Keys takes part in a local stage production, but when the leading man is murdered, his partner Detective Heath Barrington is thrust into the limelight to find the killer. (978-1-63555-472-4)

Endangered by Michelle Larkin. Shapeshifters Officer Aspen Wolfe and Dr. Tora Madigan fight their growing attraction as they work together to destroy a secret government agency that exterminates their kind. (978-1-63555-377-2)

Incognito by VK Powell. The only thing Evan Spears is focused on is capturing a fleeing murder suspect until wild card Frankie Strong is added to her team and causes chaos on and off the job. (978-1-63555-389-5)

Insult to Injury by Gun Brooke. After losing everything, Gail Owen withdraws to her old farmhouse and finds a destitute young woman, Romi Shepherd, living in a secret room. (978-1-63555-323-9)

Just One Moment by Dena Blake. If you were given the chance to have the love of your life back, could you ignore everything that went wrong and start over again? (978-1-63555-387-1)

Scene of the Crime by MJ Williamz. Cullen Mathew finds herself caught between the woman she thinks she loves but can no longer trust and a beautiful detective she can't stop thinking about who will stop at nothing to find the truth. (978-1-63555-405-2)

Accidental Prophet by Bud Gundy. Days after his grandmother dies, Drew Morten learns his true identity and finds himself racing against time to save civilization from the apocalypse. (978-1-63555-452-6)

Daughter of No One by Sam Ledel. When their worlds are threatened, a princess and a village outcast must overcome their differences and embrace a budding attraction if they want to survive. (978-1-63555-427-4)

Fear of Falling by Georgia Beers. Singer Sophie James is ready to shake up her career, but her new manager, the gorgeous Dana Landon, has other ideas. (978-1-63555-443-4)

In Case You Forgot by Fredrick Smith and Chaz Lamar. Zaire and Kenny, two newly single, Black, queer, and socially aware men, start again—in love, career, and life—in the West Hollywood neighborhood of LA. (978-1-63555-493-9)

Playing with Fire by Lesley Davis. When Takira Lathan and Dante Groves meet at Takira's restaurant, love may find its way onto the menu. (978-1-63555-433-5)

Practice Makes Perfect by Carsen Taite. Meet law school friends Campbell, Abby, and Grace, law partners at Austin's premier boutique legal firm for young, hip entrepreneurs. Legal Affairs: one law firm, three best friends, three chances to fall in love. (978-1-63555-357-4)

The Last Seduction by Ronica Black. When you allow true love to elude you once and you desperately regret it, are you brave enough to grab it when it comes around again? (978-1-63555-211-9)

Wavering Convictions by Erin Dutton. After a traumatic event, Maggie has vowed to regain her strength and independence. So how can Ally be both the woman who makes her feel safe and a constant reminder of the person who took her security away? (978-1-63555-403-8)

A Bird of Sorrow by Shea Godfrey. As Darrius and her lover, Princess Jessa, gather their strength for the coming war, a mysterious spell will reveal the truth of an ancient love. (978-1-63555-009-2)

All the Worlds Between Us by Morgan Lee Miller. High school senior Quinn Hughes discovers that a broken friendship is actually a door propped open for an unexpected romance. (978-1-63555-457-1)

An Intimate Deception by CJ Birch. Flynn County Sheriff Elle Ashley has spent her adult life atoning for her wild youth, but when she finds her ex, Jessie, murdered two weeks before the small town's biggest social event, she comes face-to-face with her past and all her well-kept secrets. (978-1-63555-417-5)

Cash and the Sorority Girl by Ashley Bartlett. Cash Braddock doesn't want to deal with morality, drugs, or people. Unfortunately, she's going to have to. (978-1-63555-310-9)

Counting for Thunder by Phillip Irwin Cooper. A struggling actor returns to the Deep South to manage a family crisis, finds love, and ultimately his own voice as his mother is regaining hers for possibly the last time. (978-1-63555-450-2)

Falling by Kris Bryant. Falling in love isn't part of the plan, but will Shaylie Beck put her heart first and stick around, or tell the damaging truth? (978-1-63555-373-4)

Secrets in a Small Town by Nicole Stiling. Deputy Chief Mackenzie Blake has one mission: find the person harassing Savannah Castillo and her daughter before they cause real harm. (978-1-63555-436-6)

Stormy Seas by Ali Vali. The high-octane follow-up to the best-selling action-romance, *Blue Skies*. (978-1-63555-299-7)

The Road to Madison by Elle Spencer. Can two women who fell in love as girls overcome the hurt caused by the father who tore them apart? (978-1-63555-421-2)

Dangerous Curves by Larkin Rose. When love waits at the finish line, dangerous curves are a risk worth taking. (978-1-63555-353-6)

Love to the Rescue by Radclyffe. Can two people who share a past really be strangers? (978-1-62639-973-0)

Love's Portrait by Anna Larner. When museum curator Molly Goode and benefactor Georgina Wright uncover a portrait's secret, public and private truths are exposed, and their deepening love hangs in the balance. (978-1-63555-057-3)

Model Behavior by MJ Williamz. Can one woman's instability shatter a new couple's dreams of happiness? (978-1-63555-379-6)

Pretending in Paradise by M. Ullrich. When travelwisdom.com assigns PR specialist Caroline Beckett and travel blogger Emma Morgan to cover a hot new couples retreat, they're forced to fake a relationship to secure a reservation. (978-1-63555-399-4)

Recipe for Love by Aurora Rey. Hannah Little doesn't have much use for fancy chefs or fancy restaurants, but when New York City chef Drew Davis comes to town, their attraction just might be a recipe for love. (978-1-63555-367-3)

Survivor's Guilt and Other Stories by Greg Herren. Award-winning author Greg Herren's short stories are finally pulled together into a single collection, including the Macavity Award nominated title story and the first-ever Chanse MacLeod short story. (978-1-63555-413-7)

The House by Eden Darry. After a vicious assault, Sadie, Fin, and their family retreat to a house they think is the perfect place to start over, until they realize not all is as it seems. (978-1-63555-395-6)

Uninvited by Jane C. Esther. When Aerin McLeary's body becomes host for an alien intent on invading Earth, she must work with researcher Olivia Ando to uncover the truth and save humankind. (978-1-63555-282-9)

Comrade Cowgirl by Yolanda Wallace. When cattle rancher Laramie Bowman accepts a lucrative job offer far from home, will her heart end up getting lost in translation? (978-1-63555-375-8)

Double Vision by Ellie Hart. When her cell phone rings, Giselle Cutler answers it—and finds herself speaking to a dead woman. (978-1-63555-385-7)

Inheritors of Chaos by Barbara Ann Wright. As factions splinter and reunite, will anyone survive the final showdown between gods and mortals on an alien world? (978-1-63555-294-2)

Love on Lavender Lane by Karis Walsh. Accompanied by the buzz of honeybees and the scent of lavender, Paige and Kassidy must find a way to compromise on their approach to business if they want to save Lavender Lane Farm—and find a way to make room for love along the way. (978-1-63555-286-7)

Spinning Tales by Brey Willows. When the fairy tale begins to unravel and villains are on the loose, will Maggie and Kody be able to spin a new tale? (978-1-63555-314-7)

The Do-Over by Georgia Beers. Bella Hunt has made a good life for herself and put the past behind her. But when the bane of her high school existence shows up for Bella's class on conflict resolution, the last thing they expect is to fall in love. (978-1-63555-393-2)

What Happens When by Samantha Boyette. For Molly Kennan, senior year is already an epic disaster, and falling for mysterious waitress Zia is about to make life a whole lot worse. (978-1-63555-408-3)

Wooing the Farmer by Jenny Frame. When fiercely independent modern socialite Penelope Huntingdon-Stewart and traditional country farmer Sam McQuade meet, trusting their hearts is harder than it looks. (978-1-63555-381-9)